A STICKY SITUATION

A MULBURY MYSTERY

JUNO HARVEY

mp
mandurang
press

First published by Mandurang Press 2021

Book cover by Melissa Williams Design

ISBN: 978-0-6452604-1-0 (ebook)

ISBN: 978-0-6452604-2-7 (paperback)

To the Nanas

ONE

Rosemary Exeter woke at the first magpie murmur. It was not yet light, and stars twinkled through the half-open curtains. She sat up and felt down the bed for the reassuring lump of the large cat at her feet, who raised her head as Rosemary put her hand on her. The dream had been vivid, like a short video shot in high definition. Alasdair had glanced up from pounding the blood-red leather and smiled at her like he used to, all teeth and a glint of mischief in his dark eyes. Then he'd put down his hammer and walked out the door, the finished shoe abandoned on the bench.

Rosemary shivered. She waited a moment to allow the armour to re-harden around her heart, then slid out of bed, donned a thick dressing gown and sheepskin-lined boots, and headed to the kitchen. Once the overhead light was on, she felt better. Bowls of autumn fruit covered her bench, not shoe leather. Sweet yellow quinces, scarlet apples and chestnut-toned pears coloured the kitchen. The residents of Mulbury were harvesting their trees and buckets of produce turned up on the doorstep of *The Preserved Mulbury* with almost overwhelming regularity. She glanced at the fruit as she switched the kettle on. 'It's never ending,' she said to Sunny as the ginger cat sauntered into the room, pale orange tail arched elegantly over her striped back.

Sunny rubbed herself against Rosemary's leg. *You like it that way*, her expression read. *Now, where's breakfast?*

Rosemary ate a bowl of Rakisha's home-roasted granola while Sunny tucked into a handful of kibble. The granola was satisfyingly crunchy. 'It's about the only thing edible from *The Sweet Potato*,' Rosemary told Sunny. She got a flick of a tail in response.

The sun still hadn't risen by the time Rosemary finished breakfast and prepared for the day. She showered, dressed in a neat navy shirt and jeans, and brushed her long dark hair with its one grey streak down her right temple before braiding it. Back in the kitchen, she lifted her biggest saucepan onto the stove and measured out berries she'd stored in the freezer.

The little frozen bodies clattered noisily as they tumbled in, and she paused. The faint hum of radios in the buildings either side of her signalled her neighbours were already up and hadn't been woken by the berry cascade. Mrs Lionel's first job when the sun rose was always to sweep the town Square opposite them. Jasper Lu, though, was much more subdued in the morning, at least he had been since his return from hospital. Rosemary turned her ear to his bookshop but heard nothing more.

When Mr Arthur had owned the bookshop, he made it his mission to complain about the noise and smells Rosemary's business created. At the slightest rattle of a pan, he'd bang heavily on his side of the divide, making ancient plaster dust fall like soft rain onto Rosemary's sideboard. One particularly spicy pickle mix had him setting up a row of pedestal fans on the footpath under their connecting verandas to send the *hideous odour* back her way. Nothing he'd done worried Rosemary. His red-nosed indignation hadn't touched her, not even when he'd yell abuse through the walls. When he'd sold the shop, Rosemary didn't even know it had a new owner until Jasper Lu had pushed open the door of her shop, making its bell jangle cheerily, and bought a bottle of that very same pickle. 'I use it with my curries,' he'd said, pushing his chest-length black hair over his shoulder.

She'd nodded.

He'd waited, as if she'd failed to do something, then headed for the door. As he jangled out, he called back over his shoulder, 'Do you read? I have books.'

'Good for you,' she'd said, and saw his face warm to ripened-tomato red.

'I mean, I own the bookshop now. *The Read Mulbury.* You know? Next door? It joins you on one side and *Patricia's* on the other.'

'I know it.'

He'd paused a moment longer.

She'd dredged up some good manners. 'Welcome.'

He'd smiled as if she'd passed a test before giving a slight bow, jangling outside, and loping towards his shop.

Rosemary poured sugar into a bowl and set it next to the heater to warm. Jam-making would wait until after opening the shop. In the meantime, there were jars to label, accounts to do, and plans to make for the harvest accumulating on her kitchen bench. There were also chickens to feed, gardens to water, and clothes to hang out on the washing line, but it was still too dark, and the nip of frost felt sharp even through the window. Rosemary turned her own music on and worked at her table, waiting for the rest of Mulbury to shake off the night.

MRS LIONEL HEARD the faint rattle of Rosemary's berries as she ate her bacon and egg breakfast. She nodded to Percy, who still snoozed in his bed near the fire. 'Rosemary's working,' she said to the fox terrier. 'We should be, too.' But she passed the time until the sky lightened by knitting patiently seated on the couch. She stood stiffly, throwing the half-finished sock on a cushion, then entered the back of *The Green Mulbury* and pulled its bamboo blinds up to let the rising sun fill the shop with expectation. She took her broom and Percy and went outside to sweep the gravelly surface of Goldmarket Square.

That's how Mrs Lionel was the first to see the old man under The Exceptional Tree. Sunny watched from her windowsill, her tail flicking slowly from side to side.

The old man lay on his back, arms and legs out like a starfish. *Like a sand angel,* thought Mrs Lionel, *if he'd been lying on the beach. Or a snow angel if Mulbury could ever have snow.* Instead, he lay in the dirt, eyes slightly open, with his double-breasted suit coat buttoned up neatly and his feet pointed one each way at a forty-five-degree angle.

Percy sniffed the man's face. 'Leave it,' said Mrs Lionel, and the terrier backed away with a soft growl. She crouched near the man and took his hand in hers. Stone cold, it was, and nothing to do with the autumn chill. She leaned forward, put two fingers on his neck, pressed, but no life thumped under her fingertips. 'Peace be with you,' she said as she stood, pulling the phone from her pocket.

By the time the police came from Big Town, many of the residents of inner Mulbury had gathered in a respectful half-circle around the old man's body.

'Do you recognise him?' whispered Holly Hubbard to

her sister, Hannah, but she shook her head. Holly looked around, but no one seemed to know the man, not even Rakisha who tried to find out something about everyone.

A police officer waved them away except for Mrs Lionel, who was recounting her morning. 'Come on,' said Kelly, heading for her café. 'Coffee's on me.'

By the time Kelly had opened and started her machine, Mrs Lionel was free. She walked over to where Rosemary Exeter stood, the only resident not crowded into Kelly's shop and not caring that she wasn't. 'Well?' said Rosemary.

'No obvious signs of harm but I didn't turn him over.' Mrs Lionel shook her head. 'Poor dear probably lay down to sleep and slipped away in the night.'

Rosemary gave a curt nod.

It did not fool Mrs Lionel. Rosemary Exeter was not the nodding type, certainly not the sort of person who would assume a man no one had ever seen before could turn up in this tiny town and die in its Square without it involving a sticky sort of situation.

BY TEN O'CLOCK, Goldmarket Square was once again empty of dead bodies and police officers. Blue-and-white crime-scene tape fluttered from the Tree but had already lost its attachment to the traffic cones marking the area. Rosemary stood at her shop window, hands on hips. It was Monday, slow trade day, a day for creating stock and having tea on the back porch. From the kitchen behind the shop counter came the sweet perfume of jumbleberry jam cooking, a colourful mix of end-of-season fruit and Queensland sugar. She went back to it, stirring the mess with a large wooden spoon and calculating its setting time.

'Another twenty minutes, Sunny.'

The cat didn't stir from her cushion on the chair in the corner of the kitchen, although her ears twitched at her name.

The phone rang, a merry tune that Rosemary had claimed to identify the caller. 'Honey,' she said as she answered.

'Mum, I hear that someone died.'

'Yes.'

'Mum. Tell me.'

Rosemary smiled to herself. She could hear the hum of people in the background of Honey's call and imagined her daughter grabbing a latte and a muffin or whatever she got before heading to *Honey Blossom's Academy for Dramatic Experiences*.

'A man found in the Square. An unkempt but tidy man with no known identity.'

Honey contemplated this. 'Sounds like a case for Ronnie.'

'Yes. It won't be top priority for the police.'

'Do you know anything else?'

'What do you mean?'

'Mum. You know what I mean.'

'No, I don't.'

Another moment of silence, this time loaded with crossness.

'Mum.'

'I know nothing, Honey. Not yet.'

'Alright then.' Honey breathed in, a suck of air through the phone. 'What are you making?'

'Jumbleberry jam.'

'I can smell it.'

'No, you can't.'

'I can. A few of Hannah's strawberries, lots of Jasper's boysenberries, and a hint of gooseberries from Mrs Lionel.'

'Honey, you're thirty kilometres away. You can't smell it.'

'I don't need to, Mum. I can imagine it.' Honey laughed, a deep chuckle. 'Bye for now. Love you.'

'Love you, too.'

Rosemary put her phone on the kitchen counter and breathed in deeply. Honey was correct in her assessment. The kitchen was floating in fragrance.

The bell jangled as someone entered the shop. Rosemary gave her pot a quick stir before heading out. A tall man clad in a long black overcoat stood staring at the new windowsill display, a bowl full of yet-to-ripen quinces. 'Hello,' said Rosemary.

The man turned. He had sharp blue eyes that studied Rosemary's face. 'Morning. Lovely day.'

Rosemary glanced outside to check. The early morning had given way to one of those splendid autumn skies and soft light that Mulbury boasted about in tourist brochures. 'Yes,' she said. 'Visiting?'

'Passing through,' said the man, wandering to a shelf packed full of zucchini pickles. 'Just looking.' He pointed at the Square, where crime-scene tape waved in a light breeze. 'Bit of excitement this morning?'

'Yes.'

'Usual for this town?'

'Not particularly.'

'Do you know what happened?'

'A homeless man died overnight.'

The man nodded slowly, still watching the Square. 'That's sad. Do you have many homeless people in Mulbury?'

'There are lots of people sleeping rough in every town, but this fellow was the first I'd seen here.'

He nodded again. 'The first, eh? Perhaps not the last.'

'I'm sure it won't be the last.' Rosemary indicated the door that led from the shop into her living quarters. 'Excuse me while I check my jam.'

But the man had turned his attention back to the shelf, or so it could seem. His body angle was such that he could also have been watching the street. Rosemary ducked back inside to stir her nearly ready jam, and when she came back, the bell jangled again, and the man was outside moving towards Jasper's bookshop with his hands in his pockets.

Strangers were, of course, the lifeblood of little towns, what with their exclamations over anything cute and their pockets full of city money. This one, though, made the hairs stir at the back of Rosemary's neck. He didn't seem like the jam-and-pickles sort. He was too upright, too tense to be *just looking. Or am I tetchy because of the dead body?* she thought.

The jam was ready, a sample lying thick and lush on a cold saucer. Rosemary pulled jars out of the oven and began to ladle. Spots splattered on her bare hands, making her wince and slow down. She put a lid on each jar, screwing them home and cursing as the hot jars bit her, and took off her apron. Sunny lifted her head as she threw it on the counter but didn't follow as Rosemary jangled out the front door and walked the fifteen steps to Jasper's second-hand bookshop. A glance into the old shop revealed only Jasper at his counter.

'Everything alright, Rosemary?'

Patti Yale was out the front of *Patricia's* as she hung skirts on a rack. She held a red gingham in one hand.

'Yes,' said Rosemary.

'And what do you think about that poor old man this morning? What a way to die, all alone. Cold night, too. Can't imagine what he went through. Why, I had to have several of Kelly's coffees before I could even think clearly, it was such a shock.' Patti hung the skirt and skittered over to Rosemary. 'Do you know what happened?'

'No.'

'Oh.' Patti shrugged and stepped away, her loosely coiled apricot-coloured hair nestling in her neck. 'I would have thought you had better ideas than the rest of us, being so...' She gave Rosemary a quick grin.

'So?' Rosemary arched an eyebrow.

'*Astute*, I think the word is.'

Rosemary stared a moment at the woman in front of her, noting the carefully applied vintage look that made Patti seem from another era. There was an anxious frown, though, on Patti's face, and she had her apron on inside out. It almost moved Rosemary to pat her on the shoulder. Instead, she said, 'Why don't you sit for a spell, Patti? You appear like you need another coffee. Maybe a tea would be better.'

'Rosemary, thank you.' Patti put a hand to her forehead. 'You are quite right. I do feel a bit odd. All that excitement.'

Rosemary turned to enter the bookshop, hearing as she went Patti's last mumbled words. 'Astute, that's what I told Gerry, and I'm right. Rosemary Exeter is *astute*.' Rosemary rolled her eyes at the wonder in Patti's voice.

Jasper's shop didn't have a bell like Rosemary's. Instead, the old door—heavy with leadlight—sighed open as if moving tiredly. Jasper looked up from his computer. 'Hello, Rosemary,' he said, voice soft as ever.

'Jasper.'

'Wanting something different to read?' Jasper tapped

some books on the counter. 'Got these from a new customer.'

'A new customer?' Rosemary walked to the counter and picked up the three books there. 'Was he just in?'

'He?' Jasper frowned. 'It was a *she*. Dropped these in yesterday, among an entire box of science fiction.' He grinned and tipped his head toward the books. 'T. G. G. Duncan.'

Rosemary fanned the three books out in her hand. Their titles were new to her, but their covers suggested they were in the same series. 'Who is T. G. G. Duncan?'

'You don't know? *T. G. G.* A cult writer. Not from a nasty cult. T. G. G. was a revered writer of speculative fiction.'

'So, you've read them?'

'Of course,' said Jasper. He reached out and tapped one book. 'Everyone knows of T. G. G. Duncan. Captain Andre Kesper, who drives the spaceship *Tellurian*, is a bold and wonderful character, and his crew are full of idiosyncrasies. Despite that, there's something so, oh, I don't know, *familiar* about the plot of these books even though Space Western fiction isn't really my reading thing.'

Rosemary folded the books into the crook of her arm. 'And what is your reading thing, Jasper Lu?'

It was one of the nice things about Jasper, thought Rosemary, as Jasper's face deepened into a shade just short of crimson. A face like his couldn't hide anything. 'Well, Rosemary Exeter,' he said slowly, 'I read mainly rrrrmms.'

'Didn't hear that.'

'Romance.' Jasper stood up straight and waved at a shelf to his right. 'Historical romance. Preferably Regency.'

'Ah.' Rosemary frowned slightly. 'Jane Austen.'

'Yes. *Particularly* Jane Austen. Wish I had a first.'

'A first edition?'

'No. Well, yes. The most valuable of books are the first *printing* of first editions.' Jasper leaned forward. 'Did you know there were only three hundred copies of the first edition and first printing of the original Harry Potter?'

Rosemary eyed Jasper. 'I had no idea.'

'There you go.' Jasper's face was almost back to its usual rosy colour.

'And what is your favourite Jane Austen?'

'P and P.' Jasper wriggled. 'Can't help it.'

'Is it the fieriness of Elizabeth or the grandeur of Mr Darcy?'

'Oh, neither. I'm fond of Mary.'

Rosemary stared hard at Jasper, but he held her gaze with wide eyes until she lifted the three books in her arms. 'Mind if I take them?'

'Are you sure? You're usually a thriller reader.'

'Broadening my mind.' Rosemary patted her pocket and found it empty. 'I'll have to pay you later.'

'That's fine. Dinner tonight, anyway.'

'Yes.' Rosemary turned to leave. 'You know, I almost forgot it was Monday.'

'So, it even affected you?'

'What did?'

'A dead old man in the Square.'

Rosemary stopped. 'No. Not me.'

He blushed again. 'Well. See you at seven.'

She left through the sighing door and went back through her jangling one. Monday night was Mulbury's regular residential dinner night, at Jasper's this time, and she'd almost forgotten. She shook her head as she entered the kitchen and put the books down to tighten the jumbleberry jam jar lids. It was a momentary slip of thought and nothing to do with a dead old man in the Square.

Rosemary paused, a hand on her throat, and frowned. No, nothing had affected her for five years. She'd worked hard to make sure of that.

TWO

Jasper Lu's kitchen table seated six people. It was first in, best sat. If dinner numbers exceeded that, the rest would sit at a wobbly card table. Mrs Lionel and Jules were already drinking Roman's apple cider when Rosemary came into the house. She hung her jacket across the back of the couch, leaned down to stroke Snowy's peppery head as the old dog groaned happily in receipt, and sat at the head of the table. Jasper handed her a glass immediately.

'Roman is on his way,' explained Jules about her husband. 'He's preparing some cuts for tomorrow. It would be a good night to come to the restaurant.'

'Cuts of what, dear?' asked Mrs Lionel.

'Goat,' said Jules. 'Local buck kids. Delicious.'

'You are so lucky Rakisha isn't here,' Jasper said.

Jules huffed good-naturedly at him. 'As if I'd mention meat in Rakisha's presence. It wouldn't be worth my life.'

Rosemary watched Jasper as he settled a plate of cheeses on the table and sat down beside her. He gave her a wan grin. 'Still not feeling well?' she said quietly.

'I'm fine.' Jasper smiled again, but Rosemary didn't see it in his eyes. 'I get exhausted.'

'You should have skipped dinner night. I would have done it.'

'But it's my turn.' He sipped at his cider. 'It makes me feel normal to do the things I would have done before I got sick.' He waved his glass around.

'Yes.' Rosemary gave him one last look before turning to Mrs Lionel, who was once more describing her find that morning, this time to Jules.

'There wasn't much to see,' Mrs Lionel said after she'd run through her description. 'Only a man, alone.'

'Poor fellow,' said Jules, shaking her head. 'I hope he didn't notice.'

'Notice what, dear?'

'That he was alone. Lonely.' She shrugged. 'Some people like being by themselves.'

'Even when they're dying?'

'I imagine so.' Jules leaned over and touched Mrs Lionel's arm. 'Perhaps especially when they're dying.'

'Well,' said Mrs Lionel, 'the police didn't seem too concerned. They asked their questions, did their forensic science business, and went on their way.'

'They'll have to follow it up.' Jules reached for the cider bottle and refilled her glass. 'It's what they have to do. Right, Rosemary?'

'They do.'

The door went again and Roman came in, ducking his head so it wouldn't touch the top architrave, and peeling his coat off at the same time. Three tiny dots of blood decorated his shirt, but Rosemary assumed that no one else would notice them among the dancing flamingos that covered the rest.

'Roman,' said Jasper. 'Good to see you.'

'Thank you.' Roman took the offered glass. 'It's been a while.'

'Three weeks, Roman,' said Mrs Lionel.

'I know, I know.' Roman sat in a chair opposite Jules and clinked his glass against hers. 'Business. It has been booming. And all that autumn produce.' He rubbed one hand through his thick, dark hair. 'Courgettes, aubergines, tomatoes. I have been feeding herds.'

'Hordes,' corrected Jules, clinking her husband's glass again.

'And herds.' Roman shook his head. 'But I don't complain. Soon it will be winter and our little town's visitors will slow down to a trickle.'

Mrs Lionel nodded. 'And that will give us a chance to plan the Mulbury Gala for spring.'

'That's right,' said Jules. 'Plenty of time.'

The door opened again, but stayed empty. Rosemary recognised the high-pitched jabbering of Patti and the low agreement of Gerry. A moment later, they both appeared, trying simultaneously to fit through the doorway. Patti managed first, leaving her diminutive husband to stagger in after. He closed the door with his hip as he struggled with a box in his arms.

'Hello Patti,' said Jasper. 'Welcome, Gerr-'

'We *would* have been here on time,' said Patti, 'but he wanted to bring it along and I said it wasn't appropriate, but he doesn't always listen to me, so he has.' She paused as she saw Rosemary. 'He said that you would want to see it.'

'Rosemary understands the significance of these sorts of things,' Gerry said, slightly too loud.

'What is it?' Jules half rose from her seat. 'A treasure chest?'

Gerry set the box on the end of the table in front of Rosemary. He brushed at its surface and a cloud of dust curled lazily upwards. 'Treasure of a sort. See?'

As the lid lifted, heads craning to see, Rosemary reached in and lifted a pile of photographs which cascaded back into the box almost immediately. 'Slippery,' she said, lifting more up and gripping them. 'What are they, Gerry?'

'Mulbury. They're photos of one hundred and fifty years' worth of our town.' The little man smiled happily. 'Perfect for putting up at the Gala.'

'Is that all?' Jules sat back and swept up her glass. 'I thought you'd found the Hand of Hela.'

'The Hand of Hela is a myth, my beautiful lady.' Roman held his glass out to Jasper, who refilled it without comment. 'It doesn't exist, Jules.'

'It does. It *did*. My grandfather held it.'

'A story told by a loving family to their-'

'-beloved children. Roman. I know what you think, but I *know*. The Hand is a family legend, and its truth is out there. It *exists*.'

'Well,' said Mrs Lionel. 'I think it's lovely, Jules. You keep that legend close to your heart.'

'You believe me, Mrs Lionel?' Jules rolled her eyes. 'Please let me know someone believes me.'

'I believe in the power of story.' Mrs Lionel reached for the box of photos and tipped it towards her. 'I believe there would be hundreds of stories if we searched through these photos properly. Where did you find them, Gerry?'

'In our cellar.' Gerry sat in the nearest chair and put his elbows on the table. 'I'd always wanted to know if there was anything behind the wooden wall at its end. Well, time has unfortunately taken its toll. When I went down there to fetch a bottle of wine, I saw that some rotting boards had fallen away and *bingo*. There was the box.'

'Our shops along Goldmarket Road all have cellars, dear,' said Mrs Lionel. 'Mine didn't have a wall, only shelves. I don't go down there now. It's too hard on my knees to use the ladder.'

'Mine has a cupboard,' said Rosemary. 'I put it there when I started *The Preserved Mulbury* to keep my pickles cool. Otherwise, there was nothing but brick walls.'

'My cellar is full of boxes,' said Jasper. 'Mainly books.'

'Of course,' said Jules. 'What else would be in there?'

Jasper picked up a photo from the top of the pile. 'Stuff from Mr Arthur. Nothing as interesting as these. Why was a box of photographs hidden in your cellar, Gerry?'

'I suspect someone stored rather than hid it. I found a receipt dated 1983, which was the year of Scarlet Tuesday, Mulbury's most terrible bushfire. I assume they thought a cellar was safe, even behind wood. There was a box of toys down there as well. You know, a couple of trucks, some plastic bricks and a jigsaw tube. Treasures of a kind.' Gerry folded his arms across his chest and shook his head sadly. 'I'll get Barry to take the toys into Big Town for the op shop.'

'Lots of things were hidden to be kept safe from the fires,' said Jules. 'Some places survived the flames, some didn't.'

'Entire families didn't survive that fire,' said Mrs Lionel thoughtfully. 'I remember well.'

'It's a significant find,' said Rosemary, flicking through the box's contents. 'They're in surprisingly good condition. Lots of photographs of the old buildings, some of which are still around.'

Mrs Lionel leaned over to see. 'Before the bushfire burnt others to the ground.' She pointed to an image. 'That's the bank where your restaurant is now, Roman. Oh, this one is Goldmarket Square with a much smaller Exceptional Tree.'

Jasper reached out for another photo. 'This one shows our shops. You can see the original veranda running across them.'

Rosemary reached out to run her finger down the image. The shop fronts were dark under its shadow, but she could just make out the rectangular outlines of their doors: the haberdashery that was now *Patricia's*, the printery that became *The Read Mulbury*, the sweet shop she now owned, and the tinker's shop before *The Green Mulbury*.

'The shops survived the fires,' said Mrs Lionel, 'but not all the shop owners. Mrs Tasher, the haberdasher-'

'*That* was her real name?' said Jasper.

Mrs Lionel silenced him with a frown. 'Mrs Tasher, who was a renowned expert in antique fasteners, perished. As did the owner of your sweet shop, Rosemary.'

'Mr Pevensey, renowned for his eucalyptus lollypops.'

'What's that building?' Jasper plucked a photo out. 'It looks magnificent.'

Mrs Lionel squinted at it. 'That's the mayoral residence, back in its heyday.'

'It's all boarded up now.'

'Yes, dear. It's certainly seen better days. Do you know they used it as an emergency centre after the fires came through? So many people suffered burns and heat stress and broken bones. They couldn't all go to Big Town or the city at the same time. They nursed people in that house.'

'Did you nurse them, Mrs Lionel? That's what you used to be.'

The older woman shook her head. 'No, dear. I wasn't a nurse by then. I was a dairy farmer. But I do remember the chaos of the time. So many people lost their homes. Mulbury swarmed with refugees.'

Rosemary sighed and tapped the photos into a neat pile to hand back to Gerry. 'The historical society in Big Town would have been very interested.'

'Shame it doesn't exist any more. It was another casualty of the fires, and no one's had enough interest to start it up again.' Gerry put the box's lid back on it. 'Rosemary, you go through them. You've got a keen eye and might find something of interest.'

'He doesn't mean now,' said Patti.

'Oh no, of course not. Some time in the future.' He tapped the box. 'I know, not the sort of thing to ponder when we're trying to have dinner.'

'Yes, put it away for now,' Patti said. 'Oh, did we get the card table?'

'We could put it up to join this table.' Jasper pushed his chair back and rose a little unsteadily.

'We'll do that,' Gerry said immediately.

'We'll help you in the kitchen,' Rosemary said with a nod to Mrs Lionel.

'Yes, dear, we'll help you.'

Rosemary lifted the box from the table and put it on the couch next to Snowy while Gerry and Patti fussed around joining tables together. Mrs Lionel followed Jasper to his kitchen and was exclaiming over the eggplant lasagne that he'd prepared on the old wood stove when Rosemary came in.

'This kitchen always reminds me of my Aunt Lilibeth,' said Rosemary as she slipped on oven mitts ready to carry the hot pot to the table.

'Especially with that old-fashioned bench.' Mrs Lionel had bread on a board and was shaking her head at Jasper's offer to take it. 'Aunt Lilibeth was a good general cook and a whiz at preserving?'

'She was resourceful. A child of the depression, she always said.'

Mrs Lionel frowned. 'It made women very resilient.'

'Yes.' Rosemary hefted the pot from the stove. 'Resilient is a good way to describe the women in our family.'

She led the kitchen procession back to the dining room where Patti and Gerry sat like children at the card table, making them lower than everyone else by a good thirty centimetres. She tried not to smile at the sight and had just put the pot down when the door opened once more.

'Kelly,' said Jasper. 'Welcome.'

Rosemary took her time to straighten and turn to the newcomer. They eyed each other for a moment before Rosemary said, 'Kelly.'

'Rosie.'

'Mary. Rose*mary*.'

'I think Rosie is so much prettier, don't you? Rosie-posey.' Kelly unwound the scarf from her neck and draped it over the couch where it lay across a snoring Snowy. 'Still, Rose*mary* does suit you better.'

'Right,' said Jasper, frowning, 'enough talk. Now we eat. Is everyone happy for me to serve?'

'Let me do it, my friend,' said Roman. 'You have prepared this delicious dish and I am very much looking forward to eating something that I haven't cooked myself.'

'I suppose you mostly eat leftovers from *The Leftover Restaurant*?' Gerry laughed.

'Tell me about it,' said Jules. 'Some nights, the customers eat everything, but mostly we manage on what they don't eat. Not that I mind.' She smiled at Roman. 'My husband is an excellent cook.'

'As Jasper is.' Roman handed the first bowl down to Gerry. 'The aroma... is it sweet basil? A hint of oregano?'

'Yes. A touch of coriander root, too. This is the first time I've made this particular recipe.'

'I also detect those bush tomatoes you grew.'

'Yes.' Jasper passed a bowl to Rosemary. 'They survived, despite my absence.'

'They probably didn't get as much water as usual.' Rosemary thanked him with a nod. 'But they grew well.'

Mrs Lionel passed the bread and there was an extended quiet as people tucked into dinner. Jasper sat on Rosemary's left next to Roman, who was next to Kelly. Mrs Lionel was on her right next to Jules, with a gap before Gerry and Patti's little table. A quorum of Mulbury residents, she thought. Franco rarely attended, but there was one more to arrive who would be there (she glanced at her watch) in two minutes.

Two minutes later, right on cue, the door opened to Barry Holden. He hadn't changed out of his mechanic's overalls, but then he had never changed out of his overalls for any Monday night dinners he'd attended. And he was always thirty minutes late to any event. Mrs Lionel joked that Barry's watch was set incorrectly, but Rosemary suspected that Barry's sole aim was to eat and not socialise.

'Barry,' said Jasper.

'Jasper,' said Barry. He sat at the corner set for him and started eating immediately.

'Any news, Barry?' asked Gerry, continuing to eat as if he didn't expect an answer.

Barry ploughed his way through half his dinner before putting his fork down to take some bread. 'Actually,' he said, 'I have some news.'

Gerry swallowed badly, causing a coughing fit that was

only assuaged by hard thumping on his back from his wife. The rest of the dinner party paused with forks suspended.

'What did you say?' said Kelly.

'News,' said Barry. 'I have some.'

'Well, out with it, dear,' said Mrs Lionel. 'Tell us.'

'I got to work this morning and found a car blocking the workshop.' At that, Barry started eating again.

Patti put her fork down with a clatter. 'Barry. You can't leave it there.'

'Well.' Barry wiped his mouth with the back of his hand. 'That's it. I rang the police, and they had it towed away.'

'You rang the police?' Gerry swivelled his chair around. 'That was quick. What if someone had accidentally parked where they shouldn't have? It might have been one of those city tourists who thinks they can park anywhere there's a patch of ground.'

Barry shrugged. 'No, it wasn't. I thought I'd better contact them straight away. You know. Because.' He took a bite of bread.

'Because, Barry?' Rosemary frowned. 'Because *why*?'

'The blood.' Barry held out his glass to Roman for a refill. 'I rang because of the blood on the back seat.'

THREE

The dinner party ground to a halt. Forks stilled as the Mulburians around Barry waited for him to continue. He wiped his bowl with the last of his bread and glanced up. 'What?' he said.

'Barry, dear,' said Mrs Lionel. 'When someone tells a story that ends with the discovery of blood covering the back seat of a car, we remain curious for more information.'

Barry's eyes widened. 'Oh. Really? Not much to say. The car had no petrol in it, so they towed it away.' He frowned. 'Mind you, they were very quick to the scene. Must have driven well above the speed limit to get to Mulbury so fast.'

'How long did it take them?' asked Gerry.

'Oh, well, can't have been more than five minutes.'

Gerry shook his head. 'Barry, no one could drive from Big Town to here in five minutes. You couldn't even helicopter it.'

Barry scratched his chin. 'Fair point.'

'They were already here, Mr Holden,' Jules said loudly.

'They were already in Mulbury because of the dead old man.'

'Eh?'

'The old man that Mrs Lionel found in the Square this morning.'

'There was a dead man in the Square this morning?'

'Yes, there was.' Kelly put her fork down into her empty bowl. 'You now see why we would like to know the complete story about the car.'

'Yes, yes, I can.' Barry scratched his chin. 'You think there might be a connection between the two events.'

Jasper put his hand up to stop Jules from saying anything more. 'Don't you think it's strange, Barry, that we needed the police twice in one morning?'

'Now I think of it, strange. Very strange.'

'Tell us the whole story, dear.' Mrs Lionel poured Barry more cider. 'From the beginning.'

'From the beginning?'

'From the time you got to work,' Rosemary said quickly, envisaging a tale of Barry's early-morning hygiene routine.

'I got to the garage at about seven-thirty and tried to pull into the drive but there was the car, smack-bang in the middle of it and hard up against the gate.'

'What sort of car?' Jasper asked. 'Old? New?'

'Early model sedan. Good one, too. Don't make them like that any more. I've worked on a few of them in my time. Good solid cars, not like these new ones with their electronic innards-'

Rosemary leaned forward. 'Had you worked on this one?'

Barry shrugged. 'Not that I can remember, which isn't saying much with my noggin.' He tapped his head and

Rosemary half expected it to ring hollow. 'Anyway, it needs a service.'

'Why do you say that?'

'Soot around the exhaust.' Barry shook his head. 'Either hadn't been serviced for a long time or some other mechanic had been taking this bloke for a ride.'

'Bloke? You mean, the car belonged to a man?' Patti laughed. 'How on earth do you know?'

Barry sat up straight. 'I've been working on cars for nearly forty years, Patricia Yale. I know these things. Men's cars, especially old ones, have a layer of dust, bits of rubbish on the floor, and old catalogues or papers or clothes on the back seat. Women's cars are full of tissues and sweet wrappers and shopping bags.'

Jules crossed her arms. 'Really, Barry, that's very sexist of you.'

Barry's face tightened. 'I don't mean that women don't drive men's cars. Or the other way around. I'm saying that, in this case, you can tell who *owns* it. This car was a man's car.'

'Why?' said Rosemary. 'What could you see?'

'General filth everywhere. Dirt and stones on the driver's seat floor. Old takeaway food wrappers. A smelly blanket. Also, a couple of sweet wrappers and a hairbrush.' He glared at Jules. 'A woman had *driven* the car, but it was *owned* by a man.'

Rosemary tapped the table, and Barry turned back to her. 'You said it had blood on the back seat.'

'That got me.'

'How did you know it was blood?'

'The colour. You know? Blood has that true red. Nothing else like it.'

'Not paint? Ink?'

Barry frowned. 'Looked like a very bloody patch to me.'

Rosemary sat back. 'There could be a logical explanation.'

'Not saying that there wasn't, but I'm not leaving a strange car blocking my driveway, filled with blood or not. I needed to get working.'

'So, Barry,' said Kelly, 'you really noticed nothing happening in the Square this morning?'

He shook his head. 'Once I got that car sorted, I went straight to work. Full day of services, you know.' He scratched at his chin again. 'Missed all that excitement having some of my own.' He picked his bowl up. 'Any more where that came from, young Jasper?'

Young Jasper, all fifty-five years of him, scooped out the last of the lasagne to Barry and stood to take the empty dish back to the kitchen. Rosemary half-rose to help him, but he shook his head. He was walking better, she noted. Still shaky but at least without a walking stick. Fatigue was his biggest problem, she knew. The more he did, the stronger he'd get, but it was a gradual business.

Patti took over the conversation with a discussion of a new bag of vintage clothes for the shop that had come her way. Rosemary let the talk wash over her. Clothing, even vintage, was not in her top ten of interests, but she appreciated Patti's passion and ability to mend the most mangled of donations to become wearable again. *Patricia's* was a place fashionistas plagued on the weekends.

After ten minutes, during which Barry had also eaten the rest of the bread, Rosemary gathered up dirty plates and took them out. Jasper was lifting a chocolate self-saucing sponge from the oven and its heavenly scent caught Rosemary as she came into the room. 'Rich,' she said approvingly.

'My order of organic cocoa arrived today.' Jasper put the dish down. 'I couldn't resist. The good news is that I even feel like eating it.'

'Good news indeed.'

Jasper paused, his hands now on the table on either side of his pudding. Rosemary waited, watching the top of his head as it bowed down as if giving grace to the cocoa. 'I don't know, Rosemary.'

'Don't know what?'

'The old man. I have a sudden feeling that it has sullied the town.'

'Jasper.' Rosemary took one step towards him. 'You aren't thinking straight. You're tired.'

Jasper pushed himself upright and ran both his hands through his long hair. 'I am trying very hard to be logical about it. I am trying to be like *you*, you know.'

'What do you mean?'

'Logical. When I think the curse is following me around, I try to be like Rosemary Exeter.'

'What curse?'

Jasper shook his head. 'You'll think I'm an idiot.'

'Possibly. Tell me about it anyway.'

He ran a finger around the edge of a dessert plate. 'Bad things happen to me.'

'Like what?'

'Like the fact that I got pneumonia and no one else did.'

'That's not a curse. That's because you went to the city when there was a particularly virulent outbreak and pneumonia was the result.'

'Rosemary, no one else in this part of the state got sick and I'm sure others went to the city during those bad days.'

Rosemary shook her head. 'Really, Jasper. My logic tells me that getting sick was a matter of viral infectiousness.'

She took the oven gloves and nudged him aside to pick up the pudding. 'My logic also demands that we should eat this delicious dessert before it goes cold. You bring the bowls.'

She caught his sad face as she carried the pudding to the table and sighed quietly. It would take more than stern words to make Jasper logical. She had noticed his morbid moods when he was tired, even before he got sick. So, he thought curses were like loyal dogs following him around? In the morning, he'd be rested, and the idea would dull. He had only to get through the night. That was a trick Rosemary had learned long ago.

With buildings that leaned towards each other in equally failing states, *Patricia's*, the bookshop, Rosemary's preserves empire and *The Green Mulbury* were like ancient siblings. The back porches of each extended out in parallel and slightly towards each other, overlooking patches of ground that ran down to the creek. Rosemary's was full of fruit trees and vegetables, while Jasper's was a huddle of berry canes and weeds. It also meant that, when Jasper couldn't sleep, he spent part of the night leaning over the balcony rail staring into the dark in full view of Rosemary from her bed. He'd never acknowledged that she was there. Perhaps he didn't realise that she left her curtains open to let the morning light in. Anyway, she'd never told him. *And I never will,* she thought.

'What do you think, Rosemary?'

Rosemary let her thoughts return to the room to find the table's occupants watching her. The pudding bowl was empty, and so were their glasses. 'What do I think about what?'

'I told you she wasn't listening,' said Jules across the table to Roman.

'She doesn't always have to listen to your sweet prattles.'

Jules frowned and turned to Rosemary. 'What do you think about having an arborist assess The Exceptional Tree next week?'

'We'd decided to have the assessment before the Mulbury Gala.'

'That's right, we had.' Jules tipped her head. 'Kelly's brother, Darren, could do it next week.'

Rosemary felt her jaw clamp and tried to relax it before anyone noticed. 'We'd already organised someone else from Big Town.'

'Oh.' Kelly touched her lips with her serviette. 'Yes, I had heard that, but Darren can do it sooner and we might as well get it done now as later.' She touched Roman's arm. 'Don't you think?'

'That Tree...' Roman sighed. 'It is the most magnificent example of nature I have ever seen.'

'Not so magnificent if a branch breaks off and lands on someone's head,' said Jules.

'Do you think that might happen?' said Patti from the depths of the card table.

'I bet it has at some stage in its thousand years.'

'We will get it assessed,' said Rosemary. 'We had an arborist booked.'

'I'll cancel him,' said Gerry.

'What if this Darren bloke says to chop it right down?'

'Barry,' said Patti, her hand on her chest.

Gerry chuckled. 'It's protected, Barry, as you know. It's number four on the National Significant Tree Register. I think they'd rather close the whole Square than have anything drastic done to the Tree.'

'Darren won't recommend anything untoward.' Kelly pushed her chair back and stood. 'He's known that Tree for as long as anyone here except for Mrs Lionel. He'll see in an instant if it needs a little trim.'

'You're leaving?' Jasper began to rise, but Kelly waved him down.

'I have an early start tomorrow. The senior cyclists are coming through at seven and they'll all want eggs. It pays to be prepared.'

'Thank you for the coffee this morning, dear,' said Mrs Lionel.

'My pleasure.' Kelly tugged her scarf out from Snowy, who had rolled onto it. 'Thank you, Jasper, for a delicious meal.' She waved to the chorus of goodbyes, ignored Rosemary completely, and left.

'That was good of her, getting Darren so promptly,' said Patti to Jasper.

He smiled. 'Very nice of her, of course.'

Under the table, Rosemary felt the warmth of his knee against her thigh. She shook her head slightly. There was nothing particularly *nice* about Kelly, but her brother was even worse.

FOUR

Rosemary arrived home a few minutes before ten o'clock. Sunny stirred from her cat bed next to the firebox and wandered over, sniffing her human's leg thoughtfully before stroking her cat cheek firmly down it.

'Sunny, you should be asleep.'

So, said the look in Sunny's green eyes, *should you.*

'I'm going now.'

But *now* was a long time in reality. Rosemary went into the shop and checked stock for a while before heading back inside and planning the next day. The last of the tomatoes sat on the bench, ready for chutney. There were pears, too, to mull and bottle. And apples to dry. So much to do.

Midnight came and Sunny was once again curled into a crescent moon on her bed while Rosemary sat up in hers trying to relax with a London thriller. It was hard to concentrate, and she couldn't quite work out why. It was less to do with dead bodies and more to do with Kelly and Darren. She hadn't seen Darren since Alasdair's memorial, not at close range anyhow. Not that she would need to see him close up next week, but her view of The Exceptional Tree was front and centre from the shop. She wouldn't be able to help noticing his lanky figure as it roamed around the ancient, twisted trunk.

She put the book down with a clunk. Darren was not the issue. Too much time had gone by to be very concerned about past humiliation. The real problem, the reason sleep seemed so remote, was that a reminder of Darren was also one of Alasdair. After her bad dream the night before, she didn't want to dwell on her husband any further.

Rosemary lay down, switched off the light, and put a pillow over her head to muffle noise as she did every night. Sleep came eventually, thankfully full of dreams of bubbling tomatoes and nothing else.

MRS LIONEL JANGLED EARLY into *The Preserved Mulbury*, genuinely seeking a jar of jumbleberry jam. 'Haven't even had breakfast yet,' she said as Rosemary handed her one.

'Neither have I. I'm still full of Jasper's delicious food.'

Mrs Lionel paused, giving her friend a firm look. 'I don't open until ten o'clock. I'll bring you back some toast, dear. My bread, your jam. Lovely.'

Rosemary nodded, but Mrs Lionel had already jangled out the door.

The tomatoes were bubbling on the stove, sending a steaming, opulent fragrance around the kitchen. It was a deep, earthy smell. That of deepening days, thought Rosemary, as the planet slowly turns away from the sun. She stirred thoughtfully and almost didn't hear the ring tone of her phone that heralded Honey Blossom.

'Mum,' said Honey as soon as Rosemary accepted the

call.

'I'm good, thanks.'

'I haven't asked you how you are yet.'

'But you will.'

'Mum. Stop it.' Honey gave her low chuckle. 'I'm glad you're good, but I wasn't really ringing for that. Are you doing anything after you close?'

'Only the usual. Gardens and kitchens and cats and-'

'Yeah, I get it. You're busy, but all that can wait. Not Sunny. She'll have to be fed. But can you help me with the tots?'

'Why?'

'Always so suspicious.'

'Yes. You normally cope quite easily with ten four-year-olds pretending to be trees.'

The silence at the other end made Rosemary lay her wooden spoon down and swap the phone into her other hand. 'Honey?'

'I haven't been feeling that well, Mum.'

'In what way?'

'In a sort of sick way. In a sort of sick *morning* way. Only it happens at night.'

This time it was Rosemary who was quiet.

'Mum? Do you get it?'

'You and Ronnie are having a baby.'

'Yes.'

In the next pause, Sunny stalked across the room, her tail straight in the air. She stopped next to Rosemary, who bent absent-mindedly to stroke the cat's lightly striped head.

'Mum?' Honey's voice had tears drenching it.

'Honey, no. It's not what you think.'

'You're not happy? About the baby?'

'On the contrary.' Rosemary sighed. 'Have you passed *that* time?'

'Yes, Mum. I didn't want to tell you until I did.' Honey was quiet for a moment. 'Mum? Are you happy for us?' she finally said in a trembling voice.

Rosemary tickled Sunny's chin. 'Honey, it's the best thing I've heard in so many years I've lost count.'

'Really?'

'Yes. Really.'

'I'm so glad. I thought for a moment that...'

'Don't be ridiculous. How could I be anything other than ecstatic about news like that?'

'Well, I suppose.' Honey had her smile back. 'So, you'll help me? This afternoon at the hall? Please, it's like I've been on a roller coaster by mid-afternoon. Any slight movement makes me chuck.'

'I was the same. Morning sickness is a misnomer.'

'That's great, Mum. Not the sickness, you helping me. I'll try to work out something else for next week.'

'Hannah might help you. She trained as a teacher, remember, before she went into the store with her sisters.'

'She's so busy with *Mulbury Feeds*. I'm thinking of stopping these classes, anyway.'

'Probably wise. You have enough of the classes for older children.'

'That's for sure.'

'I'll see you later, then.'

'Mum?'

'Yes?'

'What are you making?'

'Tomato chutney.'

'The one with the pears?'

'That's it. Aunt Lilibeth's recipe.'

'I can smell it.'

'Honey…'

'I can. The tomatoes are almost over ripe, so they smell like a hot February day. If you breathe in hard, you just get the tinge of sweetness from the pears. You put in malt vinegar. I caught that, too.'

'Honey, you're impossible.'

'Love you, Mum.'

'Love you, too.'

Rosemary slid the phone onto the bench and stirred pensively, looking up as Mrs Lionel came in holding a plate of sourdough toast. The older woman stopped in the middle of the room. 'Goodness me, Rosemary, what on earth has happened?'

'Honey's pregnant.'

'Oh.' Mrs Lionel beamed. 'What wonderful news, dear.' She stepped forward and gave Rosemary a one-armed hug while holding the toast high in one hand. When she moved back, she studied Rosemary's face. 'You don't think so?'

'Yes, I do.'

'But…?'

Rosemary shrugged.

'Ah.' Mrs Lionel put the plate down on the counter. 'There were complications last time.'

'That doesn't mean it will happen again.'

'Is there something else, dear?'

Rosemary regarded Mrs Lionel's kindly face. 'Alasdair will not know.'

Mrs Lionel's eyes softened further. 'No, he won't, and that's that.' She put a hand on Rosemary's arm and gave it a little squeeze.

'I dreamt about him.'

'Again? It's understandable.' Mrs Lionel squeezed again

and removed her hand. 'It will be a very long time before Alasdair is completely out of your thoughts. Have some breakfast, dear.'

Rosemary picked up a bit of toast and took a bite but before she could compliment her friend for the fine bread and herself on the slight tartness of the jumbleberry, the door slammed open revealing a tall man almost consumed by the bulk of his puffy, olive-green jacket.

Mrs Lionel bobbed a greeting then whisked the breakfast plate away to the kitchen, leaving Rosemary swallowing last crumbs. 'Can I help you?' she said pleasantly to the man.

He walked part way into the room and put both his hands into the pockets of his jacket. 'No, thank you. I'm just looking.'

Another one, thought Rosemary. She raised an eyebrow but politely turned away and stood at the counter scanning her stocktake results. In her peripheral vision, she watched the man walk slowly to the pickles shelf, take a jar of relish from the shelf, and finally come over to where Rosemary was immersed in multitasking.

'There is one thing,' he said.

Now that he was standing close, Rosemary saw worried creases on an otherwise smooth face and scorching blue eyes that were large and somewhat familiar. He couldn't have been much older than Honey, and yet there was an aura of unhappiness that aged him. His shoulders hunched forward slightly, and his arms were stiff. 'What would that be?' she asked, watching him closely.

'I've lost something.' The young man waved one hand towards the Square. 'I was in Mulbury the other day for the Mulbury Band Festival, and something fell from my pocket.'

Rosemary considered him. They held the Mulbury Band Festival at the football oval, but attendees often wandered into town to search for all-things-cute-and-country from the shops surrounding the Square. 'What was it you lost?'

The man started to answer, but the words caught in his dry throat. He coughed and tried again. 'A postcard.' He pulled an envelope from his pocket. 'It must have fallen out of this.'

Rosemary took what he was offering and turned it over in her hands. It was a plain white envelope like that which would hold a birthday card, only the bottom had worn through. It was easy to see how something could fall out of it. She gave it back. 'Can you give me any more information? We have postcards all over town advertising this, that and the other.' She pointed to a stand of tourist information near the door. 'It's a popular way of marketing Mulbury, especially as they show the town as it was in the Goldrush. Lots of photos of the old buildings, as you can see.'

He put the envelope back in his pocket and contemplated the stand without going over to it. The silence stretched on. Rosemary could hear Mrs Lionel stirring the chutney and humming to herself. She twitched to get back to it herself.

When it was clear she had lost the young man in some sort of lengthy daydream, she tapped him on the shoulder. He jumped.

'I'm Rosemary Exeter,' she said. 'You are...?'

'Marc Cambridge.'

'Marc. I haven't found a postcard in this shop that didn't belong to that rack over there.'

'Oh.' Marc turned to the pickles again. 'Would anyone else? I mean, I've already asked the lady in the clothes shop and the man with the books. Maybe someone found something out there?' He pointed out the front to the Square. Police tape still waved from The Exceptional Tree.

'Possibly. If so, it may have ended up in the bin.'

The young man's face blanched. 'The bin?'

'The recycling bin. In this town, we encourage everything to be recycled.' Rosemary tapped the note pad she kept on the shop counter. 'This, for example. Mrs Lionel made it out of used Christmas wrapping.'

Marc frowned again. 'Mrs Lionel?'

'Yes, dear?'

Rosemary smiled to herself. Of course, her friend wouldn't be listening deliberately to a conversation that didn't involve her, but it was hard not to hear in the echoes of the old building. 'Marc has lost a postcard. You didn't pick one up in the last week and turn it into a blotting pad?'

'A postcard.' Mrs Lionel came back into the shop. 'Not that I recall, dear. What sort of postcard? Old? New? Written on?'

'It was old,' said the young man. 'Faded. It was a picture of old buildings.'

'May I ask,' said Mrs Lionel with a kind smile, 'what was so special about it? You seem a little distressed by its loss.'

Marc rubbed a hand over his face. 'It was part of my Granny's collection. I had it safely in my pocket.'

'Your Granny won't be happy.'

His face scrunched. 'She passed away recently.'

'Our condolences, dear,' said Mrs Lionel.

Rosemary studied the man. 'I am surprised that you think you could find a small piece of card days after you lost it.'

'I want to know what happened to it.' He wriggled in

his jacket.

'I doubt you'll find out now,' said Rosemary. 'Would you like to purchase that relish?'

'Pardon?'

'The jar you put in your pocket.'

Marc pulled his hands out of his jacket pockets. 'Oh. Sorry. I forgot.' He placed the jar on the shop counter. 'No, thanks. I'll leave it for now.'

Rosemary said nothing.

Mrs Lionel frowned as the young man turned to leave. 'If we find the postcard, dear,' she called, 'could we ring you?'

Marc reached the door and pulled it open, so it jangled furiously. 'If you find it, could you please keep it for me? I'll be back.' He slipped out, making his way swiftly down the street to a red sedan parked nearby.

'Well,' said Mrs Lionel, heading back to stir the chutney, 'what do you think of that?'

'Absolute bollocks.' Rosemary took the spoon from the older woman and checked the thickness of the brew. 'A young man does not search for an old postcard for days on end, no matter how important it was to his grandmother.'

Mrs Lionel took the spoon back while Rosemary fetched jars to sterilise in the oven. Once they were stacked, Mrs Lionel gave a last stir and put the spoon on its rest. 'Maybe it wasn't only his grandmother who thought the postcard important?'

Although Rosemary didn't answer, after the jars were full and Mrs Lionel had taken her breakfast plate back home, she considered what her friend had said. There had to be a potent reason for such a postcard quest. Marc Cambridge had said he would be back. She'd be waiting for him.

FIVE

Hannah Hubbard wheeled her bicycle into the back of the produce shed and leaned it up against a stack of oaten hay. The smell was breathtaking in this corner, so fresh, sweet, and golden. She pulled a strand out of the nearest bale and stuck it in her mouth to chew as she took her helmet off. It splintered under her teeth and tasted of light bran. *Quite delicious,* she thought, *but I'm glad I'm not a horse.* She spat the blob out before heading into the office with her helmet under her arm.

'Good ride?' Holly didn't look up as her sister entered.

'Not bad. Took the High Road hill a bit fast but got to the top without stopping.' Hannah rubbed her hand through her short, pale hair. 'I think I need a new bike.'

'You've been saying that since Dad left.'

'Don't you think I deserve a new one?'

'You can do what you like.' Holly finished tallying up figures on chicken feed and tapped the pencil on her mouth, frowning. 'We need to do an order today.'

'Heather can do it. Gives her something to do besides stuffing birds.'

Finally, Holly frowned in her sister's direction. 'Give it a break.'

'Sorry. But I meant it. Sort of.' Hannah reached for the jacket hanging on a trolley and slipped it on. 'She should have other things to do each day. Even Dad said so.'

'And she does.' Holly held up a piece of paper. 'I give her a list of jobs every morning.'

'You're so good, Holly. Heather's lucky she has you for a sister.'

Holly stepped away from the counter and gave her head-taller sister an awkward hug. 'It'll be alright. *Heather* will be alright. You know why? Because she has *us* as sisters.'

Hannah squeezed Holly back. 'I know. Got crazy there for a moment. I don't suppose you've found her necklace?'

Holly shook her head. 'Nope. Lost forever, probably when she was out walking the paddocks. She's pretty upset about it.'

Hannah sighed, then stood up and peered over Holly's blonde curls. 'Hey, did you make pancakes for breakfast?'

'It's Tuesday. Pancakes on Tuesday.'

'Since when did that rule come in?'

'Monday.'

'Yesterday?'

'Yep.'

Hannah smiled. 'I love those sorts of rules.'

'How about you have a shower and I'll cook the rest of them?'

'Are you saying I stink?'

'Hannah, you've finished riding sixty kilometres-'

'-seventy.'

'-seventy kilometres on a clapped-out pre-carbon-fibre racing bike. You stink.'

'Thanks a lot.'

Holly put an arm around Hannah's synthetic-clad waist. 'And hurry up because the lucerne truck's coming and we need to unload.'

'I don't think I'd better help with that.'

'Why not?'

'I'll get stinky again.'

Holly pushed her towards the house that stood outside the produce shed. 'Not half as much as you are now.'

Hannah put her hands up in defeat and left the building.

The truck was half an hour early, so by the time Hannah emerged again, Holly was unloading, with Heather singing by her side. 'Hello, little sister,' said Hannah, swinging in to help.

'Han, Han, Hanny,' said Heather, tucking long strands of golden hair behind her ear. 'Hannah just got up.'

'I've been up for ages. I've been for a ride.' But Heather had turned away to heave a bale up on the stack, humming to herself again.

'This looks good, Paul,' said Holly to the truck driver as the last bale fell neatly on the rest and he came to have his consignment checked off.

The man grinned. 'It's been a good year in that district.' He took back the paper chit. 'Keep out of trouble, girls.'

'Why does he always say that? We aren't *girls*,' said Hannah as the truck pulled away. She puffed her breath up to blow back her spiky fringe.

'He thinks we aren't old enough to run the business.' Holly grunted as she heaved a chaff bag to display in front of the lucerne.

'Stupid man,' muttered Hannah.

'Lovely man,' said Heather. She held out her hand to

show the others a little doll twisted out of blue hay bale twine.

'You know,' said Holly thoughtfully, 'we could sell those in the shop. Rustic farm charm, that sort of thing.'

'Twine dolls will not sell to the people who come in to buy chook, dog and horse food.' Hannah shifted another chaff bag to lean against the first.

'I'd buy one,' said Heather, standing the doll up in her palm.

'You would, wouldn't you? Although you don't have to.' Hannah put her hand out to smooth her sister's hair away from her face. 'People would give it to you, anyway.'

Heather smiled at her sister. 'When's Dad coming home?'

Hannah cast a swift glance at Holly.

'We don't know,' said Holly gruffly. 'He said he'd be back in autumn and we're only in the middle of it.'

'He hasn't called me.' Heather drifted off towards her taxidermy room that adjoined the office with her sisters in tow.

'He hasn't called any of us for ages,' said Hannah.

'We shouldn't expect him to call at all.' Holly flicked a hair tie off her wrist and pulled her curls back into a rough ponytail. 'Doesn't matter, we're fine as we are. We run this place just as good as he did.'

Hannah laughed, her roughness upsetting some magpies that investigated the shed. 'As *good* as he did? We are *so* much better at this than he was. It's ridiculous.'

Holly scowled. 'You're right. We are *fantastic* at running this business.'

'Dad's good at other things. Music. Singing. Disappearing. Reappearing when he runs out of money.'

Holly opened her mouth to reply, but Heather came out

of the office, pointing at something in the corner of the shed. The twine doll was now pinned in her hair, looking like a child lost in a cornfield.

Holly caught her arm. 'What is it, Heather?'

'See?'

'See what?' said Holly and Hannah together, following the pointing finger.

'There.'

There was a row of pallets usually stacked with chicken feed in tight white bags. The pallets were nearly empty, with the bags at the front missing here and there like a row of boxer's teeth. 'We need to order more,' said Hannah.

'There-ere,' said Heather in a singsong voice.

'Okay, we're going to see what we can find.' Holly stopped Heather with an outstretched arm. 'You stay there.' She motioned Hannah forward.

'It's another of her *imaginings*,' said Hannah quietly as they walked towards the pallets.

'Even so,' said Holly, barely moving her lips. 'We have to go along with it.'

They reached the pallets and peered over the bags.

'Nothing,' said Hannah.

'Wait.' Holly scrambled over the remaining bags and crouched down so that the others could barely see her.

'What is it?' Hannah followed, careful to not slide onto her sister, whose attention seemed to be on the floor between the wooden slats.

Holly leaned back, pulling something up with her. 'It was tossed down there.'

'Give me a look.' Hannah took it from Holly and spread the item out. 'A sleeping bag?'

'There's more.' Holly crawled forward to the back of the pallets. 'A coat and a blanket.'

'Someone's stashed their things here?'

'It's pretty messy, like stuff's been thrown in there.' Holly held up a drawstring bag stuffed full of clothes. 'A pillow.'

'I don't want people sleeping on our feed.'

'People have to sleep somewhere. At least it's out of the wind in here.'

'You don't think they're that dead man's things?'

'Could be.'

'Hannah? Holly? Dead man?'

Both women looked up at their sister, who still stood near the office but with her hands folded over her chest. Even from that distance, they could see she was shaking.

'Did she know about the old man?' said Hannah quietly to Holly.

'I didn't tell her. Did you?'

'No.' Hannah chewed her lip. 'We should have broken it to her more gently.'

'It's okay, Heather,' called Holly. 'Someone's clothes are back here. A poor old homeless man died today under The Exceptional Tree. They could be his things.'

'Joe.'

'What did she say?' Holly turned to a grim-faced Hannah.

'I think she said "no".'

They scrambled back over the chicken food and rushed to Heather. 'It's okay. The poor old fellow is at rest now.'

Heather trembled. 'Nooooo.'

'Oh, crumbs,' said Hannah. 'She's going off again.'

Holly nodded towards the street outside. 'I think we need Mrs Lionel.'

'I'll go.' Hannah was already halfway out of the shed when Holly called after her. 'And Rosemary.'

Hannah didn't have to go far to find Mrs Lionel. She was in the shop next door, calmly melting yellow soap into laundry liquid. She stopped stirring as Hannah crashed through the shop door, making the croaking frog at the door do its thing. 'Mrs Lionel, it's Heather.'

Mrs Lionel turned off the stove and made for the door, beating the younger woman out. She hurried to the shed as Hannah went to *The Preserved Mulbury* to find Rosemary.

'Rosemary, it's-'

But Rosemary didn't need to hear. Chutney finished, she was thinking about figs, but Hannah's alarmed appearance meant only one thing.

'Where is she?'

'In the shed.'

They left the shop together and ran down the path. 'What happened?'

'We found stuff behind the bags. Someone's been living there, probably the old homeless man.'

They reached the shed and slowed to a walk at Holly's waving arm. Mrs Lionel had Heather's head on her shoulder and the young woman was sobbing noisily into it. With some difficulty, Rosemary shepherded them into the office and sat Mrs Lionel and Heather on the little couch next to the kitchenette.

Holly whispered the tale of the morning so far to Rosemary as Mrs Lionel listened in over Heather's noisy distress. 'She heard us say the old man was dead and got upset.'

Rosemary nodded, more to show she had listened than in agreement. 'Anything to identify the clothing as the man's?'

'I don't know. We left it over there.' Holly tipped her head towards the pallet.

Hannah beat them to it, running over and leaping the

feed bags to pull the sleeping bag and other things out for Rosemary to inspect. The sleeping bag was an older style, thick but not warm, and definitely not waterproof, as the dampness was obvious to Rosemary, the material spongy under her fingers. The drawstring tote held an array of threadbare shirts, socks with holes in the toes, and an equally thin tailored suit with the scrap of a hanky in its coat pocket. Nothing identified the owner and even the clothing labels were too worn to be decipherable. Rosemary drew the strings again.

'What do you think, Rosemary? Why is Heather so upset about an old man she doesn't even know?' Hannah's hair spiked high on her head in unhappiness as she trawled her fingers through it. 'It's been a while since she's been like this.'

'When was the last time?'

'Dad had an accident up north, but we didn't know about it for a month, when he finally wrote us a letter. Heather cried for twenty-eight days, and we had no clue why. Once he wrote and we found out that he was alright, she stopped. She feels things more deeply than anyone else.'

Rosemary tied a loose knot in the drawstring. 'These clothes could be the dead man's. They'll have to go to the police.'

The howling from the office continued, and Hannah's shoulders drooped. 'Heather didn't even know the man. What does it mean that she's so upset?'

'It means,' said Holly, 'that we have to put up with this until we find out what it all means.'

Rosemary said nothing.

Holly put her hands over her face. 'I'm not sure I can stand it. She can go on like this for ages.'

Hannah bit her lip. 'Maybe Mrs Lionel will have her again.'

'We can't fob her off to poor Mrs Lionel.'

'Yes, we can.' Hannah turned to Rosemary. 'We could, don't you think? Sometimes?'

But Rosemary thought it wouldn't matter whether Heather was with Mrs Lionel, at home with her sisters, or being treated in a centre for distressed young women. Heather Hubbard knew something that no one else did, and until it sorted itself, the young woman would stay upset.

SIX

Wednesday was the second busiest day of the week for Mulbury because of the senior citizen buses. Why every senior citizen club in the vicinity had bus trips on a Wednesday had puzzled Rosemary from the first day it happened. Then she decided she didn't care. Sell a lot on Sunday, restock, sell nearly as much on Wednesday. She'd heard that many senior citizens didn't have two coins to rub together, but this was not the fate of those who boarded the buses. Coins—and notes, and plastic cards—slipped through their fingers as if covered in olive oil.

The buses began their arrival at about morning teatime. This meant that crowds came off their transport and made beelines for either Rakisha's vegetarian café, *The Sweet Potato,* or Kelly's *Mullings of Mulbury.* After about thirty minutes, they emerged revitalised and split into groups making for Jasper's *The Read Mulbury* bookshop, Rosemary's *The Preserved Mulbury* or Mrs Lionel's *The Green Mulbury.* If they were fashionistas, they made a beeline to Patricia's. Closer to lunchtime, *Franco's Patisserie* and *The Leftover Restaurant* started filling up, and there was peace in Goldmarket Square for about an hour. Then one bus would honk its horn, followed by the pod of others, and the visitors would make last-minute dashes to shops they hadn't yet visited before climbing on board and exiting for the week. By three o'clock, Mulbury was quiet again and shop-keepers took a tally. Even Hannah, Holly, and Heather's *Mulbury Feeds* store did well on a Wednesday, at least in the budgie and gourmet cat-food lines.

Rosemary kept her eyes open for Marc Cambridge. His tall youthfulness would have stood out in the sea of day trippers, but he didn't appear.

At five minutes past three o'clock, Honey rang. 'Hello, Mum. Quiet again?'

'Yes. All gone.'

'Good day?'

Rosemary scanned the shelves, noting the gaps where her apricot and strawberry conserves had been. 'At first glance, yes.'

'That's good.'

'How are you feeling, Honey?'

'Okay. Better now since I cancelled those tot classes. Thanks again for helping.'

Rosemary closed her eyes briefly at the memory of the overjoyed scrabble of little children careering around the hall like banshees. 'That's quite alright.'

'I know, it was dreadful.' Honey laughed. 'The classes are always like that. Usually, I like them, but you can see that they're currently a bit exhausting.'

'You've done a sensible thing, closing them for now.'

'I'd stop them over winter anyhow.'

'Yes.'

There was a pause. 'Mum, they've got Ronnie working on the old man's death.'

Rosemary nodded, forgetting for a moment that Honey was on the phone. Of course, the police would use Ronnie. An old man's death with no obvious signs of a misdemeanour was not a priority for ordinary police work so Ronnie's private investigator company had another job.

'Mum? Did you hear me?'

'Yes, Honey. Ronnie has the job. That's good for you?'

'Yes, and it makes a change from insurance fraud. When Ronnie started this business, he thought it would be more...'

'Exciting?'

'Exactly. Not much fun stalking people with a long lens who are going about their own business.'

'Sounds degrading.'

'To Ronnie and the person being stalked alike. They warned him when he did his PI course that the work was mostly drudgery.'

'Lucky he has his Uncle Geoffrey then.'

'*Detective* Geoffrey. He's been able to put a bit of work Ronnie's way. I like him. He's gruff, but nice.'

'What's the main issue with this case?'

'They're waiting on the coroner's report to see whether death is from natural causes, but Ronnie's job is to identify the man. He's not foremost in the missing persons database, meaning he could have been reported a long time ago, if at all.'

'That will keep Ronnie very busy.'

'Especially as he still has his other jobs.'

The door jangled and Mrs Lionel entered the shop, Heather clutching her arm. Mrs Lionel saw Rosemary on the phone and pointed into the kitchen. Rosemary waved her in. As Mrs Lionel walked past, she rolled her eyes. Rosemary gave a small smile. Heather was leaning hard on the older woman's arm, and it was clearly time for a break.

'I need to go, Honey.'

'Okay, Mum.' A beat passed as Honey paused. 'What are you making now?'

Rosemary glanced through the kitchen door to the rows of drooping figs sitting in their egg carton confinement. 'Fig and vanilla jam. It's not on yet.'

'Oh. I can smell it though.'

'Honey, you definitely can't smell something that isn't even cooking.'

'I can. The figs are rich and golden, and they have the scent of yellow gum honey mixed with an intoxicating sweet liqueur. You don't have to add the vanilla, Mum. Only lime juice. It'll be better.'

'I already have fig and lime.'

'You said you'd nearly sold out. Make more.'

Rosemary narrowed her eyes at her shelves. 'You're right.'

'I know. Love you, Mum.'

'Love you, too.'

Rosemary put her phone in her pocket and went in search of Mrs Lionel. She was easy to trace. From the couch came a long, low moaning, a bit like a cow pining for her calf. Mrs Lionel had Heather on her shoulder, patting her back in an endless, patient rhythm.

'How long has she been making that noise for?'

Mrs Lionel strained to see Rosemary over her shoulder. 'She's alright during the night, falls asleep quickly, poor love. As soon as she wakes, though, she gets more and more miserable. By lunchtime she's crying, by now she's moaning. Then she falls asleep for a bit and wakes up blank-eyed but silent.' The older woman wriggled Heather away until the girl had her head on a pillow. 'I thought the walk might make her stop, but she was leaning on me too heavily. Hope you don't mind.'

'Leave her there for a bit. I'll make you a cuppa.'

'Thanks, dear. I'll go and lock up the shop while you boil the kettle.' Mrs Lionel heaved herself from the couch. 'I'll take her back to her sisters tonight for a bit of a rest myself.'

Rosemary sliced a teacake she'd made earlier and had pieces on a tray with the teapot by the time Mrs Lionel came back in. They went out on Rosemary's balcony, leaving the door ajar to keep ears on Heather. Mrs Lionel bit into the cake with delight. 'Delicious.'

'Aunt Lilibeth's recipe. She sifts her flour thrice.'

'Thrice?' Mrs Lionel chuckled. 'Haven't heard anyone say *thrice* in a long time.'

They ate in silence for a while, looking out over Rosemary's garden acreage. Sunny came out of nowhere and curled herself on the seat beside her mistress, equally contemplating the placid autumn garden with its decorations of plump fawn chickens and slim white ducks. Each night, the poultry wandered back into their houses and Rosemary locked them up against foxes. They rewarded her with so many eggs she could almost keep Roman and Jules completely in restaurant ingredients for the entire week.

'Do you think, dear,' began Mrs Lionel, 'that the sisters are managing while Richard's away?'

'Yes, they're fine.'

Mrs Lionel pressed her lips together momentarily. 'What about Jasper, then? Is the bookshop too much for him at this stage?'

'He closes early if he has to. Sometimes for lunch as well. He's managing.'

'And the others? Are they alright?'

Rosemary turned to her friend, collecting Sunny onto her lap in the same motion. 'Why are you worrying? Everyone is fine.'

Mrs Lionel shrugged and tilted her head towards the inside of the house. 'It's Heather, I suppose. When she gets upset like this, it rattles me. I have strange dreams. I see problems in everyone's life.'

'You shouldn't look after her then.'

'I promised their mother I'd keep an eye on the girls.'

'They're grown. You don't need to any more.'

'This one isn't grown.' Again, Mrs Lionel indicated the house.

'She's twenty-one.'

'Only in years.' Mrs Lionel put a hand to her cheek and shook her head. 'She won't ever be *grown*, not in the usual sense. She's of another time, another parallel perhaps.'

'That makes little sense.'

'It's not meant to. *Heather* makes little sense. She's one from a fantasy novel with its plot full of magic. If she was in King Arthur's time, she'd be Morgana's apprentice.'

Rosemary gave a brief nod. Not that she believed in magic, but she could see what Mrs Lionel meant. Heather was one of those in the wrong place and time, but where she was meant to be was difficult to say. 'You should stop feeling the responsibility that should be Richard Hubbard's.'

'Richard knows he can't cope. That's why he leaves, dear. His music is his excuse, but his reason is that it's too hard.' Mrs Lionel sighed. 'It'll all work out, I suppose.'

'Ronnie has the old man's case.'

'For what reason, dear?'

'To identify him.'

Mrs Lionel chewed thoughtfully. 'I'm glad Ronnie's on

to it. Maybe once they identify the poor fellow and reunite him with his family, Heather will find some peace.'

'Do you think that's what the issue is?'

'What else could it be?'

Rosemary stroked the deep orange line that ran from Sunny's head to the middle of her back. The cat purred in satisfaction.

'You don't think it is, do you, Rosemary?'

'Why would she get so upset about an old man's death?'

'You don't think he died naturally, do you?"

'No.'

'Keeping your mind open, dear?'

'Always.'

From inside, Heather gave one deep groan and then resumed her lowing. Mrs Lionel took another slice of cake. 'I've always admired your mind, Rosemary Exeter. It doesn't allow emotion to blur your thoughts.'

'I try not to let it.'

The noise of a sliding door opening made both women turn their heads. Jasper Lu appeared on his balcony, walking right up to the edge and putting both hands on the rail as if finding it difficult to breathe.

'Jasper?' called Mrs Lionel. 'Are you alright, dear?'

It took Jasper a moment to locate the voice, but a smile brightened his face when he saw them. 'Oh, sorry, I had a coughing fit in reaction to a box of particularly dusty books. A senior brought them in. Said he wanted nothing for them. Now I know why. They're filthy.'

'Come and join us for a cup of tea. We have plenty of cake.'

'Cake? Well, I'll be over.' Jasper waved his hand and went back inside.

'He hasn't got his appetite back,' Rosemary said.

'I know, dear. But he needs company.' Mrs Lionel reached out and put one hand on Sunny's warm back. 'Perhaps he could do with a cat?'

'He has Snowy.'

Mrs Lionel pursed her lips and drank the rest of her tea before saying, 'Old dogs that sleep all day and night are company of a kind but not quite like a dog that's at your side all the time.'

Rosemary looked at her friend. 'You miss Percy? He died over twelve months ago.'

Mrs Lionel poured herself more tea. 'I don't miss him as much as you think.'

'What do you mean?'

The older woman put a dot of milk into her cup. 'Don't think less of me.'

'I would always think nothing but the best of you.'

Mrs Lionel stirred the milk in. 'Well, dear, Percy is still with me.'

Rosemary folded her arms. Mrs Lionel picked her cup up and sipped.

'Percy is still with you.'

'Yes, dear, that's what I said.' Mrs Lionel sat the cup back down. 'I see him.'

'A ghost dog?'

'I don't know. It doesn't matter what you call him, the fact of the matter is that he's here.' Mrs Lionel lifted her head and stared at Rosemary. 'With me.'

'Now?'

'No, dear. He's at home, waiting for me.'

Below the balcony, ducks quacked, and a chicken heralded a new egg with a long cackling song. Rosemary let her arms relax. 'Alright.'

'That's all you can say?'

'Do you want me to say more?'

'No, I don't want you to say anything else.' Mrs Lionel gave Rosemary a quick grin. 'I'm not mad.'

'I know.'

'But, please, don't mention it to the others.'

'They would understand.'

'Perhaps.' Mrs Lionel finished her tea. 'I don't want that tested. I can trust you.'

Rosemary reached across and grabbed her friend's hand. 'That you can.'

'Thank you.' Mrs Lionel squeezed Rosemary's hand back. 'Now, where's that Jasper?'

After quite a few minutes in which Jasper Lu did not appear, Mrs Lionel looked pointedly at Rosemary, who stood up, tipping Sunny gently on to the seat. 'I'll go.'

'Thank you, Rosemary.' Mrs Lionel shook her head. 'I do worry about that man.'

Rosemary jangled out from her shop and creaked her way into Jasper's. It was dull in there; the curtains drawn and only a desk lamp on. She stood still for a moment until she heard the squeak of a chair across floorboards coming from the kitchen. She walked on. There was Jasper, a box of old books on the kitchen table and a broad smile on his face.

'Rosemary,' he said when she came out of the gloom into the light. 'You'll never guess.'

'First edition?'

Jasper shook his head, making his long hair dance across his face. 'First *printing* of first edition.' He held up a thick, hardcover book.

SEVEN

When Jasper Lu first took over the bookshop, he was what Roman called a 'dark hearse' until Jules corrected him. After their first almost-awkward interaction, Rosemary thought she should see what he'd done to eradicate grumpy Mr Arthur's presence. Gone were the plastic shelving and matching rotating wire stands. Instead, hardwood bookcases and enticing wooden crates with rows of spine-up best-sellers crowded the room. Jasper kept newer titles to a minimum, and spruiked forgotten ones, displaying his stock online as well, as business boomed. He had collections around all topics, fiction and non-fiction, but his speculative fiction section was renowned. *The Read Mulbury* was the place for geeks, Arthurians, and cosplayers.

Jasper also had an eye for good deals.

Rosemary couldn't read the book title from where she stood. 'What's it called, Jasper?'

Jasper put the book down carefully on the table and reached behind him for a pair of white cotton gloves. He pulled them on slowly, tucking each finger in carefully, and picked the book up again. Just as cautiously, he took the dust cover off to reveal a perfect-condition, hardcover edition.

Rosemary peered at the cover. 'Why does that title ring a bell?'

'You took a copy of it the other day.' Jasper turned the book over lovingly. 'A Space Western by T. G. G. Duncan?'

'*Forces and Horses*. I remember now. I've got that one.'

'Not *this* one. Not this first.' Jasper caressed the cover. 'Not this beauty.'

Rosemary refrained from commenting on Jasper's overly lavish petting, but he saw her face and flushed that Jasper-tone of embarrassed crimson. 'It must be an excellent find.'

'Rosemary, my display magnet worked. I've had loads of speculative fiction books come in since Monday, but I truly was not expecting this.' He stroked the cover again. 'They published this book in 1959. Only fifty first edition first print copies. This is one of them.'

He's going to swoon, thought Rosemary, and stepped forward to get him a glass of water. Jasper put the book carefully down inside its dust cover and tugged off his gloves. He stood up and took the water well away from the table, drinking it all in one gulp.

'Mrs Lionel worries about you,' said Rosemary.

'She worries about everyone in this town.'

'Yes.'

'Who worries about her?'

'I do.'

Jasper smiled and hooked dark strands of hair behind an ear. 'Yes, I believe you do. I think that's wonderful. Do you worry about *everyone* in this town?'

'No.' From the chagrined expression on Jasper's face, Rosemary knew she'd answered too quickly. 'Not everyone needs worrying about, Jasper. You know that perfectly well.'

'Do I?' He smiled and put the glass down. 'That's the biggest difference between you and me, Rosemary. I think that, at times, *everyone* needs to be worried about.'

Rosemary humphed. 'Come to my place and have cake with Mrs Lionel.' She turned without checking he was following and went back out the way she'd come. As she walked through her lounge room, she noted Heather was now awake and staring at the wall in front of her. Rosemary paused to tuck a rug around the young woman's shoulders and by that time Jasper was in the house as well. She pointed to the balcony and let him go ahead, flicking the kettle on again as she passed.

Jasper told the tale of the first book to Mrs Lionel, who recognised the author and was much more impressed than Rosemary had been. The sun was low in the sky by the time the teacake and storytelling had finished.

'I'd better go, dears.' Mrs Lionel stood up stiffly. 'I'll take Heather back to the girls.'

'I can help you, Mrs Lionel.' Jasper bounded up, then staggered backwards. Rosemary caught his arm to steady him.

'You don't need to be doing anything extra, and it could take me a while to extricate myself from the poor girl's clutches.' Mrs Lionel smoothed her skirt down and put her shoulders back. 'You get home, Jasper Lu, and have a rest. Wednesdays are very busy, and you need to take it easy.'

'Well,' said Jasper as Rosemary let him go, 'I'm mostly okay, but by the end of the day I find myself exhausted.'

'It's being on your feet all day. It does it to us all, even the toughest ones.' Mrs Lionel gave Rosemary a cheeky grin.

'I'll help you with Heather,' said Rosemary.

'Thank you, dear.'

Jasper left with a slight bow, and Rosemary took Heather's arm to guide her from the couch. The young woman stood willingly enough but then noticed who it was touching her and started moaning again, looking around for Mrs Lionel. At last, one woman on either side of the distraught girl, they walked out the door and down the pavement to *Mulbury Feeds*.

'She's back,' Rosemary heard Hannah yell to Holly.

'Sound a bit more enthusiastic, can't you?' Holly came out of the office with a concerned frown. Hannah walked behind, yawning and rubbing her face.

'Here she is, dears.' Mrs Lionel took Heather's hand and gave it to Holly, who clasped it in both hers.

'Any change?'

'No, still the same.'

Rosemary didn't miss the desperate glance Holly threw at Hannah, but to Hannah's credit, she took Heather's hand out of her sister's and said, 'Hello, little sis. I've got something for you. Apple pie with custard, your favourite. I've spent all day slaving in the kitchen making treats for you...' Her voice trailed off as she led Heather toward the house tucked behind the huge produce shed.

Holly sighed. 'I don't know what to do.'

'You've got two choices,' said Rosemary. 'Put her in hospital or leave her here.'

'I've got one choice, you mean.' Holly shook her head. 'She's okay here where we can watch her. I don't trust that they'll look after her anywhere else. I don't know how long this is going to go on for.'

'We're by your side,' said Mrs Lionel. 'You aren't alone, you and Hannah.'

'I know. The whole town is great. We get leftovers from Kelly and Rakisha all the time, and Jasper makes sure we have enough to read. You give us all the jam we can eat, Rosemary, and Mrs Lionel...' Holly smiled wanly. 'Well, I really don't know what we'd do without everyone.'

'You would actually be fine, you know.' Mrs Lionel patted Holly's shoulder. 'You three are very strong women.'

Holly stood a little taller. 'Thank you. Thanks for everything.'

'It's my pleasure.'

Mrs Lionel and Rosemary left the three sisters to their evening and walked away from the fresh grassy smells of the produce shed. 'Take a turn around the Square with me, Rosemary,' said the older woman. 'I haven't paid homage to The Exceptional Tree today.'

'You swept the Square this morning?'

'No, I didn't. I was too worried about leaving Heather by herself.'

Rosemary nodded, not wanting to repeat she thought it too much to care for Heather. They walked into the Square and stood under the massive Tree, marvelling at its ancient fused and twisted branches. Mrs Lionel stepped up to its truck and put her hands flat against its silver skin, spreading her fingers wide. Rosemary waited a moment, then joined her, placing her hands in the same way. The Tree was warm, thrumming with life despite the chilly evening. Rosemary closed her eyes.

'Magnificent old thing, isn't it?'

Rosemary snapped back, her hands at her sides in fists. She hadn't needed to see who it was that spoke. 'Kelly,' she said.

'Rosemary.' Kelly shrugged her fur-lined hood over her head a little more. 'Mrs Lionel. Saying hello to the Tree?'

'Paying our respects to it, dear.' Mrs Lionel gave the trunk a gentle pat and turned to the other woman. 'How was trade today?'

'Wonderful Wednesday, I call it.' Kelly smiled. 'They're so hungry when they get here it's like they've walked all the way from Big Town instead of being driven. Greedy things.'

'They just enjoy being out.' Mrs Lionel tugged her cardigan around her shoulders against the growing chill. 'Many of them eat alone and it's a real treat to be out.'

'Yes, well, so many of them are overweight. I suspect they eat all the time, alone or not. Still,' Kelly shrugged, 'I think it's great.'

'You put your most expensive items on the Wednesday menu,' said Rosemary evenly.

Kelly frowned. 'That's a dreadful thing to say.'

'I have that wrong?'

'My menu depends on what I have available, Rosemary Exeter. Wednesday is mid-week and I have to decide on what to serve to allow a range of items across the week.'

Rosemary said nothing, but one eyebrow went up.

'You have delicious items every day,' said Mrs Lionel with a stern glance at Rosemary. 'If you'll forgive me, I'll be heading back. It's quite cold, isn't it?'

'Might even be a frost tonight.' Kelly tilted her head at Rosemary. 'I hope you've harvested all you can, for it might get bitten.'

'I've got it under control.'

'Good for you.' Kelly hunched her coat up again. 'Of course you have. Goodbye, ladies.'

Mrs Lionel took Rosemary's arm as they crossed the gutter. Not, Rosemary thought, because she needed steadying, but as a reminder not to be stirred up by Kelly Flanagan. She let it go once they had crossed the road.

'What are you doing this evening, Rosemary?' Mrs Lionel asked as they parted ways on the footpath.

'Fig jam tonight.'

'With lime?'

'You've been talking to Honey.'

Mrs Lionel smiled. 'I rang her to see how she was going.'

'She's fine.'

'Yes, she is.' The older woman waved goodbye and opened the door of her shop, the frog croaking in greeting.

Rosemary went inside and locked the front door. The blind gave her a little grief as she tried to pull it down over the window, so it wasn't until she'd fought with it and won that she noticed the rectangular piece of cardboard lying a metre from the door as if pushed hurriedly underneath. She picked it up, brushing a little dirt from its surface.

It was a postcard.

EIGHT

Rosemary waited impatiently for Marc Cambridge to return, but more time ticked on, and the only visitors were the rest of the weekday crowd—wandering nomads, plenty of time on their hands—and the steadfast regulars who frequented *Patricia's*. She kept the postcard at the back of her till but not before studying it carefully first.

The postcard was dirty and scuffed, with ragged edges and brown splotches decorating its underside. Nonetheless, Rosemary recognised the picture as a reproduction of one from Gerry's box of photographs, a common enough image in Mulbury's marketing. The picture might have dated back to the gold rush, but the postcard's manufacturing was more recent, and it was addressed to a Mrs Cambridge in the city. What interested Rosemary most was the indentations of a cross pressed into the front directly over the doorway to the sweet shop, which was now *The Preserved Mulbury*.

On Friday, the door jangled, and Ronnie tripped in. Rosemary was lining the shelves with her recently finished fig jam and smiled at the sound. She didn't need to turn around to know who it was. The mat outside the door was

Ronnie's nemesis. *I hope*, she thought, *that the baby has Honey's grace.*

'Hello, Rosemary.' Ronnie straightened his shirt over his belly and swept hair from his eyes.

'Ronnie. You've got a new job, Honey said.'

'Yes. Trying to find out who John Doe is, besides being John Doe because John Doe isn't...' he stopped at Rosemary's frown.

'It will be good to find out who the dead man was.' Rosemary pointed to the door to the kitchen. 'Tea?'

'No, but thank you. I got a coffee from *Sweet Potato*, although I'm not sure it was coffee.' Ronnie rubbed his stomach. 'It tasted gritty.'

'Rakisha makes her own beverages. I believe she uses dried legumes for her coffee.'

'Not coffee beans then?'

Rosemary shook her head. 'Something much more sustainable. Probably a pea of some sort.'

Ronnie's red face drained. 'Perhaps I will have a cup of tea. Peas and I, well, we don't always mix well.'

Rosemary made her grandchild-to-be's father a decent cup of black tea and watched the colour come back to his face. Not that colour was ever away from Ronnie's face for long, but he could change shades like a chameleon. It set off his strawberry blonde hair in interesting ways.

Once he'd settled and had eaten three oat biscuits, he pulled a notebook from his oversized jacket. 'I thought I would start by interviewing those who saw the man on the day he was discovered. You, for example, Rosemary. If you don't mind.'

Rosemary didn't reply. *The crash test interview dummy,* she thought to herself.

Ronnie coughed and scribbled his pen on a page to

make sure it worked. 'What did he look like when you saw him?'

'Start with the day and time, Ronnie. It breaks the ice and makes people think back to that moment.'

'Oh, okay.' Ronnie coughed again and held his pen up. 'What day and time did you see him?'

'It was Monday just gone, at about seven-thirty in the morning.'

'And what were you doing in Goldmarket Square at that time?'

'Mrs Lionel came to my door and asked me to the Square to see what she had found.'

'And who is Mrs Lionel?'

'You know who Mrs Lionel is.'

Ronnie lowered his notebook. 'Please, Rosemary. I'm practising.'

'Practising is a great idea.' Rosemary sat up straight. 'Mrs Lionel is my best friend, my next-door neighbour, and the owner of *The Green Mulbury*.'

'And she came to your door and asked you to the Square to see what she had found?'

'That's what I said.'

'I know,' said Ronnie in a whisper. 'I remembered it word for word.'

'Keep going.'

'Right. And what had Mrs Lionel found in the Square?'

'A dead man under The Exceptional Tree.'

'What did this dead man look like?'

'Dead.'

Ronnie went to lower his notebook again and Rosemary raised her hand to stop him.

'He was lying on his back with his arms straight out on either side. He wore a suit coat, frayed at the elbows, double-breasted. His shirt buttoned to his neck and had once been light blue, although was now rimmed with dirt. His trousers matched his jacket and were pleated, probably from the 1980s era. His shoes were newer, though, with the shine still around the laces. They were too big because there were gaps around his ankles. They were black but dusty.'

'You see?' Ronnie's grin revealed straight, square teeth, the best feature of his colourful face. 'You notice so much, Rosemary. More than anyone else.'

'You haven't interviewed anyone else.'

'They won't tell me anything more useful.'

'Hmmm,' said Rosemary. 'Also, there was a feather in his top pocket.'

'A feather?'

'Yes. Black and white. Possibly a magpie's.'

'What does that mean?'

'He collected feathers.'

Ronnie stared at her.

'I don't know what it means, Ronnie. I'm surmising. Mrs Lionel will tell you about the man's past.'

'How?'

'She reads faces well.'

Ronnie tapped his pen on his notebook. 'Well, before I get to her, is there anything else you can tell me?'

'He was cold.'

'Cold?'

'As in very dead.'

'So, he died during the night because he wasn't there in the evening.'

'Or they shifted him.'

Ronnie frowned. 'The coroner will work on that bit. I'm meant to find out who he was.'

Rosemary moved the empty teacups to the sink. 'Let's go and see Mrs Lionel. She'll be of more use than me.'

They didn't have to go far. Mrs Lionel was sweeping the footpath free of leaves. The plane trees lining the street had decided it was indeed nearly winter and begun a flurry of leaf disposal. She stood straight as Rosemary and Ronnie jangled out of the shop and propped the broom against her shop window frame. 'Ronnie, dear. I hear congratulations are in order.'

'Yes, I think the police are really finding me useful.'

'Pardon?'

Ronnie's forehead creased in puzzlement until Mrs Lionel's words sank right in. 'Oh.' he said. 'You mean the baby.' His face glowed crimson. 'Yes, we're really stoked. Can you imagine me a daddy?'

Rosemary tried hard not to catch Mrs Lionel's eye who, she glimpsed from the edge of her vision, was trying hard not to catch her eye. 'It's wonderful news, dear. You know you can count on me as a babysitter.'

'Thank you, Mrs Lionel.' Ronnie flipped open his notebook and lowered his voice. 'I'm here on official business.'

'Yes, dear. Do you want to come inside, or will we keep standing in the street?'

'Could we go inside? It's cold today.'

The wind was bitter, thought Rosemary, despite the sunny day. She followed Ronnie and Mrs Lionel into the shop, making the frog launch into a frenzy of electronic croaking, and inspected the shelves while Mrs Lionel settled on the stool she kept behind the counter. Ronnie placed his notebook carefully on top of a stack of vinegar bottles.

'Mrs Lionel, I believe you know this woman?' Ronnie pointed his pen at Rosemary.

'Ronnie, you know I do.'

'For the record?'

Mrs Lionel's sigh echoed around the shop. 'Yes, I know this woman. She is Rosemary Exeter, my best friend, next-door neighbour, and owner of *The Preserved Mulbury*.'

Ronnie nodded seriously. 'Ms Exeter tells me you found the man's body in Goldmarket Square on Monday morning.'

'That's right, dear.'

'Could you tell me what you saw?'

'A man, lying on his back, face turned up to peer into The Exceptional Tree except, of course, he was dead.' Mrs Lionel shrugged. 'At least his last view of this world was our beautiful Tree.'

'Unless,' said Ronnie with a glance at Rosemary, who was now inspecting a range of bamboo cleaning brushes behind him, 'he had died somewhere else and had been moved.'

'There is always that possibility.'

'Mrs Lionel.' Ronnie leaned closer to the older woman. 'Rosemary said that you read faces.'

'Did she just?' Mrs Lionel peered around at her friend.

'You do,' said Rosemary, moving on to a row of euca-lyptus oil bottles.

'It's not a special skill. You only have to be observant.'

Ronnie tucked his pen behind his ear. 'What did you see, Mrs Lionel?'

'What did I see?' Mrs Lionel sighed and stared for a moment at her hands. When she lifted her head, there was a distant look in her deep blue eyes. 'I saw a frail old man whose face told me he'd spent years outside. Decades, even. He'd had surgery on his cheeks and ears. Skin cancer removal is my guess, but not for a while. He had signs of more cancers on his nose.'

'She was a nurse,' said Rosemary from near the goats' milk soaps. 'As well as a dairy farmer.'

'A very long time ago.' Mrs Lionel straightened her back. 'His top teeth were missing and some of his bottom ones as well. It would have made it hard for him to eat properly and perhaps that was why he was so thin. I couldn't see much of his eyes, but what I could were bright blue but opaque. Cataracts, my guess. All in all, I saw an elderly man who had taken little care of himself for some time.'

Ronnie's face paled. Even Rosemary felt the weight of what Mrs Lionel was suggesting. An old man alone, a lonely man perhaps. One whose self-care had gone, who had no one to care for him. The air in the little shop seemed heavier than before.

'And, of course, there was the scar he had.'

Rosemary grabbed the bottle of tea tree oil she'd knocked over and set it upright. 'Scar?'

'Didn't you notice, dear?' Mrs Lionel's eyes twinkled. 'On the side of his head.'

'A surgical scar?'

'No. I'd say it was from an accident.'

'Recent one?'

Mrs Lionel shook her head. 'No. It was too ragged.' She put a finger to her cheek. 'Hard to say without having another look, but there could have also been some skull indentation.'

Ronnie's face mottled. 'That sounds nasty.'

'Yes.' Mrs Lionel shrugged. 'He may have had some brain damage along with it. But it wasn't what he died from.'

Ronnie wrote in his notebook while Mrs Lionel

watched. Rosemary arrived at the drying herbs hanging from a frame above the entrance into the house. She crumpled some thyme, the fragrance strong in its concentrated form.

'Okay,' said Ronnie at last. 'Is that all you can think of to say about the scene?'

'Yes, dear.' Mrs Lionel stood up. 'My guess is that this man's family will be very hard to find even if you discover who he is.'

'I would start at his jacket,' said Rosemary, peering into the canopy of herbs.

Ronnie clutched his notebook in both hands. 'What do you mean?'

'It was well made, too big for our man now, but may have fitted once. Tailored.'

'You don't see many people getting a tailored jacket these days, dear.'

'But,' said Ronnie, 'it may have been secondhand.'

'Something for a private investigator to find out.'

At Rosemary's words, Ronnie straightened. 'Yes. That's right.' He slipped his notebook away. 'Thank you both. I'm going to have one last look at the scene before heading home.'

'How is Honey, dear?'

Ronnie grinned, showing those good teeth again. 'She's beautiful.' He left the shop, waving goodbye.

'When Honey first introduced Ronnie to me,' said Mrs Lionel thoughtfully, 'I wondered if she'd made a big mistake. He's very...'

'Uncertain,' said Rosemary.

'Something like that.'

'He isn't the sharpest tool in the shed.'

'Rosemary...'

'He loves Honey, though. He's devoted.' Rosemary put a hand on her cheek before letting it drop. 'That means much more than I used to think it did.'

Mrs Lionel's eyes widened. 'Oh, yes, dear. It does. And she loves him back.'

'Yes.'

'He is loyal, and that is most commendable.'

Rosemary watched Ronnie through the window as he climbed into his old utility and rumbled down the road towards Big Town. 'Indeed it is,' she said.

'Tea?' said Mrs Lionel kindly.

'Yes, thank you.'

Mrs Lionel left the room to boil the kettle, leaving Rosemary staring pensively after her son-in-law.

NINE

Rakisha always found it hard to get out of bed on Fridays. Friday, day of goddesses, was traditionally one of garden harvest in her former life when the household would spend long hours stripping crops and relishing in the bounty they had grown. At least, that was what Rakisha liked to remember. Fridays in the warm sun, with friends dressed in cotton and wearing straw hats with long satin ribbons. From the depths of her warm bed, Fridays like that were easily conjured. They certainly outstripped the Fridays of Rakisha's current reality where the chilly café needed the fire lit and another day of grinding grains awaited her.

Still, it wasn't all bad.

On Fridays, at approximately a quarter past ten, Barry came for his coffee.

At first, she wondered how he knew that Friday coffees had her special added ingredients, a little spice that the household used to utilise to make the days flow. The first addition had been an accident. The spice spilled into her dried peas as she was grinding, knocked over by a pesky raven that liked to walk through the shop as if she owned it. By the time Rakisha noticed, the spice had ground up nicely, making the somewhat earthy aroma of peas morph into something sweeter. She'd kept the recipe to herself, for Fridays, and then for Barry, who confessed one day that he'd found her barista skills the best in Mulbury.

His actual words were, 'Gee, love, this is beaut.'

Rakisha slid out of bed and piled the blankets into a heap. She dressed quickly and warmly in thick, home-spun wool jumpers. Her hair was annoying today, hanging in long grey ringlets over her face, so she piled it up on her head, a mass to rival any raven's nest. Fire lit and sandwich board out, and it was time for her whole grains before the day really began.

By ten o'clock, no one had been in. The Gregorian chant on her player pounded in her temples, so she swapped it for Gillian Welch, feeling a calm descend. By the time Barry threw back the door (*I should get that hinge fixed*, she thought), Rakisha was humming to herself and contentedly making granola.

'Hello, Keesh.'

'*Rakisha*, darling. I'm not made of eggs.' Her laugh faded as Barry stared at her with a slightly open mouth. He seemed, she thought, even less responsive than usual. What had happened in Barry Holden's week? She smiled winningly to cheer him up. 'Flat white?'

'Just a coffee.' Barry peered into the glass-fronted cabinet. 'And one of those brown squares. Are they chocolate?'

'Carob, darling.'

'But it's got plenty of sugar?'

'Date paste. Sweet and wholesome.'

'I want sweet. Don't care about wholesome.'

She blushed as she bent to retrieve the cake. 'Would you like anything else, Barry?'

'No. All good.'

Rakisha observed Barry over the top of the coffee machine. He reminded her of Peter Petal, one of the householders from an era ago. Something about his stature or the way he walked because it certainly wasn't his clothes. Peter Petal was resplendent in tie-dye, whereas she'd never seen Barry out of flannel. Still, they stood the same, one foot slightly in front of the other, and the set of their shoulders-

'Keesh, can you hurry? I've got customers.'

Rakisha blinked and poured the too hot, steaming soy into her legume mix. A slurp of yacon syrup and she handed it to Barry in a keep cup along with his brownie. 'Barry, darling, you need to bring your own cup with you.' She smiled. 'I can't keep giving these away, can I?'

'Bring my own cup?'

'Yes, darling. It's better for the environment.'

'Okay, if you can't afford cups, I'll bring my own.'

'Now, it's not a matter of cost, darling, it's a matter of *ethics.*'

Barry paused at that. She could see the word swirling in his head and not landing anywhere. He shrugged, raised his cup, and made for the door.

Yes, she thought, *and the way they walk. Large steps, a meaningful gait, a way of stepping-*

'Keesh, can I ask you something?'

The meaningful steps had stopped at the door and Barry turned towards her.

'Yes, darling, anything.'

He came back into the shop and rested the cup and cake on the bench. 'Do you think...'

She waited, but Barry had gone on pause. 'Barry, darling, you wanted to ask me something?'

'It's embarrassing...'

'Perhaps it would be better if we sat down at the table?'

Barry studied the little table for two set against the window. 'I've got customers, mind.' He picked up his morning tea again. 'Well, okay, but it'll only take a minute.'

Rakisha wiped her hands on her floral apron and came out from behind the counter. Barry had sprawled on the nearest chair, meaning she had to squeeze past him to the other. She noted that, like Peter Petal, he was warm. A large, warm man-

'It's like this, Keesh.' Barry took a deep drink of his coffee. 'If you knew something about someone that wasn't good, but it was none of your business, then would you tell someone else about it?'

She blinked. 'I'm not sure that I understand you, darling.'

'I've found out something about someone. It's not good.'

'Something about someone in Mulbury?'

'Yeah.'

'Oh, well, that is a troublesome matter. You probably shouldn't say anything, darling.'

Barry slurped his coffee again and stood to go.

Rakisha shot her hand out to grab his arm. 'Unless, of course, it's causing you sleepless nights or pain. Then it's best to share.'

'I'm sleeping okay and the only pain I get is in this dicky shoulder.' He shrugged one up.

'Oh.' She stood as well. 'If you need to share, darling, then I'm always here.'

'You are, you know.'

'Sorry, darling?'

'Always here. The shop is always open, you don't take holidays.' He frowned. 'Why is that?'

'Where would I go, Barry, darling?'

'The city? I don't know. Anyway, got customers.' He peeled back the paper bag and took a bite of brownie. 'You make great cakes, Keesh.' Raising the cup once more, he left.

Rakisha watched him trundle across the Square, diverting around a low branch of The Exceptional Tree, and onto the footpath that led to the garage. He was so like Peter Petal, and yet Peter Petal shared all his secrets with her. Well, Peter Petal shared all his secrets with whoever was listening to him. In that way, Barry Holden was *not* like Peter.

She frowned and went back to counting lavender heads to prepare for making cookies. Their sharp fragrance gave her a headache almost immediately, which, she thought, was odd for a herb that alleviated the same when rubbed into the temples. After a few minutes, she shoved the bowl of heads away, touched her hair to make sure it was still under control, and left the shop.

Halfway across the Square, she ran into Kelly.

'Hello, Rakisha. No customers?'

Rakisha peeked into *Mullings* where the casual girl Kelly employed was busy serving a carload of tourists. 'I've finished a run of them,' Rakisha said. 'Now I'm off to do a few chores.'

'Well,' said Kelly, folding some straight dark hair away from her face with one long finger, 'hurry back in case someone goes into your shop. I won't have the chance to explain that you're out at the moment.'

Rakisha felt her lip curl and covered it up by pointing at *Franco's Patisserie*. 'Franco's outdoing all of us.'

A minibus disgorged passengers who made a beeline for

the bakery. Rakisha recognised them as the Friday mob that travelled through on their way to a fishing spot on the river. Hungry business, fishing, and they needed to stock up.

'Franco's delicacies are lost on those men.' Kelly folded her arms and watched the crowd.

'Strange, then, that they prefer his place to mine. Or yours.'

With that sting, Rakisha walked away from Kelly with a straight back and her head high. She felt the other woman's gaze on her and veered away from her course to the garage to see Patti instead. Only Gerry was there, though, looking lost among the neat rows of fashion excitements. He sat in front of the counter polishing a pair of red shoes. Patti's work in restoring their lustre and replacing the heel was clear. 'She really is a whizz,' said Rakisha.

'Who?'

'Your wife, Gerry darling.' Rakisha nodded at the shoes. 'I remember when they came in. Scuffed and dreadful. It seemed someone had worn them to do the ploughing. With a team of horses.'

'Hmmm.' Gerry held the shoe up. 'She does do a good job.'

'Is she here, darling?'

'Gone to Big Town to pick up a load. I'm here by myself.' He looked at Rakisha hopefully. 'Got time for a cup of tea?'

'No, darling, sorry.'

Gerry put the shoes down. 'It's not much fun, is it, sitting in an empty shop.'

'Darling, put some music on. Hello to Patti and I'll see her later.'

Rakisha hurried out, leaving Gerry to contemplate the

music idea, and crossed the road to the garage. There was no one in the office, so she tapped at the counter bell.

It was at least three minutes before Barry appeared. He had brownie crumbs on his unshaven chin and Rakisha baulked a little. Peter Petal never had a crumby chin, and he was always clean-shaven. Well, not so much clean-shaven, as in almost hairless, his face boyish with patches of fine beard hair that weren't worth the razor-

'Hello? Rakisha? What's the problem?'

Rakisha blinked. 'Barry, darling, I've been thinking about what you said.'

He frowned. 'That I'm busy with customers?'

'No. And, darling, you are not.'

'You're a customer. I'm busy with you.'

'Well, yes, but I'm not a customer.'

'Yes, you are. You bring your van to me every six months. Clockwork, you are. Unnecessary, I say.'

'Yes, that's right, I am your customer. But not today. I am your *friend* today.'

He scowled. 'Friend?'

'Yes, Barry, and I've been thinking about what you said, and I think it would really help you to share that little secret with me.'

'Secret?'

Rakisha wriggled irritably. 'Yes, Barry. Darling. About knowing something about someone. In Mulbury.' She lowered her voice. 'It's better that you let it all out.'

Barry stared at her without speaking. After a minute or so, she felt herself shrink. *I'm here now*, she thought. She squared her shoulders and waited.

Finally, Barry sighed. 'You could be right. It might be better to spit it out.'

'That's right, darling.' Rakisha smiled encouragingly. 'Out with it.'

'It's a secret, mind?'

'Yes, darling, I know what a secret is. I won't tell anyone.'

He paused a little longer, then came over and bent down towards her. She smelt oil and carob and a wisp of Mrs Lionel's camomile shampoo. 'Keesh, Heather Hubbard has blood on her hands.'

TEN

Unprecedentedly, Rosemary Exeter did not open her shop on Saturday. Instead, she took a selection of her preserves and stacked them in *The Read Mulbury* next to the front counter. 'I might buy them all myself,' said Jasper.

'You don't need to buy anything of mine.'

'We'll barter exchange then.'

'Yes.' Rosemary touched the nearest jar. 'I haven't paid you for those books yet.'

Jasper's face coloured nicely. 'It's a small favour.'

'A favour, nonetheless. I'll collect the leftovers later.'

'Whenever you're ready.'

Rosemary gave a curt nod and turned to go.

'Rosemary?'

'Yes?'

'I hope Honey's okay.'

She didn't nod this time, just left.

Ronnie had rung a few minutes after seven o'clock. 'I don't know, Rosemary, but she doesn't seem right to me.'

Rosemary put Sunny, who'd been on her lap, gently on the floor. 'In what way?'

'She's been up most of the night, prowling the lounge room. She says she's not sick. How do I know if she's telling the truth?'

'Does she have pain? Fever? Numbness?'

'No. She's pacing.'

'She sounds restless.'

'But why, Rosemary? Could you come and talk to her?'

'I'll be there soon.'

In fact, it took an hour to get ready by the time Rosemary had organised the deal with Jasper, checked on Mrs Lionel (Heather had stayed the night), and placated Roman who was relying on the last of her zucchinis to make fritters but had been too late to collect them (they were now pickles). Finally, she climbed into the car and headed to Big Town.

Honey and Ronnie lived on the outskirts, but it still was a thirty-minute drive from Mulbury. The paddocks on the way were autumn brown with a flush of green in the lower regions after recent rain. Sunlight stretched low across the ground and lit a mob of horses grazing by the fence as she rattled past. The blue car had been Alasdair's pride but had received no such love since he'd gone. Barry serviced it and that was all the attention it got. Rosemary glanced at the floor of the passenger side and swore, once again, that she'd vacuum it one day.

Ronnie's ute was parked out the front of their cream brick veneer house. Rosemary pulled into the drive and got out swiftly. The door opened as she reached it.

'Mum,' said Honey, 'what are you doing here?'

Rosemary gave her daughter the once-over. Taller than she was, but willowier, Honey showed no sign of her pregnancy yet. Her polished-leather-brown hair was pulled back into a hasty ponytail and an oversized pullover sloped from one shoulder. Her face was a healthy pink, her eyes bright, although with blue under shadows.

'Mum, is everything okay?'

'That's what I'm here to ascertain.'

'What on earth does that mean?'

'Where's Ronnie?'

'Here.'

Rosemary looked over Honey's shoulder and saw Ronnie beckoning her in. 'Let me talk to him.'

Honey stepped away from the door and let her mother go by. She closed the door and followed. Rosemary listened carefully as she did, but heard nothing to show Honey wasn't her usual, light-footed self.

'Okay, you two.' Honey swung onto a kitchen stool and picked up the mug she'd obviously been drinking from a few minutes ago. 'What's going on?'

'I'm worried about you, Honey Blossom,' said Ronnie, twisting his hands together.

'Why?'

'You hardly slept last night.'

Honey took a sip of her drink and kept her head down.

Rosemary reached over and plucked the mug from her hand. 'Are you alright?'

Honey sighed and folded her hands across her stomach. 'I'm great. A bit of nausea, lots of sudden tiredness, but apparently that's normal.'

'You've had a recent check?' Asked Rosemary.

'The midwife says everything's on track. Nothing to worry about.'

Rosemary studied Ronnie and then went back to Honey. 'Nothing to worry about. Is that right?'

'Really, you're both fussing for no reason.'

'Are we now?'

A silence stretched on. Even Cuddles, Ronnie's Golden Retriever, knew better than to disturb it. He stood outside at the glass doors to the backyard wagging his tail but not barking a word.

'Honey?'

'I'm having a little trouble sleeping, that's all.'

'Why?'

'Mum, you know I don't sleep well.'

'You don't stay up all night, though.'

'No.'

Rosemary pulled a stool out to sit next to her daughter. 'Out with it.'

Honey contemplated Ronnie, chewing her lip as she did. 'I'm fine, really, Ronnie. But maybe I haven't told you everything about me and my past.'

Rosemary crossed her leg and swung her foot back and forth gently. 'You haven't told him?'

'No.'

'I see.'

'I don't. Told me what?' Ronnie put both his hands to his face. 'You aren't going to tell me you suffer from a terrible disease and I'm going to lose you?'

'No, Ronnie.'

'If it isn't that, then there's nothing that can be as bad.' He let his hands drop, but the pressure of his fingers had left marks on his cheeks. 'Oh.' His hands went back up. 'You don't love me any more and you stayed up all night thinking of ways to say you're leaving.'

'No. Jeepers, Ronnie, why would you think that?'

'I don't know. My head is swirling with all the bad things that might happen that means we won't be together when Tallulah is born.'

'Tallulah?' Rosemary put her linked hands around her

knee, letting the name swirl around her head and deciding that it was beautiful.

'It's what he calls the baby.'

'My Grandmother's name. I've always loved it.' Ronnie put his hands down again. 'Honey, please, tell me that everything is alright.'

'It is, Ronnie. Calm down.'

'How can I calm down when you haven't told me something that might affect me for the rest of my *life?*'

'For all our sakes, Honey, tell him.'

Honey leaned forward, her hands on her knees, then sat up straight. 'Ronnie. This is not the first time I've been pregnant.'

'Not the first... oh.' Ronnie pulled a chair from the dining table and sat down heavily. 'We've been pregnant before?'

'Not *we*. Me. *I've* been pregnant before.'

Ronnie looked at Honey then Rosemary. 'You have a child already?'

'No.'

Rosemary reached out to squeeze Honey's shoulder.

'I don't understand,' said Ronnie, face as pale as milk.

'I lost the baby.'

'Lost?'

'Ronnie,' said Rosemary. 'She means the baby died.'

'I was twelve weeks pregnant.' Honey shuddered quietly.

'Oh, Honey.' Ronnie took the two steps to her and wrapped his arms around her. 'How awful for you.'

'Awful for everyone,' said Honey at Rosemary over Ronnie's shoulder.

Rosemary shrugged. 'Not a good time.'

The house was quiet while Ronnie rocked Honey, and

Rosemary looked politely out the glass door. Cuddles had sensed the emotion and was sitting, tail still and ears down.

'It got me last night.' Honey's eyes were dry, but her voice caught. 'Couldn't stop thinking about it.'

Ronnie stepped back a little. 'What's worrying you, Honey? Do you think Tallulah's not going to make it?'

'I'm nearly thirteen weeks now and I've been okay.' Honey sighed.

'There were extenuating circumstances,' said Rosemary.

'What like?' Ronnie's mouth opened in horror. 'You don't mean that the father of the baby-'

'No, he was a nice boy, but simply that. A boy. We would never have lasted.'

'What did you mean, then?'

'It was when Alasdair disappeared.' Rosemary stood up suddenly and opened the door to Cuddles. 'This dog needs attention.'

'Here, boy.' Honey patted her leg, and the dog inched gratefully towards her. She glanced up at Ronnie. 'I'm sorry to worry you. I don't think it will happen again. I got to wondering what that baby would be like now.' She shrugged. 'It's not useful, thinking things like that, but even I can't help it now and then.'

Ronnie's colour had returned to normal. 'Gosh, Honey, I had no idea.' He chewed his lip for a moment. 'Is there anything else I don't know? That you want to tell me, that is. I'm not prying. I don't mind if you have secrets you don't want to share. I do completely understand-'

'Ronnie.' Honey brushed the dog's nose off her leg, stood, and enveloped Ronnie in a bear hug. 'You are the most beautiful person I know.'

Rosemary took over patting the dog, partly to avoid the

intimate scene in front of her and partly because Cuddles looked offended at Honey's rejection.

After a few moments, the lovers broke up. Rosemary slid from the stool. 'I'll leave you two now.'

'No, you won't, Mum.' Honey let Ronnie go and took her mother's hands. 'Do you know how hard it is to get you out of Mulbury? You haven't been to our house for ages. I'm making cups of tea. I haven't had breakfast, either, so you'll have to put up with that as well. I've got eggs left over from the last batch you gave me. I'll scramble them.'

'Let me,' said Ronnie.

'No. I'll do it.' Honey had already rounded the bench and was hunting for a saucepan in a drawer. 'You talk to Mum about the case.'

'I shouldn't talk about it to anyone.'

'It's *Mum*, Ronnie. Not *anyone*. She's useful. She could be part of your team, you know.'

'I'm quite happy with the shop,' Rosemary said quickly.

'Still.' Honey gave Ronnie a sharp look. 'Tell her what you've found.'

'Not much, actually,' Ronnie said as the saucepan hissed on the heat. 'The coroner's report will be awhile but my source at the morgue said they found a wound on the old man's side.'

'Meaning?'

'He didn't die of old age. He was killed.'

'That would be why they shifted him,' said Rosemary.

'Why would someone kill an old man?' said Honey.

'Rage?' said Rosemary. 'Revenge? Being in the wrong place at the wrong time?' She turned to Ronnie. 'Did your source say what caused the wound?'

Ronnie shook his head. 'No. It wasn't noticeable until

they had him at the morgue apparently, which is why you and Mrs Lionel saw nothing.'

'How could a wound not be noticeable?'

'Something about a tamponade? I didn't know what they meant.'

'It means something staunched the wound. Perhaps it was the way he was lying.' She was quiet for a moment. 'Have you found out who he was?'

Ronnie shook his head. 'I'm no closer. I followed up with what you said about the suit. There was a tailor's label on it, but his shop closed last century. I reckon the tailor himself might be dead by now, but I'm still looking.'

Honey clattered plates on to the table. 'Eggs, people.'

Honey's cooking skill must have come from Aunt Lilibeth, thought Rosemary. The eggs were delicious, fluffy and exquisite on wholegrain bread Honey had baked the day before. For the first time in an age, Rosemary felt herself relax completely. She sat on longer than really needed, following the eggs with strong coffee that Ronnie brewed, and listening to the pair of them chat about Tallulah's nursery that was under construction.

It was after lunchtime when Rosemary climbed into the iridescent blue car, waved goodbye to Honey and Ronnie standing with their arms around each other in their doorway with Cuddles poking his head out between them, and headed back to Mulbury.

She was nearly home, singing along to a Paul Kelly tune, when she passed a car pulled over to the side. A man stood at its open boot, reaching in for something. He straightened as she went by and she saw his face momentarily, a glimpse of vivid blue eyes under a fringe of black hair. It was vaguely familiar.

She'd left the car and was unlocking *The Preserved Mulbury* when it came to her, triggered by the bowl of quinces in the front window that were destined to be tomorrow's jelly. The man at the car had been the stranger in her shop on the day the old man had been killed.

ELEVEN

Jasper Lu had sold all her preserves, or so he said when Rosemary came to pick them up. 'They're really popular,' he said as he handed her the box with a bag of sale money inside. 'Especially the jumbleberry.'

'It reminds people of summer,' said Rosemary, tucking the box under one arm.

'I suppose it must. I guess it's a bit like how people read beach stories in winter.'

'That's called escapism.'

'Escapism is the foundation of my sales.'

'Yes. I could see that.' Rosemary swapped the box to her other arm and reached for a book displayed on the counter. 'You said you weren't into Space Westerns?'

'I'm not, usually.' Jasper nodded at the book Rosemary was holding. 'That first, though, got me thinking. If there was one first in the district, there may be others.'

Rosemary turned the book over to read the back. What Jasper had said was good sales sense, and that was something he had quite a lot of. She would've believed his tale about selling all her preserves if she hadn't spied the edge of a jumbleberry jam jar hiding just out of sight on his kitchen bench.

'Are you going to open for the last hour of the afternoon?'

She hesitated. *I should,* she thought. *Every hour open is a potential sale.* The afternoon had dimmed, though, and there was something appealing in keeping the blinds closed on the shop, lighting a fire in her little lounge room, and having some quiet time with Sunny. She felt tired. Honey's story had brought back some of the drama of years ago, and with it a flash of exhaustion. 'No,' she said. 'That'll do for today.'

'Well, perhaps you'd like to have dinner with me, Rosemary?' Jasper fidgeted with the brown wrapping paper on his counter. 'I was only tossing some tofu through some veg. You're welcome to join me.' His face had deepened to a velvet red.

She studied him for a moment, running through the image of sitting at Jasper's kitchen table listening to Snowy's snores from the couch. It was a pleasant image, a warm one. She sighed quietly. 'Very kind of you, Jasper, but I will say no tonight.'

Jasper straightened the paper. 'It was only a thought. I'll have to go the tofu alone.' He gave a short laugh.

'Thanks for this.' She held the box aloft as she headed for the door.

'Goodbye, Rosemary Exeter.'

His voice trailed after her as she let the heavy door close. Her legs didn't falter as she walked the few steps to her shop, although her mind did. A bit. Dinner with Jasper was a comfortable affair, sort of like lounging on a best friend's couch while they made bread and butter pudding because it was your favourite. She suspected Jasper did not think of her as a frumpy best friend, but more as a poten-tial... someone.

And what do you see him as? said a voice in her head that sounded a lot like Mrs Lionel.

A friend, answered the other half of her brain. *One with book benefits.*

Rosemary pushed the jangling door open and closed it immediately, headed through the shop, and shut the connecting doorway. Sunny was on the windowsill in the dining area and jumped down to arch herself against Rose-mary's leg while she prepared a cat dinner of sardines and rice. She lit the fire, closed the curtains against the cooling night air, and curled up on the couch with a pot of Darjeeling and a pre-dinner Yo-Yo.

The coffee table in front of her was the dumping ground for all things she had yet to do. Bills, letters, and jar labels littered a central ceramic dish that she once bought in Tuscany. A basket of shirts was there to be mended. Under it was a scrapbook of new preserve recipes to try. Next to them were the books she'd borrowed from Jasper on the same day.

Rosemary picked up the first one. Its front cover showed the crew of a spaceship standing on its lowered ramp, their expressions solemn and with Stetsons jammed on their heads. It was a busy cover, with glimpses of an outlandish city in the background and cargo on a pallet spilling from its containment. The title, *Forces and Horses,* slanted across the feet of the crew, with the author's name in a bold blocked font at the bottom.

She opened to the acknowledgements—*to H, I, J and K*—then read the first chapter. And the second. Only Sunny jumping up to curl next to her made her pause. A few strokes of the lean tabby's head, and a third then fourth chapter flew by. The house darkened around her as she reached the end and closed the book.

'Plot-driven adventure starring a courageous captain and his eclectic crew,' she said to Sunny, who opened her eyes disdainfully. 'Just what was needed.' The cat's head nodded as she went back to sleep.

Rosemary stood up from the couch to stretch. The room was delightfully warm, and the alluring fragrance of quince and cinnamon wafted from the kitchen. It would have been all too easy to read the next two books on the table. Slim though they were, that would have seen the end of the evening and she couldn't go without food. Instead, she cooked herself a simple risotto, stirred in mozzarella, and garnished it with basil and a few drips of balsamic vinegar. Taking a steaming bowl and a glass of local Riesling back to the couch, she shoved the cat over and sank into the cushions to eat, balancing the second Space Western on her lap to read.

She didn't hear the first knock on the glass door leading to her balcony. Crazed outcasts of the planet Nowra had captured Kesper, who was about to be zapped. The second lot of knocking crescendoed and she put the book down with a start. It was well after ten o'clock and, had it been a normal day, she would have been in bed. She put her hand reassuringly on a very alert Sunny's head and went to the porch door, switching off the light so that she could see better through the crack in the curtains. 'Who's there?'

No one answered for so long Rosemary thought they had gone away. She pressed her face against the glass and scanned the deck. Empty except for the outdoor table and chairs. She waited, then stepped back as a third lot of knocking sounded. This time, she saw who it was. She pulled the curtains aside and pushed the door open. 'Heather.'

The girl stood shivering in shorty pyjamas and no shoes. Rosemary ducked outside but slowed as Heather flinched away. 'Come into the warm, Heather. It's too cold out here.'

Slowly, as if her legs weren't working as well as they should, Heather crept in the door. Rosemary shut it firmly behind them and tugged the curtains across before reaching for a long-sleeved cardigan she had on the back of a chair. She wrapped it gently around the girl and steered her into the armchair closest to the fire. As a second thought, she picked up Sunny and sat her on Heather's knee for extra warmth.

'That will be better.'

Rosemary knelt to knead the cold out of Heather's feet. They were white and damp. Rosemary pulled her own lambs wool slippers off and tugged them on to Heather. 'I'll get you a warm drink.'

Rosemary put milk on the stove, watching from the corner of her eyes as Heather put one hand out to rest on Sunny's head. The cat purred loudly and pushed her crown into the girl's palm. Rosemary stirred honey into the milk, poured it into a large mug, and came to sit next to them.

The residents of Mulbury knew about Heather's sleep-walking. She rarely left the house when she did it, but it had happened before. The first time, she was eight years old. Her mother had died, her father stayed drunk for a year—it was no wonder, said everyone. It was a reaction to the stress of it all. Holly and Hannah knew to lock all the doors of the house, and Heather didn't make it out again until she was fifteen. That time, she was away all night and there'd been a frantic search among the old abandoned mine shafts. She'd reappeared at dawn, dirty and cold but uninjured. The cause, said her father, was Holly going into hospital to have her appendix out.

But what was going on this time?

Rosemary frowned. It was Heather's night to stay with her sisters and not Mrs Lionel, but to get to the deck as she had meant climbing up the trellis in the dark. If she'd been at Mrs Lionel's, then it was simply a matter of leaping over the rails of one deck to another. If she'd been at Mrs Lionel's, then Holly and Hannah were not taking their fair share of caring for the troubled Heather. Rosemary felt irritation rise.

'Sunny,' said Heather suddenly, moving her hand down Sunny's spine.

Rosemary handed Heather her drink. 'Have this now.'

Heather drank obediently, her cheeks returning to pink with the warmth.

'What were you doing outside, Heather?' Rosemary said as she took the empty mug back. 'It's a cold night.'

Heather looked at her for the first time, her clear blue eyes also the colour of her sisters'. But neither Holly's nor Hannah's had ever appeared so frightened.

'It's alright. You're safe now.'

Heather shook her head. 'No,' she said in a firm voice, as if she was debating politics, 'I'm not.'

Rosemary studied her. 'Why not?'

'Because,' said Heather, reaching out for Rosemary and tapping her fingers on her arm, '*he's* here.'

TWELVE

Although Rosemary applied liberal amounts of warm milk drinks and Sunny's charms, Heather didn't say another word. Rosemary rang Mrs Lionel reluctantly to tell her of Heather's abscondence, and the older woman reacted in the horrified way Rosemary thought she would.

'It's my fault,' said Mrs Lionel, tying the cord of her dressing gown as she came in the front door. 'I forgot to latch the French windows. Well, I never latch the French windows. I should have been more careful.'

'What was Heather doing at your place at all?'

Mrs Lionel tucked a curl of her silver hair behind one ear. 'Sleeping, Rosemary Exeter.' She held a hand up. 'I know. You think the others should care for their wee sister, but they need their rest as well. They are running an extremely busy business.'

'As are you.'

Mrs Lionel waved her hand. 'Not as busy as them. I have enough stock made for a month's trade and I'm only fiddling around with my concoctions as usual. Hannah and Holly are feeding the town's livestock and, after the nasty dry summer we've had, they need to be on top of their orders.'

Rosemary frowned as Mrs Lionel took a seat next to Heather and gathered one of the girl's hands in both of hers. 'I'm not convinced that you should do the brunt of care in this situation.'

'I don't need you to be convinced.' Mrs Lionel glared at Rosemary. 'I'm quite capable of making my own decisions. Now get me a cup of that good night-time tea you have and tell me what happened.'

Midnight came and went as Rosemary administered tea and they talked about the meaning of Heather's words. The girl's eyes closed with their softly voiced chatter, and she curled up with Sunny to sleep. Rosemary covered her with a rug, gave Mrs Lionel one as well, and stoked the fire. It had already been a long night with no end in sight.

'Well, I have no idea what she meant,' said Mrs Lionel eventually. '*He* could be anyone. Her father, maybe.'

'It could be someone not related.'

'It could be. Someone who's done something wrong by the sisters.' Mrs Lionel shook her head. 'I'm having trouble thinking who on earth that would be.'

'We don't know everything about the Hubbards.'

'No. But I know a lot. Louisa was a good friend of mine, even though we were decades apart. I went to most of the girls' important events: their awards at school, sports days, equestrian competitions.'

'It's someone that none of us knows.'

Mrs Lionel sighed and reached for her teacup. 'That's what I'm most afraid of. Heather's imagination is scary. It's like she's currently living in yet another alternative world, but where, I can't start to guess. I think it would be full of people, some unsavoury.'

Rosemary nodded. A world that no one else could imagine would explain a lot about Heather.

Eventually, Mrs Lionel returned home. Rosemary covered Heather with another blanket and stretched herself out on the couch. She managed a few hours before the dawn light woke her. Heather slept on, twitching now and then. Sunny stayed firmly in her lap.

Rosemary started on some quince jelly, setting the fruit to boil for some hours before she could strain the juice to set. The street was unusually quiet, perhaps because of the overcast day, with only one older couple jangling into the shop to buy a gift box of pickles and trying a sample of jam. Just before lunchtime, Holly and Hannah entered, their clothes dusty and bits of hay littering their hair.

'We are so sorry, Rosemary,' said Holly. 'We've been flat out all morning. Special Sunday deliveries. First the oaten hay came, then chook pellets, then the bags of wheat we've been waiting for.'

'Then a whole truck-load of straw in manky square bales.' Hannah wrinkled her nose. 'I mean, we aren't a garden centre, but people love that sort of thing.' She paused, tapping her finger against her mouth. 'Maybe we *should* start a garden centre? Mulch and soil and stuff? We've got room out the back.'

'Not this month, thank you.' Holly elbowed her sister. 'How is Heather?'

Rosemary tipped her head towards her house. 'She's fine. Sitting with Sunny.'

'May we?'

'In you go.'

Rosemary followed the sisters and watched as they both kissed Heather's cheeks and rubbed her shoulders. The younger girl showed no surprise at this. In fact, she didn't react at all but kept up her slow stroking of Sunny, who was being particularly tolerant, although she regarded Rosemary with a slightly wide-eyed stare.

'We can take her home now,' said Holly, standing.

'I'll remove the cat.' Rosemary swept Sunny up, who nuzzled her neck gratefully before squirming to be put down. Once on the floor, she darted away into the kitchen and started munching her dry food.

'Come on, feathery Heathery.' Hannah tugged gently on Heather's arms and rose with her. Once up, Hannah tucked her arm around her sister and steered her towards the door.

'He's here,' whispered Heather.

'Okay,' said Hannah. She started walking, then twisted her head back. 'Who is she talking about?'

'I hoped you would know,' said Rosemary, following.

'No idea,' said Holly. 'It's not Dad. We got a text from him yesterday to say that he's working on a prawn trawler up north in between gigs.'

'Good of him to contact you.'

'He wanted some money sent,' said Holly quietly. 'Something about needing a new guitar.'

Rosemary nodded. Of course. She'd met Richard's type before. All-important musicians who couldn't manage caring for their families in case the muse left them. It was a shame that the muse didn't have ideas about where to get money other than cadging off daughters. 'No one else comes to mind?'

'No,' said Hannah. 'Absolutely no idea. I mean, we don't know many men.'

Rosemary remembered what Mrs Lionel had said. 'A grandfather? Uncle? Cousin?'

'No,' said Holly. 'Our grandparents are all dead and we

only have aunts. A few cousins, but they live in the Northern Territory, and I can't imagine they'd be down here.'

'At least, not in a sinister way.' Hannah frowned at Rosemary. 'Is that how she said it? *He's here...*' She gave a shudder.

'Yes, like that.'

'Crumbs,' said Holly. 'Should we be scared?'

Rosemary didn't answer.

'Looks like it should terrify us.' Hannah opened the door of the shop and led Heather through. 'Thanks again, Rosemary.'

Rosemary caught Holly's arm as she went to follow. 'Don't wear Mrs Lionel out. She says she's fine, but she is eighty-two years old.'

Holly's face flushed red. 'I'm sorry. We don't mean to dump Heather on her. I guess we get a bit tired, too.'

'Make it only a few nights, then. Tuesdays and Saturdays.'

'Okay, that sounds like a good idea.' Holly watched her retreating sisters. 'I don't know how long this will go on for, but I figure that if Heather is eating and drinking, she's still better off with us than in a hospital.'

Rosemary stepped aside to let Holly run down the footpath. She went back to her quinces, turned the heat down a little, and sat back at the shop counter. The autumn fruits and last of the winter vegetables were almost all in and stocks would be at a high level. With fewer preserves to make, she'd open a few jam-making classes up using fruit mainly sourced from markets rather than Mulbury backyards. Rosemary opened her diary and circled some tentative weekend dates.

She was absorbed in working out the holidays associated

with Easter and ANZAC Day and so didn't look up immediately when the door jangled.

'Excuse me.'

The voice came from a young man standing right in front of her. Rosemary eyed his olive-green puffy jacket. 'Marc Cambridge.'

'You remembered me.'

'I should forget you?'

'Oh. No. I thought you might, though. You have so many customers.'

'None that claim to be searching for a postcard.' Rosemary opened her till and lifted the money receptacle to locate the card. 'Is this yours?'

Marc's face paled. 'Yes, yes, it is.' He reached for the card eagerly. 'I was right. I dropped it around here. Where did you find it?'

Rosemary noted the way he wiped the card almost tenderly. She had no difficulty imagining that he would kiss it if she hadn't been there. 'It was pushed under the door of the shop.'

Marc froze, his fingers still touching the card. 'Pushed under the door?'

Rosemary didn't answer.

'Oh.' He brought an envelope out of his pocket and slipped the card inside. 'Someone else found it.'

'Yes.'

'Why would they have pushed it under the door of your shop?'

Rosemary said nothing.

'Maybe they saw me in here the other day? Maybe they heard me talking to you? Could it have been that old lady?'

'Mrs. Lionel,' said Rosemary. 'Not "that old lady". No, it

wasn't her. If she'd found it, she would have given it to me not shoved it under the door.'

'I'm sorry, I didn't mean to sound rude.' Marc ran his hand through his tufty hair. 'I don't understand what's happening here.'

'What *is* happening here, Marc? What does that postcard mean and why are you carrying it around?'

He looked down at the envelope in his hand as if noticing it for the first time. 'It was my grandmother's. She died this year. I found this when I helped clean up her room at the nursing home.' He shrugged. 'It's the only thing I have of hers. It devastated me when I thought I'd never find it again.'

Rosemary eyed him thoughtfully.

He shrugged. 'I suppose you think I'm a sentimental idiot.'

'No,' said Rosemary. 'It is refreshing to see a young person care so much about his grandparents.'

'Grandmother. I didn't know my grandfather.'

'He died a long time ago?'

'No one in my family knows. We think he perished in the Scarlet Tuesday bushfires that burnt so much of the state. The family looked for him, but no one has seen him since.'

Rosemary grimaced. 'There were several missing people after those fires, assumed dead. Tragic.'

They were quiet for a moment.

'Well, anyway.' Marc held up the envelope. 'Thank you very much for keeping it safe for me.'

'You haven't told me what it means.'

The young man hesitated. 'No, I haven't.'

And he has no intention of doing so, thought Rosemary as Marc nodded his goodbye and exited out the front.

Rosemary headed back to check the quinces. Sunny perched on the windowsill facing Mrs Lionel's, her tail waving back and forth, but when Rosemary went to see what she was looking at, she could only see a closed blind. She gave the cat a scratch under the chin. 'You were very good with Heather,' she said.

Sunny narrowed her eyes at her mistress as if to say, *Don't do that again. The girl nearly patted my coat off.*

Rosemary laughed. She went back to her shop counter and closed the diary, noting that dinner tomorrow night was at Roman's and Jules' house at the edge of town. Good. Of all the residents of Mulbury, no people were less stressed than them with providing a meal for a group of people. Mrs Lionel would travel with her, and she should ask Jasper if he wanted a lift.

And there he was, rushing out his back door to once again to lean against the rail of the porch and stare down into his jumbled yard. He was as he had been the other day, short of breath and sort of desperate. Rosemary frowned. There was something going on with Jasper Lu that he wasn't talking about.

THIRTEEN

Mrs Lionel knocked at the door of *The Preserved Mulbury* at exactly ten minutes to seven o'clock on Monday evening. By the time Rosemary gave Sunny a goodbye pat and collected her car keys, Jasper was talking to the older woman on the footpath. Rosemary locked the door behind her and held up her keys. 'The car is over there.'

She kept behind her friends as they chatted their way to Alasdair's car. Snatches of conversation—*I've never read Natasha Lester. Oh, you really should*—floated back to her, but she was concentrating on Jasper. He was walking fine, albeit a little slower than normal because of Mrs Lionel's gait, with no evidence of shortness of breath. When he turned his head to listen to his companion's words, his profile was normal. Sharp nose, not red. Eyes bright, not puffy or circled. Or that was what Rosemary could see in the dim streetlight before they climbed into her car.

Roman and Jules, unlike other shop owners around Goldmarket Square, did not live on their business premises. Their house was a splendid Victorian home of red brick, with a renovated interior and the largest, whitest kitchen

Rosemary had ever seen. Roman did most of the cooking at the restaurant itself, but he whipped up cakes and desserts at home. He had two enormous side-by-side refrigerators with glass fronts, which made Rosemary feel she was peering in on the intimate details of the pair's gastronomical requirements, especially when she saw prune juice on a shelf.

They parked in the street under an elm tree and walked together up the stairs leading to the house's imposing wooden door.

'Ah, Mrs Lionel. Jasper. Rosemary.'

Roman was at his best when entertaining. He had opened the door dressed in a stiff white apron with a little red and white kerchief around his neck. That, and the fact that he was growing a lush moustache, made him the caricature of a TV chef.

'Roman,' said Mrs Lionel, 'so lovely of you to have us tonight.'

'I have been anticipating my time to entertain you.' Roman bowed. 'Although it is a hard act to follow after Jasper's hot spot.'

'Hot pot, Roman.' Jules appeared behind her husband. 'Welcome. Gerry and Patti are already here.'

'Are you expecting all of us tonight?' Asked Mrs Lionel, removing her coat.

'Not Franco, as he's baking. Not the girls, either. They seem rather preoccupied.' Jules took the coat and hung it on a rack in the hallway.

Mrs Lionel and Rosemary glanced at each other. Roman would prepare take-home meals for the sisters, as he did for anyone not able to make it to dinner night. 'They'll be fed later,' said Rosemary quietly.

'Hoorah for Roman,' whispered Mrs Lionel.

They walked down the long hallway to the back of the house to find Gerry and Patti seated at a vast dining room table, sipping sparkling wine. 'Please,' said Roman, holding out full glasses, 'join our friends.'

Rosemary took a glass and sat at the head of the table with Gerry and Patti on either side. At once, Gerry leaned over to her. 'Patti sold her gilded evening dress made from unloved brocade curtains.'

Rosemary raised her eyebrows and her glass. 'Excellent, Patti. You have a real following.'

Patti squealed quietly. 'I know. I find that the more adventurous I get with my re-makes, the more people seem to love them.'

'You are the Mary Quant of Mulbury,' said Gerry, clinking his glass with his wife.

Patti blushed. 'Not really.'

'No,' said Rosemary. 'You are uniquely Patricia Yale of Mulbury.'

'Oh, Rosemary. That's one of the nicest things you've ever said.'

Rosemary shrugged. 'I only tell the truth.'

Patti's normally bright hair was nothing compared to the shade of pink her face had gone. 'Excuse me,' she said, standing and touching her cheek, 'I need to...'

'Well, that made her day.' Gerry chuckled. 'I may think the shop is boring, but clearly her fans don't. We had about twenty people go through today and it's a Monday. Mulbury is meant to be dead on Mondays.'

Rosemary sipped her wine, thinking about the previous Monday when *dead* was an apt word.

'Twenty people,' said Jasper as he slid into the seat next to Gerry. 'Do you think you could send some my way? I had two.'

'You know what you could do, Jasper, old son? You could put a display of fashion books in your window on one side, leaving the other for your normal material, and we could put a notice in *Patricia's* directing people to it.'

'That's a great idea.' Jasper smiled. 'I'll hunt through what I've got on the shelves.'

'I was going to ask you about your current display. Westerns, aren't they?'

'Not Westerns. *Space* Westerns. Speculative fiction.'

'Westerns set in outer space?' Gerry swirled his glass. 'Do people want to read about such things?'

'Oh yes.' Jasper waved his hand about. 'There's a genre out there for all readers. Space Westerns, cosy mysteries, military thrillers. You name it, someone has written it, and there's a readership for it.'

'Goodness me.' Gerry frowned. 'And what's your favourite genre, Jasper? I imagine that you're more of a literary fellow, a classics man.'

Rosemary saw Jasper's neck mottle. 'Relationships,' she said. 'Human behaviour. That's what Jasper likes.'

Jasper gave her a grateful smile.

'Life-lit,' said Rosemary. 'Writing about the everyday and its importance.'

'You do know your literature, Rosemary.' Gerry chuckled. 'Talking about business, you could do something about fashion in your window display so that I could direct customers to you, too.' Gerry tipped his glass up to get the last of his wine. 'Perhaps a display of...'

'Catwalk dolls eating pickle sandwiches?'

Gerry's guffaws brought Jules to that end of the table, half-dragging Mrs Lionel and directing her into the seat next to Patti's. 'There's too much fun going on here without me. Oh, but there's the doorbell again.' She strode off down the hall.

Roman was offering a tray of canapes when Barry and Rakisha appeared, Barry in a stained red flannelette shirt and Rakisha in an assortment of beads. Barry almost ran around the table to land next to Jasper, leaving Rakisha with Jules's arm linked through hers to sit opposite him and next to Mrs Lionel.

'Barry,' said Jasper, offering his hand.

'Jasper. Gerry.' Barry scratched at his stubbly cheek and didn't seem to notice any outstretched hands. 'Going to be cold tonight.'

'Frost, maybe,' said Gerry.

'Slippery on the roads.' Barry waved Roman's sparkling wine away. 'Beer if you have any, mate.'

Roman came back with a suitable drink and sat at the other end of the table. 'Kelly said she would be a little late. Something about having to pay a few bills online.'

Something about making a dramatic entrance, thought Rosemary, but kept her face neutral.

Roman had served soup and was clearing the bowls away when Kelly finally appeared, her face a little flustered which, as Rosemary noted, picked up the colour of her nutmeggy eyes. 'I am so sorry, Roman and Jules.' She sat with a flourish, sweeping a deep blue cape from her shoulders, and tossing it onto the nearest armchair. 'I was talking to Darren, and the time got away.'

Rosemary tensed, but only Mrs Lionel noticed. She gave Rosemary a look that said, *Settle down.*

'He's checking The Exceptional Tree tomorrow, isn't he?' said Gerry, accepting Roman's plate of roasted squab.

'Yes.' Kelly reached for a wine bottle. 'He'll be here bright and early if you want to see him.'

Rosemary did not miss the look Kelly cast down the table.

'It's been a while since we've seen your brother,' said Gerry.

'Yes, it has.' Kelly sipped daintily. 'He still feels uncomfortable in Mulbury.'

'Oh,' said Patti. 'From all that time ago? What, four years?'

'Five,' said Kelly. 'Five long years ago.'

'Five years isn't a long time.'

The table hushed at Rosemary's words. Then Jules said, tactfully, 'Tell us about your gown, Patti. Gerry started telling me and I got interrupted.'

While Patti told her story, Rosemary resolutely ate her pigeon. Monday dinners were a grand tradition, but she was always glad when Kelly didn't make it to them. The scorn Kelly had thrown in Rosemary's direction after Alasdair had gone, as if it was Rosemary's fault. *I'll never forgive her,* she thought. *As for her brother...*

Maybe, said a little voice in her head sounding quite like Mrs Lionel, *you should forgive Darren and move on?*

Rosemary caught the growl before it could escape her lips and took several swallows of wine.

Gerry pushed his empty plate forward so that he could rest his forearms on the table. 'I've been right through our old cellar now, cleaning out every nook and cranny, and Barry took away what we didn't want.' He reached over and clasped Patti's hand as she finished talking. 'Who would know that my clever wife's business would take off like it has and that we'd have to store boxes of clothes in the cellar? It can be truly tiring.'

'Oh Gerry,' said Patti. 'You hardly do a thing for it. I'm the busy one.'

'But I get exhausted watching you.'

They finished the excellent squab, with Rakisha scooping the last of her vegetarian pie up as Barry put his knife and fork down, and Roman took their dishes away. Immediately, he re-emerged from the kitchen with a blue platter mounded with a caramel-coloured pudding.

'Sticky date,' Roman explained. 'But, of course, I have plain fruit salad as well. Who would prefer that?'

'Me, darling,' said Rakisha. 'Too much gluten, I'm afraid. Sticky date pudding would only muck up my gut flora.'

Roman dipped his head in acknowledgement and went back to the kitchen to fetch a glass bowl heaped with neatly cubed fruit.

Rakisha accepted it but didn't start eating. Roman sliced the pudding and sent it around, followed by cream and yoghurt, but still she sat. 'Everything all right?' Asked Roman. 'Is the fruit to your flora's liking?'

'Yes, darling, looks delicious.' Rakisha had high spots of colour on her cheeks. Suddenly, she said, 'Barry has discovered something.'

Barry was halfway through his pudding. He inhaled suddenly, paused, then coughed a sizeable chunk of sugary date back into his bowl. 'Keesh,' he said when he could. 'That's not information to share.'

'You told me, darling, and I've been thinking.' Rakisha picked up her spoon and pointed it at him. 'I told you it would be a good idea to share your secret. A problem shared is a problem halved.'

'I did share it. With you.' Barry wiped the back of his hand across his mouth and shook his head. 'Something I won't do again.'

If Rakisha was hurt by that, no one could tell. She

continued eagerly. 'Barry has news about the car he found in the driveway.'

'Oh,' said Mrs Lionel, 'the one with the patch of blood on the back seat?'

Barry nodded. His mouth twisted this way and that until it was clear that he'd decided. 'Hard to keep any secrets in this place. Okay, I'll let it out. Remember that I told you the car belonged to a man?'

'I remember,' said Mrs Lionel. 'You were right, then?'

'Yeah, I was. Sort of. I mean, it still belongs to a man, but he hasn't got it at the moment.'

'Hurry up, Barry.' Patti twisted her serviette into a knot.

'The car belongs to Richard.' Barry sat back, sighing.

In the quiet that followed, Jules said, 'Who?'

'Richard Hubbard,' said Rosemary. 'Hannah and Holly's father.'

'More importantly, darling,' said Rakisha with a broad smile, '*Heather's* father.'

FOURTEEN

'Ah,' said Gerry, breaking the silence at the table. 'Right. So?'

'What do you mean by *so*, darling?' Rakisha threw her hair back over one shoulder, but it fell forward again in a frenzied, frizzy heap.

'We know Richard Hubbard left his car behind because he hitch-hiked up the coast.' Gerry turned to Patti. 'Actually, I can't remember the last time I saw him drive it at all. Didn't he say that the muse didn't drive, or something?'

'It was more like the muse didn't strike him while he was driving,' said Mrs Lionel.

'That's right,' said Jules, frowning. 'He used to go on about needing open spaces and no responsibilities to write his music. I guess having a car was too much of a responsibility.'

'I could list other things that were too much of a responsibility,' said Rosemary, folding her hands together on the table.

'I think you're all missing the point, darlings,' said

Rakisha with another toss of her head. 'The car was covered in *blood*.'

'There was a *patch* of blood on the back seat, Keesh.' Barry scraped his plate to get the last of his pudding. 'There it was. In my driveway. Blocking my way to work.' He shook his head. 'When the police said it was a local car, I looked it up. Must have been one of my first jobs and I'd forgotten it.' He licked his spoon. 'It's obvious how it was in my driveway.'

Gerry leaned forward. 'What was obvious?'

'Well, one of those sisters had driven the car as far as the garage and left it there when it ran out of fuel.'

'It could have been stolen,' said Jasper. 'Stolen and dumped.'

Barry shook his head. 'Stolen cars don't usually turn up parked in a mechanic's driveway. They're what you see on the side of the road with no number plate and the mirrors smashed.' He tapped a finger on his lips.

'Heather drove it there,' Rakisha said. 'Barry knows.'

'How do you know?' Jasper leaned across to see Mrs Lionel. 'Does Heather even know how to drive?'

'Oh, yes,' said Mrs Lionel. 'She knows how to do a lot of things. I've taken all those girls for driving lessons in my time.'

'But how on earth could you tell it was Heather?' said Gerry.

'I told you about the rubbish in the car, didn't I? That's how I knew it was a bloke's car.' Barry scratched his chin. 'But I'd forgotten until the coppers told me who registered the car about the sweet wrappers and the hairbrush.'

'That doesn't prove that Heather was the driver,' said Rosemary. 'Most of us have hair.'

'Doesn't prove nothing, I suppose. But then there was the blood.'

Patti put a hand to her mouth. 'What did the police say about that?'

'They haven't yet. But I know things.' Barry smiled smugly.

'What do you know?' Rosemary said, trying to keep the weariness from her voice.

'I know about Heather's crazy habits.'

Mrs Lionel pushed her bowl roughly away. 'Barry, you need to stop with the foolish innuendos.'

'What's an innuendo?'

'Barry, old mate,' said Gerry. 'I think what Mrs Lionel means is that if you've got something to say, you need to say it. But-' he raised his hand to stop Barry speaking '-only if what you're about to say is fact, and not fiction.'

'I say what I know.'

'Well then, what do you know?'

'Heather Hubbard's always been a weird sort of girl...'

Rosemary took Mrs Lionel's hand and gave it a squeeze to stop the older woman from speaking.

'... because she isn't like other girls. And I'm not talking about her sisters, they aren't so ordinary either, but I mean the other girls she went to school with. I used to see them in the street when I had the garage in Big Town. Bunches of them when I was coming home from work, all hanging around the shops after school. Then there was Heather, by herself, waiting for the bus to Mulbury, staring at the clouds or twirling around the bus stop pole like she was a little kid. I could see the others laughing at her.'

'That doesn't make her weird,' said Jasper.

'You reckon? But one day she missed the bus. I knew

who she was. I mean, who didn't? So, I rang her father, and he was too busy to pick her up-'

Jules tch-tched.

'-so he asked whether I could drive her home.'

'That was nice of you, darling.'

'He paid me, Keesh. Petrol costs a lot, you know.' Barry crossed his arms and tucked his hands into his armpits. 'Anyway, I drove her home, only she had this big school bag in the front with her and it smelled. Ponged. I said, "What you got there, Heather?" and she opened the bag, and it was full of dead birds.'

'Oh,' said Mrs Lionel. 'I suppose they were for her taxidermy.'

Barry's eyebrows shot up. 'You know she stuffs animals?'

'Of course.' Mrs Lionel lifted her head up. 'Everyone in Mulbury knows that. As does anyone who buys feed from their produce store. She's very skilled. Her father sells a few now and then and they fetch a decent price.'

'The money supports the business?' asked Gerry.

'No, dear. More like it supports Richard's music vice.'

Rosemary shook her head slightly.

'So, Barry, you think Heather drove the car to your place with a dead animal on the back seat?' Gerry reached for the wine bottle. 'Hardly a terrible thing to do if taxidermy is her hobby.'

'Good heavens, darling, it is a horrendous thing to do.' Rakisha put both her hands to her face. 'That girl is killing animals in order to stuff them. It's hideous.'

'It may not be your cup of tea, Rakisha,' said Jules, 'but it's not a crime to stuff animals.'

'It is to *kill* them.'

'She doesn't kill them.' Roman spoke quietly from his end of the table. 'She finds them already dead.'

Rakisha's face was splotchy. 'And how would you know, *butcher?*'

'I see her collecting them.' Roman waved his hand towards the far edge of Mulbury where paddocks and bushland stretched out for kilometres. 'I go to inspect my kettle.'

'Cattle, dear.'

'Cattle. The ones that I grow for my restaurant and that get cared for by that good farmer...' Roman looked at Jules.

'Justin.'

'The good farmer, Justin. I see Heather with her bag. She collects birds that have just died, usually hit by cars.'

Rosemary kept her eyes on Barry. His surprise was all over his face but the way he still had his hands jammed into his armpits was telling. 'Barry,' she said, 'what else did the police say?'

Barry shrugged.

'There was more, darling?' Rakisha frowned. 'You didn't tell me everything?'

'Nope.'

'Tell us now,' said Gerry. 'Come on.'

Barry let his hands drop. 'They found a bag behind the passenger seat.'

'Full of birds?'

'No.' Barry chewed his lip for a moment. 'Well, not that they said.'

'What did they say, then?'

'That it had tools in it.'

'What sort of tools?'

'That's all they said.'

'I guess Richard could have had a bag of tools in his car.' Gerry shrugged. 'I know I do in my car's boot.'

'I don't know.' Barry scratched at his ear. 'They sort of sounded strange when they said it. I don't think they were the type of tools you would normally carry around in a car. Anyway, they're testing them, and the blood.'

'Quite mysterious, isn't it?' Jules said, packing up the dessert bowls. 'Anyone for coffee?'

'I have a new batch of artisan beans to try,' said Roman, standing up.

It was a smooth transition, Rosemary thought. Barry's story had stretched as far as it could go. He seemed relieved, but Rakisha had her mouth so tight it was as if someone had drawn her lips on with an HB pencil and a ruler.

In the chatter about the origins of Roman's coffee, Mrs Lionel leaned over to Rosemary. 'Should we be concerned about the likes of Barry?'

'For Heather?' Rosemary shook her head. 'No. He'll drop it now. Rakisha's the troublemaker. She'll follow Heather around.'

'Not if I have anything to do with it.'

Rosemary smiled at the crossness in her friend's voice. 'Heather is well protected from sticky-noses.'

'If we can keep her from wandering.' Mrs Lionel shook her head. 'We need to find out who she's worried about.'

Rosemary gave a quick nod.

Dinner finished after coffee. Before coffee for Rakisha. She excused herself with a 'Must go, darlings' and fled out the front door, leaving a felt shug behind her. Roman gave it to Barry to return to her, but it was still there at the end of the night after he'd left. With slightly more hesitation than was usual, Mrs Lionel took it.

The night was brisk when Rosemary, Jasper and Mrs Lionel finally emerged into it. Roman and Jules waved briefly before going back inside. 'That was an enjoyable meal,' said Mrs Lionel as she climbed into the front passenger seat. 'Did you know Roman had a three-star Michelin at his previous restaurant?'

'Yes,' said Rosemary.

'No,' said Jasper. 'What's he doing in Mulbury then?'

'Jules,' said Mrs Lionel. 'She wanted to come home. Mulbury was where she was born.'

'That's the original family house?'

'No. When Jules was young, they lived above the restaurant. Only it wasn't a restaurant back then. It was a bank.'

'Mrs Lionel, you know everything about this town.'

'And why wouldn't I, Jasper dear? I have lived in this district all my life. And I keep my eyes open.'

Rosemary let a small smile reach her lips as Jasper leaned back in his seat, chuckling quietly. She could see the garage straight ahead, the now-clear driveway leading to a padlocked wire gate. It was only *just* a driveway: more a sticky, red clay patch. No one could be blamed, for example, for thinking it a patch of earth on which you could easily park a car. Places like that dotted Mulbury. It was why the local council didn't bother with marking out parking bays. In fact, there was a car parked to the side of the patch now, dark brown amongst the night shadows. So, was it coincidence that Richard Hubbard's car was parked in Barry's driveway? Rosemary wondered.

Jasper's sudden movement in the back seat alerted Rosemary even before his shout. 'Look out!'

She slammed on the brakes, but years of practice avoiding stray kangaroos meant she didn't swerve. The car's brakes shuddered and kept them straight so that the person standing in the middle of the road frantically waving their hands leapt sideways onto the verge. The car stopped in parallel.

Mrs Lionel wound down her window. 'Are you all right there?'

But Jasper was out of the car, kneeling beside the figure with his hand on their shoulder. Rosemary put the hazard lights on and went to join him.

The person lay on their side, their thick jacket hunched up almost over their head. Jasper carefully tugged it down and a pair of wide, staring eyes gazed at him before turning to Rosemary. At once, the figure struggled upright, overbalancing a little on the uneven road edge.

Rosemary caught at his jacket. 'Marc Cambridge, what are you doing?'

The young man blinked once or twice and shook his head, dazed. 'I frightened you,' he said.

'Yes,' said Rosemary. 'You were standing in the middle of the road, and I almost ran you down.'

'Sorry.' Marc brushed at his coat. 'I've been looking for you. I saw your car and thought I'd catch you now.'

'How did you know it was my car?'

He shrugged. 'No one else has a loud blue car. I could tell it was you when you went under the streetlight.'

'You do realise the time?' Jasper shook his head. 'It's late to try to catch someone's attention.'

'Is it?' Marc did a hurried skim of his phone. 'Oh, sorry, sorry. I was asleep, and I saw your headlights. I guess I thought it was a good chance to catch you.'

'You were asleep?' Jasper glanced around. 'Where?'

'In that car?' Rosemary pointed to the car parked near Barry's garage.

'That's right.' Marc plunged his hands into his pockets.

'That's not the car you had the other day.'

His breath puffed out in a little cloud. 'No, the other

one... broke down.' He shook his head. 'I'm sorry to scare you. I didn't know what else to do.'

'You said you were looking for me.' Rosemary folded her arms across her chest. 'I've been in the shop all day.'

'I came in this evening and thought you might be home.'

'It couldn't wait until the morning?'

Marc shrugged one shoulder after the other. 'It probably could have.'

'Why did you want to speak to Rosemary so urgently?'

'The postcard you gave me,' Marc said, glancing at Rosemary before letting his head drop. 'It's not mine.'

'Everything all right?' Mrs Lionel said from her seat in the car as everyone went quiet.

Rosemary turned and raised a hand to her friend. 'It's too cold to have Mrs Lionel sitting out here. How about I drop her home and then we can talk at my place?'

'Better still,' said Jasper, 'how about you drop Mrs Lionel home and I take Marc back to my place and we can talk there?'

Rosemary eyeballed Jasper, but he had his chin up and jaw clenched. 'Okay. Do you want a lift, or can you walk the twenty metres by yourselves?'

'We'll be fine.' Jasper pinched Marc's coat sleeve and marched him towards *The Read Mulbury*. Rosemary got back in her car and watched them for a moment. It seemed Marc Cambridge was getting a big lecture on leaping out at near-strangers so late in the evening.

'Do you think he's harmless?' Mrs Lionel asked as they drove around the corner and parked in front of her place.

'He's troubled, definitely. Harmlessness is hard to judge.'

'Do you need to get involved?' Mrs Lionel undid her seatbelt but stayed sitting. 'You could tell him to go away.'

'I'm curious.'

'Rosemary Exeter,' said Mrs Lionel. 'Curiosity can lead to misadventure.'

'It can also keep the brain sharp.'

Mrs Lionel picked her handbag up from the footwell of the car. 'Your brain, dear, is sharp enough.'

Rosemary gave her friend's arm a quick squeeze. 'Hurry up and get inside before I freeze.'

Mrs Lionel shook her head but got out of the car, saying nothing more. Rosemary climbed out as well, waiting until Mrs Lionel had unlocked the croaking front door and switched on an inside light before waving goodnight and heading to Jasper's.

Jasper's shop was lit with an array of reading lamps he had arranged in its middle. Rosemary walked past the packed bookshelves and into Jasper's living quarters, where Snowy lay on his back on the couch snoring quietly. Marc sat awkwardly on a stool at the kitchen bench while Jasper tried to make tea and keep an eye on the young man. 'I'll watch him now,' said Rosemary. 'You'll do your neck in.'

Jasper frowned slightly, as if to remind her the situation was no laughing matter, before turning to the other side of the kitchen and setting three mugs out.

'I can see now,' said Marc, pulling at the neck of his coat, 'how this seems terrible.'

'Good,' said Rosemary. 'I wouldn't like to think you approached every encounter with people you don't know in the same way.'

'I'm a little...' Marc waved his hand around.

'Stupid?' said Jasper, banging the kettle back on its stand. 'Reckless? Thoughtless? We could ring the police about you.'

Marc rubbed a hand over his face. 'Please don't,' he said. 'I'm desperate.'

'Whether or not you wanted us involved,' said Rosemary, taking off her jacket and hanging it on the back of a kitchen chair before sitting down, 'we are now. Tell us what's going on.'

'Sit here.' Jasper brought the teapot to the table and pulled out a chair to show Marc exactly where he should sit. 'Right,' he said once he sat as well. 'Out with it.'

'I lost the postcard here after the Band Festival last weekend.' Marc blinked at Rosemary. 'You found it pushed under the door of your shop. I thought I had it back, but it's not the right one.' He reached into his pocket and pulled out an envelope. 'See?'

The postcard slid out onto the table, picture side up. Rosemary and Jasper strained towards it.

'What's wrong with it?' asked Jasper. 'Apart from the fact that it's very faded and I can't quite work out everything on it.' He tapped the tiny cross inked on the front. 'What is that?'

'That's the problem.' Marc swivelled the card so that it faced Rosemary. 'That's not where the cross was. It was here.' He pointed to Mrs Tasher's haberdashery. 'This card is a fake.'

'Are you sure?' said Rosemary.

'Yes. And they wrote the address on the back in someone else's handwriting.'

'What are you saying, then?' said Jasper. 'That Rosemary gave you back the wrong postcard?'

'Well, no. But yes.' Marc put a hand around his tea mug and Rosemary saw how it shook. 'If you had given me the wrong card and the right one was still under your till, I'd feel better.'

'The card I gave you was the one I found under the door.'

The young man shivered. 'Someone has the original card.'

Jasper frowned at Rosemary, but she gave a little shrug. 'Listen here, Marc,' said Jasper. 'This postcard obviously means a lot to you, but I don't understand why you'd think someone would substitute another card. I mean, maybe there are lots of cards out there like yours and the crosses are all in slightly different spots?'

'No. There's only one, and it's mine.'

Rosemary picked up the errant postcard and took it over to Jasper's desk, where there was a stronger reading light. She studied the paper closely.

'See anything, Rosemary?'

'Foxing.'

'What?' Marc spilt his tea as he sat up and mopped the drops up with his sleeve. 'What's *foxing*?'

Rosemary brought the card over to the men and showed its underside. 'The discolouration on old paper is known as foxing. It's a sign of age. Unless, of course, someone did it on purpose to make it seem old.'

Marc bobbed his head. 'That's right. It's not my card. This cross is over the wrong shop.'

'But what does the cross mean?' said Jasper. 'Did your grandmother ever say?'

'No. But she kept that card very safe.'

Rosemary sipped her tea and studied the young man's face. He was very pale, and the stubble on his face was thick. 'You know what it means.'

'I'm only guessing.'

Rosemary said nothing.

Marc was quiet for a long time. Rosemary stopped

Jasper from interrupting the silence by putting a firm hand on his arm. Marc's fingers twitched an uneven beat on the table, and his leg was bouncing up and down. She waited.

Finally, Marc said, 'I didn't recognise the photo until I came to the Band Festival. I drove down Goldmarket Road, and something clicked. There were the shops, the same as on the postcard. Well, sort of different because the photo was taken of the old days. But I still recognised them.' He tapped the card. 'It was the place it happened.'

Jasper frowned. 'The place where what happened?'

Marc's eyes were a deep ocean blue in the dim light of the bookshop. 'The place where my grandfather went missing.'

SIXTEEN

Ronnie Edwards got out of bed at an uncustomary early hour. He slipped into the kitchen, patting Cuddles on the way through, and started the coffee percolator. Work documents were strewn across the dining room table in the chaos he'd left them the night before, so he sorted them out, taking care to put some straight into his satchel. The yellow dog thumped his tail as Ronnie hung the satchel on the hall coat stand next to his business coat.

'What are you doing, Ronnie?'

Honey stood at the doorway of their bedroom, all tousled hair and crumpled flannel pyjamas.

'Getting ready, you know.' Ronnie went back to the kitchen. 'I'll get you a cup of tea in bed.'

'Can't stay there any longer.' Honey put her hands on her lower back and arched it with a groan. 'Tallulah is lying on something.'

'Oh.' Ronnie put the mugs he'd just picked up on the bench and hurried over. 'Are you alright? Should you go to the doctor?'

Honey stood up straight and put one hand on Ronnie's

shoulder. 'I'm only going to say this once more, you adorable man. Stop fussing. Right? I am perfectly fine and so is Tallulah. According to the books and the ever-reliable internet, I will experience aches and pains, discomfort, indigestion, urinary urgency, fatigue, and sudden desire for fishcakes before this is over.'

'Fishcakes?' Ronnie twisted around to look at the fridge. 'I don't think we have any. I could get some when I'm out-'

'Ronnie.' Honey let him go and stomped to the kitchen. 'Fishcakes were an example. It could be liver, cheese, or caviar. That's what *sudden* means. Unpredictable.' She poured herself a tea. 'Relax.'

Ronnie rolled his shoulders and head around in a routine of relaxation. 'Sorry, Honey. I'm not really worried. Well, I am a bit. It's all so new. And there was the... you know. But I'll go with what you say. I know you hate me fussing.'

'You've got it right there.' Honey opened the cupboard and took out a cereal packet. 'Anyway, I suspect that it's not me and Tallulah that made you get up so early. You're going to Mulbury today to speak to my mother, aren't you?'

Ronnie squared his shoulders. 'I have work to do today in Mulbury.'

'You're going to tell her about the rest of the coroner's report.'

'I am conducting an independent investigation.'

'Using local sources. Very sensible, I would have thought.' Honey grinned at him and poured oats into a bowl.

'Not only your mother. I need to talk to Mrs Lionel again as well.'

'Of course. Save time, though, and talk to them together.'

'Do you think so?'

'I know so.' Honey leaned back on the bench and sipped her coffee. 'See if you can get a jar of whatever Mum's cooking up.'

'Honey, I can't ask that.'

'Say that I said so.' Honey grimaced and put her mug down. 'There's that urgency now.'

As Honey disappeared into the bathroom, Ronnie sat at the dining room table and thought back to last night's work. Uncle Geoffrey had emailed the official coroner's report with a note that said, *This will be referred to homicide. They'll want to know who this man is. We need any clue to his identity ASAP.*

'I've got urgent business to do, too, Honey,' he called.

'Well then, go and do it.' Honey emerged from the bathroom and kissed his cheek. 'Go.'

She and Cuddles waved him away from the door. The last glimpse he had of his family before he drove away was the slender Honey Blossom dressed in pink pyjamas that skimmed her tummy alongside a smiling, wagging yellow dog. He rang Rosemary on the way to Mulbury.

'Ronnie.'

'Hello, Rosemary. I was wondering whether you'd be home this morning?'

'I'm in the shop. Where else would I be?'

'Oh, well, I thought so. Could I come to speak to you?'

Rosemary's voice sharpened. 'Is it Honey?'

'No. No, Honey's fine. Great, really. It's about the man in the Square.'

'I'll be here.'

'Do you think you could ask Mrs Lionel in as well? I'd like to speak to her.'

'We've had a late night, but I suspect she's in the shop now.'

'Did something happen last night?'

'Yes.'

'Are you alright?'

'Yes. Do you have plenty of time this morning, Ronnie?'

'Oh, yes, nothing else on besides this investigation.'

'Good. There's someone else you need to talk to.'

'Oh. Righto. I'll be there soon.' Ronnie slowed to let a bounding kangaroo go over the road. 'I'll be getting a coffee. Would you and Mrs Lionel want one?'

'Would you be going to *Mullings of Mulbury*?'

'Yes, I really like-'

'Get one for Mrs Lionel, flat white, one sugar. Not for me, thank you.'

'Are you sure-'

'I'll see you when you get here, Ronnie.' The phone clicked.

Ronnie twisted his hands on the steering wheel. The sun was low, sending out long arms across the paddock that caught the frost on the grass. He thought about Rosemary Exeter and how she made him feel like a student in the principal's office. He coughed and straightened in his seat. *I'm a grown man*, he thought. *I shouldn't feel like that. A grown man and soon-to-be father...*

A smile spread over his face. A father. Something he'd never thought he'd be. Honey had come into his life like a beacon from a lighthouse, standing on that stage in Big Town with him in the audience, flabbergasted at her compelling Lady Macbeth. When she rubbed frantically at the blood on her hands, Ronnie had to clutch the side of his seat to stop him leaping on stage and hugging her. He'd hung around after the show with the groupies outside the green room and as Honey emerged—scrubbed free of makeup, her long hair tied back loosely, an oversized jumper dwarfing her slenderness—he almost swooned. Well, he did swoon a little, because when he got his bearings back, Honey had both her arms around him and was lowering him to the ground.

'Careful there, big fellow,' she'd said, and smiled.

He'd grinned foolishly back, struggled to a sitting position, and said, 'You are the most beautiful creature I have ever seen. Would you like to go for a drink?'

The rest wasn't, as they say, history. She'd let him go, given a little laugh, and said, 'No thanks.' It had taken another three months—four more Macbeths and quite a few accidental supermarket encounters—before she'd sit with him for a coffee and bee-sting pastry. Then there were another couple of months of occasional phone calls and a few more coffees before finally there was a dinner at the pub where they sat on well after other patrons had left, discovered a mutual love of dogs and, maybe, each other.

Ronnie slowed for the drive into Mulbury. He turned the corner and parked the car in front of *The Preserved Mulbury*. He could see Rosemary inside with a customer, gift packing a range of jars. Still warm from the glow of Honey memory, he left the car and crossed the Square to Kelly's.

The Exceptional Tree waved a few branches in his direction. The crime-scene tape was long gone and in the soft light of the autumn day it was hard to imagine a man lying dead—murdered—under the Tree's expansive cover. It was too nice a day, too nice a town, to have such things happen. Ronnie shook his head. Even less than twelve months as a private investigator had taught him that bad things could happen anywhere.

Kelly's café was empty except for Kelly herself placing wrapped salad rolls into the refrigerator, and a man who looked like a sapling—sinewy and thin—sitting at a table. He stared at Ronnie as he came in, gave a nod which made the wisps of his hair float around, and went back to the paper he was reading.

'Ronald,' said Kelly, wiping her hands on her stiff apron. 'What can I do for you?'

'It's Ronnie, actually.' Ronnie gave a wistful smile. 'Ronald was my father and when someone calls me that, I always think-'

'Cappuccino?'

'Oh, yes, thanks. And a flat white with one sugar for Mrs Lionel.'

Kelly went to her coffee machine. 'Visiting her, are you?'

'Yes, in a way, yes.'

'Business, is it?'

'Yes, that's it.'

Kelly pushed viciously at a lever. 'Seeing Rosemary as well?'

Ronnie saw the man in the corner stiffen. 'Well, yes, keeping her in touch with Honey.'

'How is she?' said the man suddenly.

'Honey's fine,' said Ronnie. 'Bit of morning sickness, well, afternoon nausea-'

'I meant Rosemary.'

'Oh.' Ronnie watched Kelly, who was searing the milk with a face pursed and hard. 'She's over there.' He pointed out the window at where the customers were leaving Rosemary's shop.

'I know that. I didn't ask that.' The man rubbed his long face with a spindly hand. 'How *is* she?'

'Rosemary is perfectly the same, as I told you, Darren.' Kelly slammed two lids on the coffees.

'I want to hear it from the boy.'

Ronnie bristled. Thirty-two was not a boy, he felt like saying. Instead, he paid Kelly and said, 'Rosemary is doing very well, thank you.'

'Still by herself, then?'

Ronnie felt a sudden hardness fall on him. 'She has her family. And many friends.' He went to leave, but Darren stood and beat him to the door.

'Is she still pining? Missing that horrible man? Unable to move on without him?'

Ronnie leaned back as far as was polite. Darren's pointy head was right in his face and if it wasn't because he knew Mrs Lionel loved an occasional coffee, he would've dropped them both on the floor and belted out through the door. That, and the fact that Darren had an arm across the doorway, shielding it from Ronnie's retreat.

'Darren, let it go,' Kelly said angrily. 'Rosemary Exeter is a lost cause.'

Darren shook his head slightly and kept staring at Ronnie.

Ronnie took a little sip of his scorching-hot coffee. 'Well,' he said slowly, 'I've never seen Rosemary pine. I've only ever seen her getting on with her life. And if she misses Alasdair, who could blame her? They were married for thirty years.'

'Yes, but she could have-'

'Darren,' said Kelly sharply. 'Leave it.'

Darren left it, but not before Ronnie saw how his fists clenched and his face darkened. 'Well,' said Ronnie, 'I'd better get this to Mrs Lionel before it goes cold.' He lifted the penetratingly hot cup and exited as rapidly as he could.

Through the glass of Rosemary's shop now he could see Rosemary and Mrs Lionel standing near the counter watching him. There was a young man with them as well, someone who had a thick coat on despite the decent day. Ronnie jangled through the door and went straight to Mrs Lionel. 'There,' he said, delivering the coffee on to the counter. 'Probably the hottest, most bitterly strong coffee you've ever had, going on mine.'

'In fine form, is she?' said Rosemary.

Ronnie tried another sip of his coffee and grimaced. 'You don't think much of Kelly's coffee?'

Rosemary's left eyebrow went up. 'Kelly Flanagan poisons most things.'

Ronnie put his coffee down hastily.

'I meant figuratively, Ronnie. I'm only talking about in my case.' Rosemary pointed to his cup. 'You'll be fine.'

Ronnie lifted his cup but didn't drink. 'There was this man in the shop with her. Neither of them seemed very happy.'

'Darren's here, dear,' said Mrs Lionel, taking a sip of her coffee and pulling a face.

Rosemary pressed her lips together. 'Yes. Checking The Exceptional Tree for trouble.'

'I hope that's all the trouble he encounters.' Mrs Lionel gave Rosemary a stern glance and put her cup back down. 'Now, Ronnie, I believe you want to see us but first I'd like to introduce you to someone.' She waved her hand toward the young man.

Ronnie turned just as the man looked up. 'Oh,' said Ronnie, stepping forwards to grab the man in the thick coat in a bear-hug. 'Marc Cambridge. I thought you were dead.'

Rosemary glanced at Mrs Lionel, who shrugged. Marc had his eyes closed and was painfully stiff in Ronnie's embrace. 'Ronnie,' said Rosemary, 'let him breathe.'

'Oh, sorry, sorry.' Ronnie stepped back, grinning. 'I really didn't expect to see you ever again.'

'I really didn't expect to see *you* ever again.' Marc rubbed his face.

Ronnie looked at Mrs Lionel. 'This is the person you wanted to introduce me to?'

'That's right.'

'Same with you, Rosemary?'

'Yes.'

'Well, Marc and me, we go back over ten years.' Ronnie grinned. 'We've known each other since university.'

'Yes,' said Marc.

'Madrigals.' Ronnie shook his head. 'I only joined to meet the girls. Found out I couldn't sing.'

'You lasted a semester,' said Marc.

'Only because they needed numbers. At least *you* could sing.'

'The bar wasn't very high.'

'Well, I was a long way under it.' Ronnie chuckled.

'It sounds like you have a long time to catch up on,' said Mrs Lionel.

'Yeah.' Ronnie's laughter died away. 'Seriously, Marc, I heard you lost your job. And then you sort of, well, disappeared.'

'Yeah, I did.' Marc's face grew pinched. 'I had to get away for a while after that.'

'You lost your job, dear?' said Mrs Lionel. 'That's hard.'

Marc scuffed the floor with the point of his shoe. 'Yeah, it was hard. I went away…'

'But you're back now.' Ronnie slapped a hand on Marc's shoulder. 'Maybe we could get the madrigals together for a reunion? I keep in touch with one or two. They'd love to see you. Catch up on old times. Could be fun.'

Rosemary watched Marc, noting the way his pale face whitened, making the grooves around his eyes and nose deepen into shadow. She held up her hand. 'Time for that later. Let's go into the house where we can sit.'

She led the way through the door, where baskets piled with apples meant they had to weave their way to the dining table. 'From the girls,' said Rosemary to Mrs Lionel. 'Apparently Heather helped them pick.'

'I suggested to them she would be better given a task. Once she starts, she continues until you stop her.' Mrs Lionel dabbed at her eyes. 'It's a bit like having a robot worker.'

'She'll come good.' Rosemary spoke softly.

Mrs Lionel shook her head tiredly and sat on the chair Ronnie pulled out for her. Rosemary went to the head of the table with Marc on her left and Ronnie, notebook at hand, on her right.

'I don't get why you're here, Marc,' Ronnie said, elbows on the table.

Rosemary folded her hands in her lap. 'Marc came to see me last night and stayed with Jasper.'

'But why? I mean, Mulbury means nothing to you, does it?'

'It never used to.' Marc pulled the postcard from his coat pocket and explained it to Ronnie. 'Now I've got the wrong one.'

'That's weird, but I still don't get why it's so important.'

Marc looked from Ronnie to Mrs Lionel, who smiled kindly. 'This cross on the card,' he said uncertainly, 'shows the place where my grandfather went missing.'

Ronnie's face moved through a range of red tones. 'What makes you think *that*?'

Rosemary folded her hands on the table. When Jasper had asked that same question last night, Marc had only shaken his head, keeping his mouth closed as if he was going to be sick. They'd packed him off to sleep in Jasper's spare bed without pursuing the idea, with the instruction that he was to explain more in the morning. She leaned forward now to hear what he had to say.

'My grandfather went missing in 1983, the date on this postcard.' Marc pushed himself back in his chair. 'According to my grandmother, he was a devoted family man. He was away for the day doing business and didn't come home. It was the day the fires started, and the authorities finally concluded that he had died in them.'

'I could think of other reasons someone might not return home,' said Rosemary. She didn't dare look at Mrs Lionel. 'Maybe he didn't *want* to come home.'

Marc frowned. 'His death is the only logical explana-

tion. Otherwise, he would have gone back to my grandmother. He loved her.'

'And you think the postcard shows the place he went
missing?' Ronnie twiddled his pen. 'I still don't see the
connection.'

'Granny kept this card. It was the last correspondence
from my grandfather.'

'But why would he send your grandmother a card with
a cross?'

'I think something happened to him and he sent it as a
clue. Kidnapped or worse.' Marc leaned forward and whispered, 'It could have been murder.'

In the silence that followed that, Rosemary kept her
gaze on Marc.

'Gosh,' said Ronnie. 'That's a long bow.'

'Scarlet Tuesday, dear,' said Mrs Lionel. 'That was in
1983. He could have perished in the fires, rest his soul.'

'You could ask Ronnie to help you solve the mystery,'
said Rosemary. 'He's a private investigator and quite useful.'
She didn't fail to see Ronnie's face colour.

'You're a PI?' Marc asked, his hands clenched on the
edge of the table. 'I thought you'd end up an accountant.'

'I did for a while. Honey said that life's too short to do
things that bore you, so I changed career directions.'

'Who's Honey?'

'My daughter,' said Rosemary.

Marc swallowed. 'You have a girlfriend?'

'Wife,' said Ronnie proudly. 'And we're having a
baby.'

Rosemary watched Marc nod briefly. His fingers had
started the staccato motion from last night, and his leg
movements were making the table shake. 'Ronnie is investi-
gating another mystery in this area,' she said. 'As he's doing

his official investigation, he might discover something useful for you.'

'Yeah, that's right.' Ronnie smiled gratefully at Rosemary.

'Great.' Marc tucked the postcard back into its envelope. 'What's the other mystery you're working on?'

'Mrs Lionel discovered a dead man under The Exceptional Tree last week.'

'A dead man?'

'Yes, dear.' Mrs Lionel shook her head. 'Poor man. A bitter night to die. Ronnie's trying to work out who he was.'

'You don't know who he was?'

'Not yet,' said Ronnie. 'I think I'm getting closer. The police might have a better chance of finding out who killed him if they know who he is.'

Marc drummed his fingers on the table a moment longer, then stood up so quickly that the chair nearly fell. 'It's great seeing you again, Ronnie, but I've got to go now.'

'Go?' Ronnie's eyebrows shot into his fringe. 'I've only just caught up with you.'

'Yes. Good to see you. But I've overstayed my welcome here.'

'Stay as long as you want,' said Rosemary mildly.

'Thanks, but no. I've got things to do.' Marc nodded at Mrs Lionel and Rosemary. 'I'm going to see if I can find that other postcard.' He stumbled from the table, disturbing Sunny's nap on the windowsill. 'I'll see you another time.'

'Hang on, Marc.' Ronnie went to go after him, but Rosemary put her hand on his sleeve. 'Leave it, Ronnie.'

'But... '

'I'd let him go, dear,' said Mrs Lionel. 'Something's going on with that young man. Was he like this at university?'

Ronnie sat back down, shaking his head. 'No, not at all. He was one of the confident ones. Not like me. I heard, though, that he lost his job from something wrong that he did. Perhaps he's changed since uni?'

'It happens,' said Rosemary.

'Sad.' Ronnie kept shaking his head. 'I thought *I* was going to end up the lost one.'

'There's nothing lost about you, dear.' Mrs Lionel tapped Ronnie's arm. 'I believe you came to interview us again. Have you found out the identity of that poor old man?'

Ronnie pulled his notebook from his satchel. 'I've had some luck, Mrs Lionel, but I need you to tell me something if you can.'

'Certainly, Ronnie.'

'You said you were sweeping the Square when you discovered the old man. Do you remember seeing anything unusual on the ground? Something you might then have put in the rubbish?'

Mrs Lionel frowned. 'I'm not really in the habit of looking closely at what I've swept up. I usually use the street bins because it's only a few stray leaves and the occasional sweet wrapper.'

'You don't think there was anything else in the rubbish you swept?'

'Nothing unusual. Why?'

'The man was wearing a tailored suit, as you said, Rosemary. A three-piece suit, double-breasted. It was handmade by a tailor in the city who stopped trading in the 1980s. He was known for making a pocket square for every suit and threading the client's initials into its edge. I thought you might have found the pocket square.'

'So, Rosemary was correct in saying it was the poor dear's suit.'

'Well, they say the sleeves and the legs were his length. It was big on him, but he was very thin. They concluded it could be the man's suit but made to his measurements from a long time ago. It was so threadbare that it was practically transparent.'

'He may have lost that pocket square many years ago then.'

'The squares were sewn in. A particular mark of that tailor, according to the expert dressmaker I spoke to. She couldn't remember his name, only that he was known for his good work and his collection of outfitter antiques.'

'Sewing in a pocket square is not good pocket square etiquette,' said Mrs Lionel.

'But handy for us.' Ronnie's shoulders slumped. 'If the square had been in the pocket. Or the square had been in the Square.'

'I'm sorry, I found nothing to help you.'

'Well, that was one lead. The other is the cause of death.'

'The wound?' Mrs Lionel put her hand to her mouth. 'He was stabbed, wasn't he?'

'Yes.'

'Did they say what with?' Rosemary asked.

'A thin blade, something of a specialty they're trying to identify.' Ronnie reached for his satchel and drew out the coroner's report. '"*Penetration of the myocardium resulting in almost instant loss of life.*" Apparently, it went straight into his heart.'

'No doubt severing the aorta.' Mrs Lionel shook her head. 'At least it would have been quick.'

'And he was wearing an old-fashioned elastic back brace which acted as the tamponade.'

Rosemary frowned. 'He had a long-standing back injury then, maybe from his previous occupation.'

'As well as another injury, the one that you noted, Mrs Lionel.'

'The scar I saw?'

'You were right about the head injury. Apparently old, but extensive. As you said, it would have damaged his brain. He probably didn't even know where he was.'

'Or who he was,' said Rosemary.

'Oh, the poor dear,' said Mrs Lionel. 'He'd had a rough life.'

'It seems so,' said Ronnie. 'Homicide is taking over. They want me to hand over any information I have.' He swivelled in his chair to face Rosemary. 'That's why I had to talk to you today.'

'Why? I know nothing.'

'Perhaps not directly, but you mentioned about the tailored suit, which was useful. Have you thought of anything else?'

'You haven't tracked down the tailor?'

'No. The shop was closed so long ago.'

'And you don't know the tailor's name?'

'No, but the dressmaker remembered the shop. It was called *Button Menswear*.' Ronnie shrugged.

'Go to the state library's archives. You might discover more about the business that way.'

'Oh, that's great, Rosemary. Thanks.' Ronnie pushed his chair back and stood up. 'Honey was right.'

'About what, dear?' said Mrs Lionel.

'That you would both be able to help me. I really appreciate it.'

Mrs Lionel smiled. 'How is Honey Blossom?'

Ronnie tucked his notebook into his satchel. 'She's good. Mainly.' He froze. 'Do you think I should get some caviar? Just in case?'

Rosemary frowned. 'In case of what?'

'Sudden cravings.'

Mrs Lionel put her hand out to touch Rosemary's sleeve before she could say anything. 'No, dear, I wouldn't buy caviar. It might be the thing she cannot eat.'

A commotion on the footpath made Rosemary look up. She could just see, through the doorway to the shop and beyond, the dark shapes of four people under the veranda, three of whom were talking at the same time. 'It's the sisters,' she said. 'Something's going on out there.'

Mrs Lionel was the last up from the table. Rosemary helped her with her chair, then led the way through *The Preserved Mulbury* to the street. Holly held Heather's hand tightly as the younger sister thrashed about while Hannah, one hand on Heather's shoulder and the other reaching out for the fourth person among them, simultaneously tried to soothe Heather and yell at the stranger. 'It's okay, Heather. *Who are you?* It'll be fine. *What have you done to my sister?*'

Rosemary stepped in front of the sisters. 'Is everything okay?'

'It's Heather,' said Hannah.

Heather tried to tug free of her sisters' grip. She pointed.

Rosemary turned to see Marc Cambridge on the footpath behind her. He stared at Heather, eyes wide. Rosemary turned back to Heather and gently held her arm. 'What is it, Heather?'

'Him.' Heather's eyes were wide. 'It's him. He's here.'

EIGHTEEN

Marc Cambridge twisted around as Heather spoke and, when he saw no one standing behind him, turned back with an open mouth. 'What does she mean?' he said, his face grey.

'Heather, dear,' said Mrs Lionel, walking over to the girl. 'Who do you mean?'

Heather turned teary blue eyes to the older woman. 'Him.' She shook her pointed finger. 'Joe.'

'Oh no,' said Marc quickly, 'I'm not Joey Cambridge. Joey's my father. I'm *Marc* Cambridge.'

'Wait on a moment.' Hannah folded her arms across her chest. 'Why should Heather know someone called Joey Cambridge? *We* don't know him.'

'Ask her,' said Rosemary mildly.

Hannah let her arms down to tug at Heather's sleeve. 'Who do you mean, feathery Heathery? We don't know anyone of that name.'

Heather blinked slowly and focused on Hannah. 'Joe.' She pointed to Marc.

'Hang on,' said Holly, staring at Marc, 'I think I remember. A man bought a bird right before Dad left.' She squinted at Marc. 'He looked like you. Dark hair. Bright blue eyes. Same build but older.' She shrugged. 'As he would be if he was your father.'

'I don't remember.' Hannah let Heather go and walked over to get a better view of Marc, who cringed backwards until he came up against the window of *The Preserved Mulbury*. 'This guy isn't the least bit familiar to me.'

'You were out,' said Holly. 'You had to get a load of calf milk powder in the ute.' Hannah frowned. 'This man turned up and went with Dad to see Heather's birds. I could hear them.'

'He bought a bird?'

'Yes.' Holly turned to stroke Heather's arm. 'Guess which one.'

'Not the eagle?'

'Yes.'

Hannah frowned. 'Why did Dad have to sell that?'

'It was the best of Heather's work, and he needed the money.'

Hannah stared at her sister. 'You mean it was worth the most. Dad used the money to go away, didn't he?'

Holly shrugged. 'I heard Dad playing the guitar after the man left.'

Hannah tapped her foot on the ground. 'Minor or major?'

'Yeah, minor.'

Mrs Lionel took Heather's hand and rubbed it. 'What do you mean, minor?'

'Riffs.' Hannah shifted her weight to her other leg and started tapping it. 'You could tell the mood Dad was in by what he was playing. A Blues A minor riff meant he wasn't happy. I think he felt guilty.'

'Did Heather see all this happening?'

Holly put a palm on her forehead. 'She was in her taxi-dermy room so she would have.'

'Oh, crumbs.' Hannah sighed. 'I bet she didn't even try to stop Dad.'

Heather gave a tiny whimper and Mrs Lionel rubbed her hand harder. 'What is it, love? Did you want to say anything?'

Heather closed her eyes. Her head dropped a little.

'She doesn't seem very well,' said Ronnie. 'Do you think she should sit down?'

'I think that's a good idea.' Mrs Lionel put one arm around Heather's shoulders. 'Could we perhaps have some tea, Rosemary?'

Rosemary extended her arm to show the doorway to the house, and let Mrs Lionel and Heather go first, followed by Hannah, Holly, Ronnie, and lastly Marc, whose face was the colour of bleached cardboard. She thought back to his late-night apprehension of her vehicle. Pale from lack of sleep or something else? She went in after him and headed for the kettle.

'What I'm struggling with,' said Ronnie as he plonked himself in a chair next to the couch where the three sisters and Mrs Lionel had squashed themselves, 'is why Heather seems so upset.' He put his hand up. 'Forgive me if it's none of my business, but I hear things through Honey and realise that Heather has... difficulties sometimes. You see, I've known Marc for years. Not that I've seen you for years, Marc, but I always thought you a decent guy.'

'But it's not Marc we're talking about,' said Hannah. 'It's his father.'

'I look like my father,' said Marc from the depths of another armchair. 'But that's where the resemblance ends.'

'Has he come with you to Mulbury?'

'No, no. I came here by myself. I don't know where Dad is. We don't keep in touch.'

Hannah frowned. 'He knows this place, though. He knew about Heather's birds.'

Marc shrugged. 'He collects taxidermy. I mean, he did when I was young. I bet he still does.'

'Tea,' said Rosemary, bringing a large pot to the coffee table. 'And coffee.' She handed Mrs Lionel the cup from Kelly's café. 'Don't want to waste it.'

Mrs Lionel gave her a wry smile and sipped. 'At least it's cooler now.'

Rosemary brought the rest of the tea paraphernalia over and sat down on the last empty chair. Sunny stalked over from her place on the windowsill and jumped on to Rosemary's lap. Heather lifted her head at his movement. Rosemary picked the ginger tabby up and placed her on Heather's lap, where the young woman started stroking the striped head. Sunny gave Rosemary a stare that said, *not this again*, but stayed put.

'Okay,' said Hannah, 'we'll have to go back to the shed soon, so listen. We were coming to get some of Rosemary's delicious quince syrup for our pancakes and we end up finding out that this random dude here is the spitting image of Heather's current nemesis. Anyone got any answers?'

'The quince syrup is in my fridge,' said Rosemary, pouring herself a tea. 'Help yourself.'

Hannah frowned at Rosemary. 'Anything else?'

Holly leaned forward. 'Do you have anything to say about this mistaken identity, Marc Cambridge?'

Marc balanced a teacup on one knee. 'No.' He clutched at his beverage. 'My dad and I had a falling out a long time ago.'

'That's sad for you, dear,' said Mrs Lionel.

'Don't you even know where your dad is?' Hannah said, then stopped. 'Well, *we* don't know where *our* dad is either.'

'I haven't seen my dad for years.' Marc put the teacup on the table in front of him and wriggled his shoulders.

Rosemary studied him. Marc's eyes were a vivid blue, the colour of kingfisher wings, and his wild hair was pitch black. 'I've seen him,' she said. 'I've seen your father.'

'Really?' Marc choked on his tea for a moment. 'Where?'

'He came into the shop on the day Mrs Lionel found the old man.'

'How do you know it was him?' Mrs Lionel gave Heather's free hand a squeeze.

'Because when you came in the next day...' Rosemary tipped her head towards Marc '... I almost mistook you for him.'

'What did he want, Rosemary?' asked Mrs Lionel.

'He said he was just looking. And then he left.'

Marc bowed his head, his attention on the array of items on Rosemary's coffee table. Idly, he picked up the group of Space Westerns and fanned them out in his hand. Ronnie frowned at Rosemary. 'Have you seen him since?'

'Yes. On the road to Big Town on Saturday.'

Marc dropped the books to the table. 'He was here last weekend?'

'This is all too weird,' said Hannah, frowning at Marc. 'You said you haven't seen him for years and now you both turn up in the same place? What's going on?'

'I don't know.' Marc's whisper was almost too quiet to hear.

Hannah crossed her arms. 'Well, Heather is clearly

unhappy, so I'd appreciate it if both you and your father kept away from her. Okay?'

But Marc didn't appear to hear. He rocked slightly on his chair.

Voices outside made Rosemary turn to look through the doorway and out to the street where she could see Darren—it must be him, so tall and skinny—standing under The Exceptional Tree and measuring the angle of its branches with a surveyor's instrument, watched by a group of curious tourists. He reached up to a branch and pulled it towards him, examining it for a long time as if fascinated by its bark. Rosemary put her tea down with a clunk.

At the noise, Mrs Lionel shifted on the couch, making Hannah and Holly shuffle along to give her more space. 'We'd better go,' said Holly to Hannah. 'Isn't there a load of chaff coming this morning?'

Hannah checked her phone. 'In about fifteen minutes.'

'Leave Heather here with me, girls,' said Mrs Lionel. 'I'll bring her along in a little while'

'You are a gem, Mrs Lionel,' said Holly as she stood up.

'A priceless diamond.' Hannah stood as well. 'Thanks for the tea, Rosemary, and the man-identification.'

'Any time.'

The two young women jangled out the front door as Mrs Lionel got stiffly to her feet. 'Off you go, Sunny,' she said to the cat, who sprang gratefully away from Heather's endless pats to go back to her windowsill. 'Up you get, Heather.'

Heather rose automatically. She noticed Marc again and pointed at him, but didn't make a sound. Mrs Lionel steered her towards the shop's door, Rosemary following.

Mrs Lionel paused halfway out the door. 'There are a lot of things going on that make little sense, Rosemary.'

Rosemary placed her hand on her friend's shoulder. 'They will in the end.'

'I'm curious to know when the end will be.' Mrs Lionel walked on, calling over her shoulder, 'You should see Darren before he plucks up enough courage to find his way over to you. Get it done with the least fuss.'

Rosemary shook her head, but Mrs Lionel's attention was on the golden-headed young woman by her side. Over in the Square, Darren was busily noting something on his computer. Rosemary sighed. As usual, Mrs Lionel was correct. She glanced at Ronnie and Marc sitting staring at each other in her living room, shut the door behind her, and crossed the road to Goldmarket Square.

Whatever you could say about Darren—and Rosemary had a lot of things she could say—he was a good arborist. Thorough, cautious, but sensible. He knew the value of aged trees, understood that they were irreplaceable and a lot more revered than aged people. She saw the way he checked and rechecked his calculations and even, begrudgingly, appreciated how he finished with one area and gave the ancient branch a little pat, as if to reassure it.

'Hello, Darren,' she said after standing behind him for a moment.

The device slipped from his hand as he swung quickly around, but he caught it before it could fall. 'Rosie.'

'*Rosemary*, Darren. You know that.'

'Sorry, I do.' He smiled, a familiar full-blown, all-tooth grin. 'What are you doing here?'

'Acknowledging you.'

'Got time for a coffee?'

'No.'

He slotted the stylus back into its holding spot without taking his eyes from her. 'How are you, Rosemary?'

'Fine.'

He waited. 'I think the next thing is for you to say, *how are you* back.'

'I'm not interested in how you are, Darren. I'm here to show that I saw you. Now I'm going back to work.' She turned, but he stopped her with a light grip on her upper arm.

'I know you don't want anything to do with me, Rosemary,' he said, close to her ear. 'I'm really sorry about that because I'd be yours in a heartbeat.' She pulled away from him and he put up a hand in apology. 'I know. It's not going to happen.'

'That is correct.'

His thin shoulders drooped, and she thought for a moment that he was going to collapse on to the dirt. Then he rallied, the toothy grin back on his face. 'I heard about the old man's death here last week.' He put a hand in his pocket. 'This might interest you.'

She held out her hand, and he placed a tiny metal object in it.

NINETEEN

'Rosemary!'

The shout was urgent enough for Rosemary to only scan the object before she closed her hand and slipped it into her pocket.

'Who's that?' Darren clutched his computer to his chest, his other hand forming a fist.

'Jasper Lu,' said Rosemary. 'He owns the bookshop.'

'Why is he standing there waving his arm like an idiot?'

Rosemary frowned. Jasper was glued to the footpath outside his shop front, his hand gesticulating violently for her to join him. 'Bye Darren,' she said as she walked away.

'But Rosie, Rosemary, you need to look at what I gave to you.' Darren, too, was staying where he was.

What is wrong with these men? thought Rosemary crossly. *Can't they walk?* 'Later, Darren.'

She crossed the road and saw why Jasper was stuck. The front window of his shop was broken, and he had hold of a section of the wooden cross-panelling.

'What are you doing?'

'The whole thing's going to collapse.' He panted with effort. 'If I let it go, I'm afraid it'll smash all over the books.'

'It won't hurt them.'

'Yes, it will. They might get cut.'

'So might you if the whole window goes. Here, let me.' Rosemary stepped closer, noticing the way the bottom pane was smashed inwards, and the broken crossbar splintered in the same direction. She carefully pulled off fragments of glass that were dangerously pointy and lay them in a pile on the ground. Gradually, Jasper eased his hold. The rest of the window sagged but held.

'What happened?'

'I don't know. I went to unlock the door this morning and saw it.' Jasper had a thin line of blood on his palm, and he wiped at it absent-mindedly, smearing blood over both hands. 'Did you hear anything? I was getting more books from the cellar, and I didn't.'

'No, but it's hard to hear from inside my kitchen.'

'Do you think it was an accident?'

'No.' Rosemary pointed. 'Not with that in there.'

A red brick lay amongst the broken glass and books. It was one that matched those of the shops in Goldmarket Street, and Rosemary knew that there were spare half-bricks behind the end of Patti and Gerry's building.

'Who would do such a thing?'

'The question is *why* would someone do such a thing.'

Jasper leaned down to see the brick more closely. 'Wait on.' He straightened and went back inside the shop, reaching over the books at the back of the display to collect the ones now decorated with pieces of windowpane.

Rosemary cleared what she could from the front and then went inside to help him. He continued to work in silence until they had retrieved the last book. 'Ah,' he said, using his hanky to blot more blood from his palm.

'You'll have to expand on that.'

'See?' He pointed with his foot at two paperbacks.

Rosemary squatted. 'Space Westerns.'

'Rosemary, *T. G. G. Duncan*. The ultimate in Space Westerns. There's a book missing.'

'Taken?'

'Seems like it.'

'Which one?'

'*Forces and Horses.*'

Rosemary straightened. 'That book again.'

'I found I had another tatty old copy.' He rubbed his face, leaving a line of blood on his cheek. 'Why would they take just that book?'

'Why indeed?' Rosemary studied Jasper, whose face was pale. He had the shakes, too, a fine tremor that shook his whole body. 'Time for you to sit down.'

He let himself be led back into his house and sat on a chair. Rosemary made strong tea and handed him a mug with three sugars in it. She sat next to him and waited until the mug was half empty.

'Thanks, Rosemary.' He smiled. 'That's better. Since I've been sick, I don't seem to handle shocks very well.'

'No.' Rosemary put her elbow on the table and her chin in her palm. 'We're getting a few lately.'

'Do you ever feel shocked by things that are happening?'

Rosemary stared out through the glass doors of Jasper's balcony. It was a strange sensation. They built all three of the adjoining shop houses the same, with the slight difference of window height or by including French doors. The view from Jasper's kitchen area was almost the same as hers, but skewed. Instead of seeing the neat rows of trees in her backyard and the dots of poultry tugging at the grass, Jasper's yard was a jumble of canes and neglected cottage garden plants that grew woody and straggled throughout the area. She could see her yard, and if she strained, the edge of Mrs Lionel's.

'Rosemary?'

She blinked and Jasper came back into sight, his face now warmed and his dark hair wild. 'Am I ever shocked?' She thought a little longer. 'To tell the truth, Jasper, I don't feel much of anything any more.'

It was the wrong thing to say. Jasper's face fell with such sorrow that Rosemary pulled back. He put his mug down roughly, spilling tea down its side. 'Rosemary, I'm so sorry.'

'Whatever for? It's nothing you've done.'

'And it's nothing *you've* done, either.'

'I know that.' She shrugged. 'It's what happened after Alasdair. I don't expect it will change now.'

'It will, Rosemary.' Jasper put his hand on hers. 'It's a matter of time.'

'A lot of time has passed already, Jasper.'

He shook his head and said something else, but the conversation was over as far as she was concerned. She stood up, taking her hand back from his, and fished out her phone. 'Right. Police? Insurance company? What do you want to do?'

Jasper gave her a sad smile before shaking his head matter-of-factly. 'Don't bother with the police. They aren't really going to worry about an old book.'

'It's not the book, it's the damage.'

'Well, my insurance will cover that, I hope.' He stood as well. 'I'll get my policy and give them a ring. I need to see whether I can clean it up before an inspector comes along. Doesn't look good for business.'

'I'll go out and take photos of the area.'

Jasper nodded and went to his study while Rosemary wound her way through bulging bookshelves to the front of the shop and started snapping. Outside, a tourist bus was parking in the street, so she used the shop's wrapping paper to write warning signs about the glass. By the time she'd tacked them to the remaining window, Jasper had returned. She went back into the shop to hear what he had to say. 'I can clean it up if there are photos and a witness,' he said.

She held up her phone. 'I'll send them to you. See the bus? I'd better get back to my shop. I'll help you later.'

He smiled, his eyes warm. 'Thank you.'

She creaked the door open and was about to leave when she felt his hand on her shoulder. 'What?'

But it seemed he couldn't think of what to say. Instead, he patted her a couple of times and let her escape.

Inside *The Preserved Mulbury*, Ronnie stood at the shop counter with a customer. Rosemary growled to herself at her negligence. 'Thanks, Ronnie.'

Ronnie gave her a grin as the customer picked up her bag of chutneys, smiled at Rosemary, and jangled out of the shop. 'No worries. I thought I'd wait until you came back. Everything okay with Jasper?'

Briefly, Rosemary told him about the window. Ronnie frowned, but didn't seem surprised. 'Your shops are very vulnerable because of those old glass windows. Ever thought about putting shutters up?'

Rosemary shuddered. 'No, that would be terrible. If people want to break in and steal some jam, they're welcome. It hasn't been a problem before.'

'But they took a specific book?' Ronnie tapped his fingers on the counter. 'Strange, don't you think?'

'Opportunistic, perhaps.'

'Hmmm...' Ronnie snapped upright. 'Anyway, I ought to get going. They want my report by this afternoon.' He slumped again. 'But it won't be lengthy.'

'I'm sure you did the best you could.'

His face went blotchy, something like an unfinished jigsaw puzzle. 'Thanks, Rosemary.' He lowered his voice. 'Marc is still in there.'

'Right. Did you catch up on each other's news?'

'Not really.' Ronnie chewed his lip. 'Marc's a real sad sack now. Very different from when I knew him. He hasn't talked to his father since losing his job and he hasn't had a job since. I don't think he looks after himself very well.' He lowered his voice even further and Rosemary had to strain to hear him. 'He thinks his father is searching for him.'

'Is that a problem?'

Ronnie leaned across to whisper, 'He's scared.'

'Why?'

He bent even further down. 'I don't know. He stopped talking after he said that.'

Rosemary's back started to ache, so she straightened. 'Are you going to keep in touch with him?'

'I'll try.' Ronnie stretched and put the strap of his satchel over his shoulder. 'I'd better go. Oh.' He glanced around the store. 'Honey wanted to know what you've been making.'

'She's after a jar of something.'

'Yeah.' Ronnie smiled. 'You know, she rarely eats what she takes from here.'

'What does she do with them, then?'

'She has a special cupboard where she keeps her treasures. It's full of your preserves.'

'They'll go bad if they aren't eaten.'

'Oh, she eats some. But if we have visitors, she pulls the jars out and lines them up on the bench to give to people. She calls it *promotion*.'

Rosemary felt a wave of affection for her daughter.

'But the pretty ones she keeps on the windowsill.'

'They really will go bad if she does that.'

'I know. She says your quinces glow like jewels.' Ronnie pointed at a shelf packed with quince jelly. 'They do, too.'

Light had angled onto the shelf, making the jars on it blaze like polished topaz. Around the shop, the jars took on a kaleidoscope of colour as the sun moved around or even when the overhead lights lit the shop on a dull day. 'I don't notice any more,' she said. 'I have new apple jelly. I'll get it.'

Rosemary went back into the house where the first batch of apple produce was arranged on a corner of the kitchen bench. Marc jumped up when she came in, hastily dropping a book down on the table. She narrowed her eyes at him as she picked up a jar of the translucent yellow preserve.

'I guess I'd better get going,' he said.

'Where to?'

'Home.'

'Which is where?'

Marc shrugged. 'Wherever I want it to be.' He studied his hands before lifting his head. 'Could I leave it with you?'

'Leave what?'

'The postcard. Maybe the other one will turn up.'

'Leave it with Ronnie. He's the private investigator.'

'I know that. But this one...' Marc pulled out the fake

postcard '... was pushed under your door. That could mean something.'

'Or not.' But Rosemary reached for it. 'Leave your number. I'll ring you if I have any thoughts.'

He took her phone so that he could enter his phone number. 'I'll come back soon. I'm going to keep looking.'

'Ronnie's leaving.'

'So will I.' Marc walked out to the shop.

'My phone,' said Rosemary, following closely.

'Oh, sorry.' He handed the phone back. 'Bye, Ronnie. Good to see you.'

'And you.'

'Thank you, Rosemary.'

'Don't forget Jasper.'

'I'll say thanks on the way out.'

Rosemary handed over the jar of apple jelly to Ronnie, watching Marc's exit out of the corner of her eye. He slumped in his coat, making him seem far younger than he was.

'I can't believe it's the same guy,' said Ronnie, shaking his head as he made to leave. 'Thank you for this.' He held up the jar.

'My love to Honey.'

Ronnie nodded and jangled out the door to his car, leaving Rosemary in the quiet shop. She sighed, plunged her hands into her pocket, and found Darren's gift. She pulled it out, feeling it cold and hard on her hand. It was tarnished, but she recognised it immediately. The little silver bird was from Heather's missing necklace.

TWENTY

Darren was talking to Rakisha as Rosemary once again crossed the Square to see him. She could hear the woman's high-pitched giggle floating around even before she stepped on the road. There'd been the whole busload of tourists to deal with before she could check with Darren about the pendant, and he would almost be finished assessing The Exceptional Tree. Once he left Mulbury, he was gone as far as Rosemary was concerned. Out of sight with Darren, out of mind completely.

Darren saw her over Rakisha's shoulder. Rosemary frowned as he shoved Rakisha aside, causing an *'ooooh'* of disgust, and met Rosemary halfway across the Square.

'Rosie, did you look at it?'

'*Rosemary*. Yes, Darren, it's why I'm here. Where did you find it?'

'In the Tree.' He turned to point at one of the lower branches that stretched towards the garage. 'It was caught on the bark. Do you remember it?'

'It's Heather Hubbard's.'

Darren shook his head vigorously. 'No, it isn't.'

'And what would you two have to chat so seriously about?' Rakisha was back, blinking her eyes at Darren in a way that made Rosemary think of a tic.

'Nothing that you would be interested in,' said Darren, moving to hide Rosemary's hand. 'How about that coffee you were offering, darl?'

Rakisha squinted at him. 'You just said, and I quote, "None of your crushed legume liquids for me, lady".'

'Yeah, well, I've changed my mind. Got to try something new every day, eh?'

Rakisha twirled the ends of her hair around one finger. 'Humph. What about you, Rosemary? I never see you have any of my coffee, either.'

'That's because it isn't coffee, Rakisha.'

Rakisha let her hair go, swirled effectively on the spot, mauve maxi spinning out dervish-ly, and went back to her cafe. Even from where Rosemary stood, she could hear the loud grumbles of Rakisha over her equally rumbling grinding machine.

'Wow,' said Darren. 'I thought I was the rude one.'

'Fact, Darren, not rudeness.' Rosemary held the pendant up. 'What do you mean, it's not Heather's?'

'It's yours, Rosie. Don't you remember?'

Rosemary frowned, even as she automatically corrected Darren with *Rosemary*. The necklace snuggled into her palm, a silver fairy wren. 'I don't understand, Darren. I have never owned this pendant.'

'But I gave it to you. At Alasdair's... you know. I put it in your coat pocket, in a blue velvet box. You found it because I remember you fishing it out just as you threw that rock at me.'

Now *that* Rosemary remembered. Darren, standing at the edge of the crowd holding a bunch of tangerine-coloured roses—the exact colour Alasdair always gave her—and calling out across the heads of Mulbury residents as if he was at a fish market. 'Rosie. Rosie, it's all right. You have me. You've always had me.' The rock had taken the heads off a few of the roses but, unfortunately, not Darren. Maybe the velvet box had been in her other hand, but she couldn't remember seeing it, let alone opening it. Everything associated with that day—floral tributes, well-meaning casseroles, probably the necklace—was hastily distributed by Mrs Lionel. The Hubbard sisters, alone again as their father followed his restless musical muse, most likely received the lot.

'Darren, I've never worn it. You knew I wouldn't.'

'No, I didn't, honestly. I thought you'd like it. A little bird, like you.' Darren's eyes were misty.

Rosemary closed her hand around the pendant and used one finger to poke the man's chest. 'For goodness's sake, Darren. You have me mixed up with someone else. I have *never* been birdlike.'

Darren rubbed his chest ruefully. 'Rosie, to me-'

'And don't *Rosie* me.' She jabbed him again. 'Show me exactly where this was before I slice you up and feed you to Sunny.'

Darren's long face lengthened further, but he led Rosemary to the low branch of The Exceptional Tree and pointed to a small area where bark strips dangled. 'There.'

Rosemary studied the branch carefully. One strip had torn away more recently, leaving the hard wood of the branch clean. A breeze stirred a few strands of long, golden hair caught on the bark. She scrutinised the ground. There was nothing to show now, but only days ago, the body of an old man lay almost exactly where she stood.

'Rosemary?'

She'd almost forgotten Darren was there. He stood with arms long at his sides, his face twisted miserably. Behind him, marching across the Square like it was a parade ground, Rakisha carried a large cup in one hand. 'Listen, Darren,' Rosemary said quietly, 'I'm sorry that you feel the way you do about me when I felt nothing for you. Nothing. Never had. You know how I felt about Alasdair.'

'But-'

'Stop. Say nothing. It didn't help then, and it doesn't help now.' She patted his arm. 'The necklace was a nice, but misguided, gesture. I can tell you, though, that Heather will be very glad to have it back.'

'There you are, Darren.' Rakisha arrived as he went to say something, thrusting the cup into his hand. 'Drink up.'

'That's it, Darren. Drink up.' Rosemary stepped away from the pair of them, hearing as she left Rakisha saying, 'Oh no, darling. I don't use the milk from mammals, only from nuts.' She couldn't help but glance back as Rakisha went back to her cafe, leaving Darren sipping—then spluttering—the gifted coffee.

Jasper had boarded his shop window with old chipboard. Rosemary peered through the glass at the side, but Jasper was gesticulating in front of a bookcase, with two customers nodding vigorously at what he was saying. She let him be and turned to go back to her shop, the pendant once again in her pocket.

'Rosemary. Oh, Rosemary.'

Patti was hanging garments on her outside rack. She hooked the last one on and waved to Rosemary.

'Patti. Business good?'

'Terrific, actually.' Patti scurried over to Rosemary, high spots of colour on her cheeks. 'That busload—I think they went to you as well?—were delighted with my skirts. One of them bought three.' Patti laughed, high-pitched and delighted. 'I really feel like I'm taking off.'

'You are, Patti. You have a great reputation.'

The little woman waggled her head, peachy waves bouncing on her shoulders. 'But what happened to Jasper?'

'Brick through his window.'

'Oh.' Patti went still. 'Vandals in Mulbury. Who would have thought?'

'He thinks it happened last night or this morning. Did you hear anything?'

'No, nothing. But I can't hear much over Gerry's snores.' Patti put a hand on her forehead. 'Funny, though. When I walked through the shop this morning, it felt to me that something was different.'

'What do you mean?'

'I'm not sure, Rosemary.' Patti blinked rapidly. 'Just a feeling I had that maybe someone had been in there when I hadn't.'

'Was anything taken?'

'No, nothing. I always lock our takings in the safe. I don't know, it seemed... *violated*.' Patti laughed. 'Gerry says I'm full of funny feelings, so maybe this was another one.' Her face fell. 'But is Jasper alright?'

'A little shaken.'

'Oh, of course. Poor man. Was anything stolen of his?'

'One book. Nothing of value.'

'Kids, then. A dare, maybe? Surely it won't happen again.'

Rosemary said nothing.

'Will Jasper be alright? Should I have him over for dinner?'

'You could ask him.'

'Oh.' Patti tapped her long pearl-coloured fingertip on

her mouth. 'We can't tonight. Gerry has one of his wine and cheese nights in Big Town, and I promised Jules I'd go over there. Oh well, let's see how he is tomorrow.' She glanced back at her display, where two women were exclaiming over a flared dress made from, Rosemary guessed, a tablecloth draped over a tutu. 'I'd better go.'

'Yes.'

Patti skipped off, leaving Rosemary to admire the way Patti always looked like she'd stepped from a 1950s women's magazine.

The Preserved Mulbury was devoid of customers, which was just as well, Rosemary thought, as she repacked the half-empty shelves left behind from the busload before. The bright summer preserves were thinning, leaving rich autumnal pickles and jams in their place. A sweet aroma of apple filled the shop from the slices she had set up on the dehydrator the night before—it was like being in a fragrant grocery. Rosemary pulled Aunt Lilibeth's book from the shelf behind the counter, flicking it to where the writer had captured her apple products in a sketch of a broad kitchen table laden with cider, jelly, jams and glace fruit. The page was dog-eared and sticky, pored over by Rosemary's mother and then Rosemary herself. She could almost hear her aunt's voice through the words on the page. *'Now, Rosemary. Peel and slice two pounds of firm fruit...'*

The jangle of the door startled her. The old book had taken her back to a kitchen as bright and sweet as her own, much smaller, though, and mostly taken up by the bulk of Lilibeth who believed in food as it should be, nourishing and delicious and plentiful. 'Hello,' she said, closing the book carefully and placing it back on the shelf. 'I'll just be a moment.'

When there was no answer, she turned to see the door

slowly click closed again, with no one entering. She shook her head, stopped to tidy a cascading sheaf of wrapping paper at knee height, and heard the jangle again. 'Hang on,' she said, pushing the offending paper back.

'No need to hurry. I'm just looking.'

The deep voice made the back of her neck prickle. Not that it was menacing, only that she'd heard it before and had been thinking of it that very morning. The man stood as he had before, black woollen coat unbuttoned despite the chill, blue eyes almost lapis lazuli in colour and hardness. He dominated the middle of the room and Rosemary pulled herself taller, suddenly resenting his effortless stance and proud demeanour. 'Looking for what?' she said, keeping her voice neutral.

'Something you may not have.'

Rosemary came out from behind the counter, surreptitiously feeling for her phone in her pocket. It was there, rubbing up against the silver fairy wren. 'I have a range of things.'

'Yes. I believe you have.'

'Interested in jams, are you?'

'Not really.'

'Pickles then.'

He gave a gruff laugh. 'Pickles. Very apt.'

Rosemary tried staring him down, but there was something too strong in his gaze to make him even blink. 'I can't help you then.'

'Oh, I think you can.'

There was a moment when Rosemary calculated she could have shot through the house doorway, slammed it shut and bolted it home, gaining her enough time to ring triple zero and report... what? A man in the shop joking about pickles? Besides, the connecting door was inclined to stick, so the likelihood of it being a smooth close-and-bolt was slim. In the next moment, she crossed her arms and held her ground. *The Preserved Mulbury* was her shop, and she was damned if she'd flee from some woollen-clad, handsome stranger with a clear disregard for jam.

'Okay,' she said. 'If you think I can help you, ask.'

For a second, she thought the hardness fell from his eyes, but maybe it was a trick of the light for he blinked and regarded her again with a practised steeliness. 'You know where my son is.'

She thought of Marc's recent departure. 'No, I don't.'

'You do. He's been here.'

'I have a lot of customers.'

'He wasn't a customer.'

Rosemary felt the prickle fade from her neck to be replaced by a stab of irritation at the man's indirectness. 'And who is your son?'

He took a moment to answer before he lifted his head. 'He's a conman.'

TWENTY-ONE

Rosemary said nothing, but studied the man in front of her carefully. Joey Cambridge had a silver-streaked mass of black hair that sat thickly on his head, showing signs of a good but not recent cut. Marc also had black hair, but it was longer around the ears and softened his face. Joey's hair, blunt across the tops of the ears, and his vivid, hypnotising eyes made him a sharp image whereas Marc was a blurred one.

'I don't know where your son is,' she said, crossing her arms across her chest.

'He was here.'

Rosemary didn't move.

'Where did he go?'

'Why would I answer that?' She tilted her head. 'He's a grown man. If he wanted you to know where he was, my guess is that he would have told you himself.'

Joey's jawline hardened as he ground his teeth. She could almost hear the enamel surfaces shave away. 'I need to find him.'

'That,' she said, 'is your problem. Not mine. Not Marc's.'

'Perhaps you don't understand.' Joey stepped closer to Rosemary, but she refused to budge. 'I've been looking for him for quite a while. He has something of the family's.'

'That's unfortunate.'

Joey considered her and let his arms drop to his sides. Rosemary kept her gaze on him as he moved across to the shelf of chutneys and ran his finger across the jars. 'Exquisite merchandise.'

'Thank you.'

'Your main stay of income.'

'Of course.'

His finger paused at the middle jar, hooking around the lid and pulling it towards him. The jar angled, then toppled, smashing on the hardwood floor. 'Oh dear,' Joey said, not moving, 'I am sorry.' He slid to the next jar and jerked it off the shelf, so it too crashed noisily. The sharp scent of vinegar filled the shop.

'Really, Joey Cambridge. Such juvenile behaviour.'

His eyes flashed. 'You know my name?'

'Yes.'

He stepped back from the shelf. 'What else do you know about me?'

'You have a childish temper.'

He shook his head. 'You have no idea.'

'I'm getting a few.'

He regarded her for a few moments, and she didn't blink until he lowered his head. 'I think you know where Marc is. Tell him I'll find him. It's only a matter of time.'

'I'm not your messenger.'

He scowled at that and reached over to the shelf. One hard tug and it tore from the wall, sending a cascade of jars onto the floor. He stepped away as it fell, his coat flinging out wildly in his haste. 'You already are,' Joey said as he left.

Rosemary stood still until her heart calmed and she could see the mess before her with a bit more of an objective eye. Before she could move to retrieve the one or two unbroken jars she could see, the door flung open, jangling frantically, and Jasper came in, his hair messy from his rush.

'What's happened?' He stopped short of the disaster area. 'Oh, your shelving gave way.'

'Something like that.' Rosemary reached into the heart of the smashed goods and pulled out a whole jar of zucchini and eggplant chutney. 'Saved one.'

'Is this sort of thing insured?' Jasper plucked another chutney out. 'I mean, it's ruined stock.'

'I don't know.' Rosemary stood up. 'It doesn't matter, I have plenty.'

'But you should-'

'Jasper.' She ran a hand down her braid and clutched its end. Jasper looked chastened. She opened her mouth to tell him about the detestable Joey Cambridge, but couldn't. *Maybe when he's stronger*, she thought. She tried a smile and hoped it was genuine. 'Please. Leave it.'

He sat the rescued jar on the floor away from the broken glass. 'Let me help you clean up.'

'You have your own business to run.'

'I can spare a couple of minutes. You did for me this morning.' He laughed briefly. 'We're not having much of a day.'

'No. I'll get a bucket and a scoop.'

He scanned the soggy mess. 'I'll see what I can salvage.'

There were plenty of buckets in Rosemary's laundry, some still full of apples. On her way out, she stroked Sunny's bold orange head stripe. She looked at her mistress with wide, knowing eyes, and Rosemary saw how her hand was trembling, disturbing the cat's soft hair even when she rested it on her warm crown. Sunny gave a soft miaow. 'I know,' she said, 'but I'm all right. I'm angry, not upset.'

Jasper had rescued three more jars, but the rest had smashed beyond help. He picked up the shelf and leaned it against the wall. 'Shouldn't be too hard to get it back on,' he said cheerfully. 'Not sure why it went. Maybe you'll need better screws.'

'Yes,' she said, and squatted to pick up the worst of the glass. It kept her busy for a while and it wasn't until she recognised that silence had spun its web around them that she glanced up. 'Jasper?'

Jasper stood with his nose within millimetres of a shelf of dried persimmons. His lips moved without sound.

'Jasper.'

'Oh.' He turned around, still obviously thinking about something else. 'Yes?'

'What are you doing?'

'Oh,' he said again. 'I think I've worked something out.'

'Did something need working out?'

'Yes, it did.'

He knelt beside her, and she hurried to clear a patch of glass and tomatoes. 'Careful, Jasper. It's dangerous.'

'No, no, I don't think so.'

'The glass, Jasper. *It* is dangerous.'

'Oh. Yes.' He leaned forward and plucked a section of jar up. The label drooped from it, *The Preserved Mulbury* on a background of mulberry purple. 'I've always wondered...'

'Wondered about what?'

He shrugged. 'Those Space Westerns. *Forces and Horses.*'

Rosemary sat back on her feet and scrutinised her friend. A blob of chutney hung on dark threads of his hair. 'You aren't making any sense, Jasper. *Forces and Horses* was stolen.'

'Not stolen, I think now. *Taken.*' He tapped his nose.

'What are you talking about?'

At that, Jasper's face sagged. 'I'm so sorry, Rosemary.' He threw the section of jar into the bucket and shook his head. 'Here I am, trying to help. In reality, I'm a bit caught up with my own things.'

Rosemary touched his sleeve with her fingertips. 'Are you okay, Jasper? Has something happened to your health?'

'No.' He took the little shovel from her and started scooping up the muck in front of them. 'My last tests were good, so there's no need to worry about that. Once I get stronger, I'll be right. Maybe I should have had a bit of rehab before I left the hospital.' He shook his head. 'Too late now. It's up to me. I need to do some more walking.'

'Is that what they suggested?'

'Yes, I'm meant to walk at least twice a week. It would do Snowy good as well.' He rested the shovel on the floor. 'Well, maybe not Snowy. He does nothing but sleep. Maybe *you* could walk with me?'

Rosemary considered him. Jasper had long, lanky legs in his narrow jeans. At full fitness, he would out-streak her any day, but now there was frailty in his movements, a tentative-ness that came from de-conditioned muscles and an exhausted healing system. 'I could,' she said. 'Outside of shop hours.'

'Of course.' He stood clumsily and picked up the bucket. 'I suppose this had better go in the rubbish?'

They worked together for another ten minutes before the mess was clear. The floorboards, usually a deep dull red, were patched with oils and vinegar and shone with a flare of new colour. *Quite lovely in the end*, Rosemary thought as she studied the shop.

Jasper called a regular customer of his—a crime noir addict—who was a carpenter. 'He'll be here in an hour,' Jasper said, wiping his hands on the seat of his jeans. 'I'd better go back to work.'

'Thank you. It was certainly quicker to clean up with two.'

He smiled and made his way to the door. 'Don't forget now,' he said as he pulled it open, the bell jangling furiously.

'Forget?'

'After shop hours. We're walking.'

'Today?'

He grinned. 'Any reason not to?'

Even though he didn't give her time to answer, but closed the door behind him and disappeared along the path, she had no answer anyway. There wasn't a single reason she couldn't accompany Jasper Lu on a constitutional once their work was done.

The phone call brought her back to real life.

'Mum, hello.'

'Honey. Are you alright?'

'Yes, but I'm not ringing anyone ever again if their first question is, *are you alright?* It's driving me crazy.'

'So, you are alright.'

'Yes. Mum, stop it.' Honey's voice had a smile in it. 'I rang to see if you're okay.'

Rosemary glanced at the floor. Could Honey know what had just happened? 'Of course I am. Why wouldn't I be?'

'Ronnie said there were still puzzles.'

'I would hope that we never solve all the puzzles in the world.'

'You know what I mean.' There was a pause and the background noise of magpies. 'I've got a break now and thought I'd ring. What are you making?'

'Nothing much.' Rosemary walked across to the wall and flicked the ceiling fan on to move the smell of spilt vinegar along. 'I pulled out the dehydrator and put some apples on.'

'Oh, fantastic, I love dried apples. Maybe you could do some glace ones?'

'You must be reading my mind. I have Lilibeth's book open to find the recipe.'

'Glace quinces are better. Do you have any fruit left?'

'Only my display bowl in the window.' Rosemary wandered over to it as she spoke. 'They're probably too far gone.'

'Not to glace, surely.'

'I could try.'

'I can smell those apples, Mum.'

'Honey... '

'I can. They have a light sweet tang, and it hovers close to the ceiling, just out of reach of my nose.'

'Honey... '

'It makes me think of early mornings in autumn, and dew, and how cold your Pink Ladies are when you pluck them off the tree on an autumn day.'

'Honey, you are a hopeless romantic for food.'

'Not all food, Mum. Only your stuff. And don't tell Ronnie I'm anything like a romantic. He's bad enough, all lovey-dovey.'

'He's a good man.'

There was a moment of silence before Honey spoke softly. 'Mum, you've never said anything like that before.'

'Perhaps I should have.' Rosemary cleared her throat. 'I should go. The smell in here is from a bottle of chutney I broke on the floor. Not light and delicious, more overpoweringly tart.'

'Okay then. See you soon. Love you.'

'Love you, too.'

Rosemary slid the phone into her back pocket and once again marvelled at how the sound of her daughter's voice from many kilometres away was enough to revive a waning soul. Honey was an injection of life. And perhaps she was right about the quinces?

The bowl had been on display for a few weeks. When Rosemary lifted it out, silver threads of cobweb strung from it, and it left a bare circle in a fine layer of dust. Country life, Rosemary thought as she swatted at the webs. You could spend your whole life cleaning and still the dust would seep through the old building and settle on the nearest surface.

She carried the large bowl in two hands back to her kitchen and set it down. The top quinces had yellowed, but the next layer still held a tinge of green. And pink.

Pink?

She shifted a knobbly fruit and there it was, lightly wedged in the crevices of fruit. A dirty, faded postcard with a black cross that marked the spot Marc Cambridge believed was his grandfather's last known location.

TWENTY-TWO

Patti Yale liked to lie in bed in the mornings, mulling over her designs. Gerry understood this need. He slipped quietly from the room and didn't reappear until he had her tray of breakfast. 'Pot of Earl Grey and a soft-boiled egg with wholemeal toast for my treasure,' he would say, and sit the tray on the bedside table. If she was going well, he was allowed to slip back under the warm doona and sip his coffee quietly. If the designs remained elusive, he went back out to the kitchen and read the paper at the table.

This morning, Patti reached out and grabbed his hand as he put her tray down. 'I've had an idea, Gerry.'

He took that as a good sign, went around to his side of the bed, and shuffled back in. 'Is it a good one?'

'I don't know yet.' Patti wriggled up to a higher sitting position. 'You know I've been gathering abandoned garments for years.'

'Those things you find on the roadside?' Gerry wrinkled his nose. '*Garments*, you call them?'

'Well, yes, Gerry, sweetie. Just because someone has lost

their coat or scarf or jumper, doesn't mean those items aren't garments that were once worn with love.'

'I suspect most of them have been dropped out of work utilities or car windows. Or thrown. Discarded because they're covered in oil or worse.'

'You've got a vivid imagination, my love.' Patti reached for a bag that sat at the end of the bed. 'See what I've got here.'

She upended the bag and a tumble of clothes fell onto the quilt. Gerry sat up as well and watched as she sorted the clothes into groups.

'Do you remember this one?'

Gerry took the luxurious mauve scarf she handed him. It was kitten-soft and smelled vaguely of roses. 'Didn't we find this at that roadside stop on the way to the coast?'

'That's right. It was under the picnic table and probably had been there for a while. You said-'

'I said, "Don't touch that manky thing".' Gerry nodded. 'I did. It looked someone had used it to wipe their-'

'It was mud, Gerry. I told you that.' She tugged the scarf away from him and rubbed it against her cheek. 'I had to wash it very carefully with one of Mrs Lionel's soft soaps, but eventually it turned into this.'

'Well, I would never have thought.'

'That's right, darling, you don't *think*. Not broadly enough. You see me with a discarded garment and wonder if I'm wasting my time.'

'That is exactly what I'm thinking.'

'How many times do I have to prove you wrong?'

'As many as you can.'

Patti leaned over to kiss her husband's cheek, then rolled the scarf neatly and tucked it into the bag. 'Here's another test of your memory.' She plucked a rugby top from the tumble of clothes and spread it out on the bed. 'Where did we find this one?'

'That I do not remember.'

'In Big Town, outside that pub we go to. You know, the one that has gourmet pizzas.'

'The National?' Gerry frowned. 'We haven't been there for ages.'

'At least a year. That's when I discovered this in the gutter.'

Gerry pointed at the faded fabric. 'This one looks like it's from the gutter.'

'Oh, it had been there for a long time. It was half in the drain. I think I may have torn it as I pulled it out.' Patti traced a finger over a small hole in its sleeve.

'Patti, a worn rugby top doesn't belong in *Patricia's*.'

'But that's where you're wrong, Gerry. See?' Patti fished out her design book from under the eclectic pile of clothes and turned the page to show her husband. There was the rugby top, sleeves removed, attached to a tulle skirt that flounced about its static model. 'The masculinity of the vest has now been juxtaposed against the feminine virtues of the skirt's fabric.' She smiled lovingly at the drawing.

'You seriously don't think someone's going to buy it?'

Patti laughed, a high tinkle that warmed Gerry's being.

'I'm wrong, aren't I?'

'You are often wrong, Gerry, sweetie.' She took back her design book. 'I was showing this to a customer only yesterday, and she said how wonderful it would be for her daughter. I asked what her daughter did, and the customer said, "She's in film production".' Patti reached for his hand. 'Do you know, sweetie, that I searched the daughter's name, and she's a documentary maker who's won lots of awards.'

'Well.' Gerry shook his head. 'Well, well.'

'Yes, darling. I'm waiting for her measurements.'

'I think I see what you're doing here, Patti.' Gerry took the rest of the items in his hands and studied them more closely. 'What you're telling me is that these old bits and pieces that people have lost or thrown out or worse have monetary value?' He pulled out a sock, a hanky, and a child's floppy hat. 'Even these?'

'Gerry, they have their own history.' Patti took the sock from him. 'This one. See the tiny clowns all over it? Obviously, a child's, so I'll turn it into a puppet. You can make very sophisticated puppets from socks if you try.' She snatched another piece up. 'This hanky may become part of a shirt I'm making. I'm not sure about its shape yet. I've got to find more items to go with it. Hankies are so hard to find on the street these days as most people prefer hideous paper tissues. This one has such a refined edge I think it might be a pocket square for a suit.' She held up the hat. 'And this little darling hat. Why, it's almost perfect on its own. Imagine it with a frill of washable lace and no little girl could resist.'

Gerry tried hard to see the misshapen hat as a must-have for any of the fashionistas' granddaughters pouring through the door of *Patricia's*. He nodded anyway. Really, what did it matter what he thought? He did the accounts, swept the floor, and made Patti breakfast. His use was beyond measure. 'You are a clever woman.'

Patti beamed. She smoothed down the items on the bed in front of her and flicked her design book to a new page. 'You know, darling, I've been thinking about this shirt all night.' She drew a few swift lines. 'What do you think?'

Gerry studied the page, but he might as well have been

looking at a washing line. 'I'm not the one to ask, Patti. All I see is cloth.'

Patti drew a few more lines. 'I can see it in my head if I could only find more of this material.' She gathered the hanky into her hand. 'A good linen, relatively unmarked, with a hint of previous ownership.'

'Perhaps you could use the sleeves of that rugby jumper?'

'Not helpful, sweetie.'

'Have you asked Jules? She's probably the most fashionable in town.'

'No, I didn't think of Jules.' Patti put down her pencil and stared in front of her. 'She might also have some old linen serviettes from the restaurant.' She leaned over to peck Gerry's cheek. 'You have such good ideas, darling.'

Gerry was fairly sure he'd never had a decent idea in his life except for marrying Patricia Yale, but he took the kiss well. After the breakfast tray emptied, he carried it faithfully into the kitchen and set about the household chores.

In the meantime, Patti was up and dressed and heading for Jules' house with her design book and the sample hanky. She waved away Gerry's offer to drive her and set up across the Square towards the outskirts of town. The Square was bright with sunshine and The Exceptional Tree waved the tips of its branches at her as she scooted past. A pack of anglers was at the door to *Franco's Patisserie*, patiently waiting for more pies. She gave Franco a wave, and he lifted his head to her, unable to do anything more than attend the till.

Jules and Roman had owned a restaurant in the city. Patti had read about them well before they decided on their tree change. She'd wondered, ever so briefly, whether a restaurant that prided itself on using up what people had in their gardens or that farms had discarded would be such a winner in a little country town where people knew the value of scraps of food. Leftovers were a regular weekly meal when she grew up. She'd forgotten that the residents of Mulbury and its surrounds weren't the target market. *The Leftover Restaurant* was for the city folk's romantic notions of life in the country. It was a winner from its first night.

Night being the key factor.

When Patti rang the doorbell, she had to wait long minutes before the house stirred. At the third ring, Jules opened the door in a dressing gown and bed hair. 'Patti. This is an early visit.'

'Is it?' Patti frowned at her watch; a vintage gold Rolex marred with dog teeth marks that didn't work but was very pretty. 'I'm sorry, Jules. I feel like I've been up for hours.'

'Come in, come in.' Jules stepped back to let Patti pass. 'Roman is having a lie in. There was a party of twenty last night and they wanted the full house dinner. He was on his feet until well after midnight.'

Patti tiptoed into the living area and sat on a broad, white leather couch while Jules made coffee. By the time Jules had put a cup down in front of her, Patti had the design book open with the hanky marking the shirt's place. 'I need your opinion, Jules. Do you think this will work?'

Jules picked the book and hanky up and studied the picture while sipping daintily on her coffee. Patti smiled at her. Gerry had been right. Even in her dressing gown, Jules was elegant. Her long fingers lay across the book, the nails a tasteful shade of maroon. Underneath the neck of the gown, Jules glimpsed the neckline of silk pyjamas and she blushed, thinking of her own sleepwear that was really a discarded T-shirt she'd found on a football oval.

'This is lovely, Patti,' Jules said. 'Almost pirate-inspired, but I see how you've modernised it with the stand-up collar.'

Patti nodded. 'Yes, that's it.'

Jules held up the hanky. 'Is this the cloth you're using?'

'Partly. It's the only piece I have yet. I was hoping you might have some old napkins I could use.'

'I'm sure we do. I'll look today.' Jules closed the book respectfully. 'This would be a one-off piece?'

Patti shrugged. 'All my garments are one-off pieces because they're made from what others have left behind.'

'Op shop items?'

'And roadside ones. You wouldn't believe the things I find on the side of the road or the path or strung up in trees. Not only clothes, but all sorts of things. Shoes and bags and jewellery. Sometimes I wonder if there aren't tens of hundreds of strippers running through the country.'

Jules sighed. 'Yes, I've seen all those bits and pieces on the road. *I* wonder sometimes whether they aren't crime artefacts.'

'I've never found a blood-drenched shirt yet.'

'I'm really glad to hear it.' Jules passed the book back to Patti. 'You know, I love that shirt design so much *I'll* buy the finished garment from you. If you can make it mostly out of our old serviettes, then it'll have great significance.'

'Oh, sweetie, really?' Patti hugged the book to her chest. 'It would be wonderful to have a living model. I'll need your measurements.'

'Of course.' Jules leaned back on the couch and sipped her coffee. 'I'll go into the restaurant this morning and get the serviettes to you. Then tomorrow I could drop by the shop, and you can measure me up?'

Patti grinned. Her fingers itched to sculpt the design a

little more. She jumped up, rattling the coffee table with her flared skirt. 'I'll leave you to it, Jules, and see you then.'

Jules showed Patti to the door and gave her a hug. 'Mulbury is lucky to have such a talented woman in their midst.'

Patti floated home, visions of white shirts like clouds in her head.

TWENTY-THREE

Rosemary left it until well after morning teatime to visit *Mulbury Feeds*. The day had darkened as clouds shielded the sun, and a nasty breeze whipped around her legs. She wished she'd thought to put on her long boots, but she classified them as winter wear. It was still autumn, with chances yet for crisp blue skies.

Holly was out the front of the shed with her tablet, staring at large square bales of hay and muttering under her breath. Rosemary stood a little away from her, amusing herself with trying to guess why the young woman was so displeased. The hay was in perfect condition, golden and full. Now and then, the wind whipped the sunshine scent of it Rosemary's way and she got flashes of the summer just gone when the Hubbard women had their father with them, and they had more time to laugh.

'Holly,' she said when the muttering didn't dissipate.

Holly leapt backwards, her broad-brimmed hat sliding forward on her head. 'Oh.' She pushed the hat into place again. 'Sorry, Rosemary. I was trying to work out if we'd ordered this many bales or whether Paul has given us part of someone else's delivery. It's taking up a lot of room and I don't think our tarps will cover it.'

Rosemary glanced at the sky, which was dulling further. 'You need a bigger shed.'

'I've always said that.' Holly tucked her tablet under her arm. 'Dad didn't want to hear it.'

'But you're in charge of this business now.'

Holly stared at Rosemary, her eyes a deeper shade than Heather's cornflower blue, and much more focused. 'Well, in fact...' she looked around as if the hay might conceal spies '... Hannah and I have a plan. We've worked this place up to be a top-notch business. We want to change it into our names. We'd have to pay Dad out, of course, but that should be fine. Our solicitor is working with us.'

'You've always had good business sense, Holly. The stumbling block could be your father.'

'You know,' Holly said, indicating to Rosemary that they walk into the shed, 'I don't think that's going to be a big problem. His driver in life is to have enough money to do what he likes. If we pay him out, he can spend all the time he likes faffing around on his guitar while living in a shack with his muse in remote Queensland. And he won't be on our backs all the time asking for money because he'll have his own.' She stopped and put a hand to her face. 'That sounds terrible. We do love him, Rosemary, but...'

'I understand.' Rosemary touched Holly's arm briefly. 'This isn't anything to do with love. This is *livelihood*. It sounds very sensible to me. It will protect the business and therefore you.' She paused. 'Will Heather be a partner in it?'

Holly shook her head. 'No. When she's okay, she always says she doesn't want to be part of the business. She doesn't mind working here but you know as well as anyone in this town, her definition of work fluctuates from day to day. We can care for her as long as she needs it, and she'll be happy with her birds and serving the occasional customer.' Holly's shoulders drooped. 'When she's well again.'

'No change?'

'Not really. Oh, she's not moaning and groaning quite as much, and she isn't catatonic on the bed. If she has a task in front of her, like working on a new bird, she's better. We're oh-so-grateful for Mrs Lionel having her some nights. She actually seems to sleep better there.'

'When she's not sleepwalking.'

'That's the thing, isn't it? It's so unpredictable.'

'Is Heather here now? I have something of hers.'

Holly pointed to the office. 'She's in her bird room.'

They walked together through the shed, Rosemary breathing in the rich smells of grain and hay and horse molasses. She found the shed comforting, even with the line of stuffed birds staring down with glass eyes from above the entrance to the office, and could see how the sisters loved it. It was a solid business, one that supplied essential items to the country community. Rosemary was very glad the girls had thought to take control.

Hannah was in the office when they walked in, ear buds in and rocking along to something on her phone while working on the computer. Holly tapped her on the shoulder, making her leap out of her chair. 'Holy bananas, Holly. What are you trying to do to me?'

'It's the only way I can think of to make you older than me.'

'Yeah, well, I just aged two years so you're still one ahead.' Hannah tugged the ear buds out and grinned at Rosemary. 'You're my witness.'

'Duly noted.' Rosemary smiled back at the wild-haired middle sister. 'I'm looking for Heather.'

Hannah's face fell for a millisecond, then she plastered the smile back on. 'She's been in there since she got up. I can't make her eat anything.'

'We'll tell her that Rosemary's here for an early lunch.' Holly checked with Rosemary, who nodded. 'That might work.' She pushed the door to Heather's taxidermy room open.

The light in the room was mainly from a huge skylight that took up nearly the entire ceiling, but Heather stood at a table set in the middle of the room with two small spotlights aimed at the cluster of feathers on a stand. Rosemary stopped inside the door to watch. Heather's hands moved carefully as she manoeuvred an insert into the brown bird lying on a foam bed. There was an intensity in Heather's concentration. Rosemary felt disinclined to break it, but Holly coughed and tapped lightly on Heather's table. 'Rosemary's here, Heather.'

For a long moment, Heather continued with what she was doing. Slowly, her movements stopped, and she raised her head. Rosemary bit her lip. The young woman's face was lit sharply by the spotlights that couldn't hide the blue semicircles under her eyes, and the dullness of her expression. Heather blinked slowly, as if her eyelids were too heavy, and she straightened wearily.

'Rosemary's here to have lunch.' Holly put her hand on Heather's forearm and the younger woman laid down her tools. 'We'll make cheese toasties, don't you think?'

It was like watching someone walking through a marsh. Heather obediently followed Holly, but her feet dragged, and her body slumped with effort. Rosemary came behind her, resisting the temptation to put her arm around

Heather's shoulders like you would if you were helping a wounded soldier from the battlefield. Hannah joined the line after locking the office door, walking beside Rosemary as they filed out of the shed and into the little wooden house at the rear of the property. 'I hope this stops soon,' muttered Hannah.

Rosemary said nothing.

Inside the kitchen, Holly turned on an electric heater while Hannah pulled bread from a bag. Heather went to wash her hands, then sat at the kitchen table. She'd brought a feather that she twirled between her fingers. Rosemary took the chair next to her. 'Heather,' she said, 'I've found your necklace.'

Holly and Hannah turned as one.

'You found her necklace.' Holly clutched a bag of cheese. 'We've been looking everywhere for that.'

Rosemary pulled the little silver bird from her pocket and placed it gently on the table in front of Heather. The feather-twirling stopped. Heather reached out a hand and closed it over the fairy wren, dragging it back towards her and holding it against her chest.

The kitchen was quiet. A long minute passed, then two. Finally, Heather looked up at Rosemary and a smile spread like sunshine across her face. 'Rosemary,' she said hoarsely.

'Yes?'

'She means the pendant.' Holly turned to drop a lump of cheese on the kitchen bench. 'That's what she calls it.'

'Really?'

'You gave it to her.'

'I asked Mrs Lionel to give it away. I didn't know that Heather knew it was from me.'

'You gave us lots of things that day.' Hannah dug into

the bread bag and set out eight slices. 'All that food and flowers and little gifts. You didn't have to give it all to us.'

'At the time, though, we were really grateful.' Holly dragged a forearm across her forehead. 'Maybe you didn't realise it because you had other things on your mind, but we were skint back then.'

'Dad had used the business money to buy that stupid car of his.'

'And then he hardly ever used it. It'll sit there until he gets back. Hannah has the ute, so we drive that. It's much more practical.'

Rosemary kept her eyes on Heather. 'So, you don't miss the car then.'

'Dad didn't take it.' Hannah spread butter thickly on the bread slices. 'We could drive it if we wanted.'

'The police have it.'

Hannah stopped buttering and Holly paused with the cheese slicer in mid-air. 'What do you mean?'

Rosemary frowned. 'Barry reported a strange car parked in his driveway that turned out to be your father's. You didn't know?'

Hannah put down her knife and rushed outside the house, coming back a moment later. 'She's right. It's gone.'

'Someone stole it from us?' Holly shook her head. 'I guess we didn't notice because Dad kept it right out the back and the grass ended up hiding it.'

'We never go out there.' Hannah leaned on the bench. 'We're too busy out the front in the shed.'

'Why didn't the police contact us?'

'They would have rung Dad. He has got his mobile phone, you know.'

'I suppose we should get it back.'

'They're testing it,' said Rosemary. She glanced at

Heather, then back at the others. 'There was blood on the back seat.'

'Blood?'

'What sort of blood?'

'The red kind, Holly.' Hannah crossed her arms.

'I meant, was it... human?'

'I don't know,' said Rosemary. 'I guess you'll find out in due course.'

'I'll ring Dad later.' Holly carved the cheese angrily. 'If only he'd let us know.'

'You know now.' Rosemary accepted the glass of water Hannah gave her with a nod.

Holly assembled the sandwiches and put them under the griller. Hannah sat with a thump in the chair next to Heather and held out her hand. Reluctantly, Heather handed the little bird over to her. 'Honestly,' Hannah said, turning the pendant over and over in her hand, 'we looked for this everywhere. I even pulled Heather's bed apart, thinking it might have fallen down the side. Where did you find it?'

'I didn't find it. Darren, Kelly's brother, did. It was caught up in The Exceptional Tree.'

'In the Tree?' Hannah shook her head. 'Heather, how on earth did it get in the Tree?'

Heather blinked, shot her hand out and took the bird back.

'She obviously got it caught and didn't notice.' Holly pulled the sandwiches out and served them up, then slid into a chair at the end of the table. 'Thank you for getting it back. Look at her.'

Heather was smiling as she smoothed the silver bird with her thumbs. The smile seemed to bleach the blue shadows under her eyes, and she was once again like a golden-haired angel. Even Hannah and Holly looked better, the relief on their faces lightening them. If someone had peered in the window of that little house and not known how hard the sisters had it sometimes, it could seem like a jovial group of young women having lunch with a favourite aunt.

If only, Rosemary thought, *they could sort out Heather's other problem.*

TWENTY-FOUR

Mrs Lionel was waiting on the path as Rosemary walked back to her shop. She could see her friend's hands twisting together, a sure sign that something was up. 'Dorothea,' Rosemary said, 'what's happened?'

'Oh, there you are, dear,' Mrs Lionel said, as if Rosemary had been lost. 'I was waiting for you.' She tipped her head slightly towards the inside of her shop.

Rosemary stepped closer to the window. At first, it all appeared well. The lovely green light of the shop bathed everything, making it glow like a lush conservatory. Then she spotted the patch near the house's entry door. 'Did you drop something?'

'Only the lye mix.'

Rosemary turned. 'Did you get it on you?'

'A little.'

'Show me.'

Mrs Lionel untwisted her hands and held them out slowly. Red patches decorated them.

'Let's go inside.' Rosemary put her arm around the older woman and steered her into the shop, over the spill still wetting the floorboards, and through to the kitchen. She held Mrs Lionel's hands under the tap.

'I've been doing this,' Mrs Lionel said, wincing.

'I'm doing it again.' Rosemary turned the tap on a little more. 'How long did you do it for?'

'A few minutes.'

'It needs at least fifteen minutes, as you well know.' Rosemary studied the red marks on Mrs Lionel's palms. 'Did you actually rinse them at all?'

'No.' Mrs Lionel sniffed. 'I couldn't get the tap on.'

Rosemary nodded shortly. Holding her friend's hands under the flowing water brought her in close contact with knobbly, arthritic fingers. The tap was an echo of what would have been there originally, cross-handled and stiff. Hard for many to turn on and getting near impossible if someone had burns and weakness in their hands. 'How long were you waiting for me?'

'I saw you go to the girls about an hour ago. I knew you wouldn't be long.'

'You could have come into the shed.'

Mrs Lionel nodded, then sniffed again. With alarm, Rosemary saw tears roll down her face. She put an arm around the woman and squeezed.

'It'll be alright, but I'm taking you to the doctor. Just in case.'

'Oh, Rosemary...' Mrs Lionel sniffed again and then shook her head, lifting her chin up. 'I'll be fine. I'm not quite as strong as I used to be.'

'Why were you carrying the pan?'

'I had a bucket with water and lye. That's what spilled. I was carrying it from the sink inside the shop.' She smiled briefly. 'It has a better tap. Not a brilliant one, mind. I must have tripped. The lye splashed...' She looked down at her hands. 'It could have been worse.'

There were many ways in which Rosemary thought it could be worse, but she held her tongue. After another fifteen minutes, she filled a clean bowl with water and directed Mrs Lionel into the car for the trip to Big Town and the doctor.

'Leave them in there,' Rosemary said as she pulled out onto the road.

'It's cold.' Mrs Lionel plunged her hands back into the bowl.

'The heater's on your feet. It'll warm up soon.'

They drove for a while in silence, Rosemary casting glances at her friend every few minutes. The tears had gone, but there was a deep sadness to Mrs Lionel's face that she never had.

As they turned onto the main road into Big Town, Mrs Lionel sighed. 'You know, Rosemary, I've been thinking for some time that I need a bit of help in the shop mixing my products. I'm having trouble keeping up with my soaps. I suppose I was hurrying today, and it hasn't saved me one bit of time.' She held up her hands.

'Put them back in.'

Hands lowered into the water again. 'What do you think?'

'I think that's very sensible. My only concern is whether you can afford it.'

'That's the bit I'm not too sure about. I don't make a huge living out of *The Green Mulbury,* but it keeps me happy. Sharing the profits with someone else might tip the scale the wrong way.'

'You need a volunteer.'

'Anyone with free time around Mulbury is probably my

age. I want someone young and strong to do the heavy lifting.'

'What about the Hubbard girls?'

'I thought of them, but Holly and Hannah are too busy, and Heather... well, I'm not sure she would be consistently useful. I really don't need to be watching someone all the time.'

Rosemary nodded. Heather wouldn't have been her first choice for Mrs Lionel. Love her as they did, the Hubbards already depended on the older lady and seemed to need her more than she would need them. 'We could ask around at Monday's dinner.'

'That's a good idea, dear. Someone might have a few spare hours. Or know someone who does. Where is dinner on Monday?'

'My place.'

'That's handy. Any idea what you're cooking?'

'Something with apples. I still have quite a few to process.'

'Roast pork, then. Apple sauce followed by apple crumble.'

'That's what I was thinking. Lentil pie for Rakisha.'

'Sounds lovely. I'll give you a hand.'

'Not this time. You can keep me company instead and tell me how you get your roast potatoes browned so evenly.'

'I keep telling you, dear, use duck fat. I know you won't, so you need to parboil them in boiling water first, then coat them in olive oil.'

'I keep forgetting the boiling water. I'm too used to starting potatoes in cold water.'

'For roasting, you need them cooked on the outside but not on the inside.'

The potato conversation took them into the centre of

Big Town to where Mrs Lionel's family doctor worked. She took Mrs Lionel in at once, leaving Rosemary to sit in the waiting room riffling through ancient magazines. She didn't have to read for long before her phone rang. 'Honey, I'm at the doctor's.'

'Oh, Mum, are you alright?'

'It's Mrs Lionel. She burned her hands.'

'That's why you were driving so fast down the street.'

'Not fast, Honey. At the speed limit.'

'Whatever you say, Mum. I saw you, though. Is Mrs Lionel alright?'

'Yes.' Rosemary contemplated her friend's condition. 'It's rattled her.'

'What happened?'

'She spilt the lye.'

'And she wasn't wearing gloves?' Honey sighed. 'That isn't like her.'

'No.'

'When you're finished, can you come past here? Maybe grab a cuppa?'

Rosemary noted the time. The working day was fast disappearing. Having lunch with the Hubbard family had already lost Wednesday's profits. By the time they got back, and she'd cleaned up *The Green Mulbury*, it would almost be closing time. 'Yes. I'm not sure what time we'll be there. Aren't you working?'

'I did this morning and I've got an after-school class.'

'Want me to buy something to have with tea?'

'No. I made an apple cake yesterday using the jelly you gave Ronnie. And I've got cream, so we're all set.'

'See you soon.'

The thought of visiting Honey gave the entire day an unexpected glow. Rosemary put away the ancient magazine and waited for Mrs Lionel to reappear. She did not long after, her hands wrapped in bandages. Rosemary helped her pay. 'We've got a stopover at Honey's,' she said as they made their way back to the car.

For the first time since Rosemary had met her outside the shop, Mrs Lionel's face brightened. 'Oh, lovely. Will Ronnie be home?'

'I didn't ask. He works from home, so maybe.'

Honey's little house was so close they could have walked, but Rosemary noted how shaky Mrs Lionel still was as they got out of the car. She needed tea and cake.

Honey met them at the door, with Cuddles pushing his way through to get to the visitors. He bumped his nose on Rosemary's leg and she answered with a quick pat, noting how unhappy Sunny would be when she came home smelling of dog.

'It's so great to see you, Mrs Lionel.' Honey took the older woman's arm. 'You look a bit like an Egyptian mummy.'

'I feel like one as well.' Mrs Lionel stepped inside. 'Old and wrapped up.'

'Well, at least your bodily organs are not in jars.'

Mrs Lionel laughed. Rosemary relaxed at the open mirth in it.

Ronnie was at the dining room table, papers spread in a semicircle around him. He rose to greet them, then started gathering his things together. Rosemary stopped him with a hand on the table. 'It's fine, Ronnie. We'll sit at the other end.'

'It's a bit messy,' he said, glancing at Honey, who shrugged.

'Mess is the sign of hard work, dear,' said Mrs Lionel, pulling a chair out with some difficulty and sitting down. 'I can never understand how neat people work. They must fool themselves.'

Ronnie gave her a grateful smile. 'I like my things around me.'

'Any news?' asked Rosemary, sitting next to Mrs Lionel.

'On the old man? No, nothing further to identify him, so that's what I wrote in my report. I'm still searching but I'm working on an insurance case as well which is all this paperwork.'

'It's good to see jobs coming in for you.'

'They haven't, really.' Ronnie sat back down again. 'After these two, I've got a bit of a lull.' He dragged a hand down his face. 'I thought I might get busier. I guess I have to prove myself first. If I could find out who this man was...'

'It's fine, Ronnie,' said Honey briskly as she plonked a plate of cake on the table. 'They did not build Rome in a day.'

'No, but...' He glanced at her slightly bulging tummy.

'We'll be fine. Help me with the tea things.'

Rosemary offered some cake to Mrs Lionel before helping herself to a slice. It was a masterful work. She marvelled once again at Honey's talent.

'Have you heard from Marc?' asked Ronnie as he took a slice of cake.

'I left him a message about the second postcard on his phone. He hasn't rung back.'

'You reckon this is the original postcard?'

'The cross is on the old haberdashery, so yes.'

Ronnie frowned. 'You know, I've been talking to one of the other madrigals in our group. She said Marc left his job because he stole money. And it was his father's business. He's been looking for him ever since to make Marc repay.'

Rosemary picked at her cake. 'That's why he disappeared. For the same reason, recognising Mulbury, they've ended up in the same town.'

They ate quietly for a minute, the only sound being Cuddle's occasional whining reminder he was in the room as well and needed sustenance. Honey slipped him some crumbs, then turned to Mrs Lionel. 'Seems like you could do with some help for a few days. It's going to be hard with your hands like that.'

'I'll manage, dear.'

'Ronnie could help you.'

Ronnie sat up. 'I could?'

'He could mind the shop for you, Mrs Lionel. His work is fully transportable. He could work from your place.'

Mrs Lionel smiled. 'Oh, I'm sure Ronnie-'

'Honey's right.' Ronnie tipped his head toward his piles of paper. 'I could set myself up on a table behind the counter tomorrow and when customers come in, I can help you. And if you need more help than that, I'm there.'

Mrs Lionel's face went a slight shade of pink and the deal was done. She was humming as Rosemary drove home, and her hands were quiet in her lap. When Rosemary glanced at her, she smiled back. 'Nice young man, that Ronnie.'

Nice, yes, thought Rosemary. *And perhaps persistent enough to continue his investigation.*

TWENTY-FIVE

Rosemary settled Mrs Lionel at home, promising to bring her an evening meal later. 'You are a good friend, Rosemary,' said Mrs Lionel as she settled herself on the couch.

'As are you.' Rosemary put a gentle hand on the older woman's shoulder before leaving through the front door of the shop, stepping over the patch of newly scrubbed spillage, and locking the door behind her. The frog croaked appreciatively.

'Hello, Rosemary. Ready?'

Rosemary took a moment to realise it was Jasper in front of her on the path, an over-large beanie on his head, complete with jaunty red pom-pom that was so heavy it lay to one side.

He gave a little bow before registering her stare. 'Too much?' A hand crept up to touch the pom-pom.

'Not at all. It looks very warm.'

'I thought we could walk on the outskirts path.'

Inwardly, Rosemary sighed. What she really wanted to do was to spend time alone, to think about the day. She noted Jasper's expectant dark eyes and nodded. 'I'll get a jacket.'

He stayed on the path as she slipped inside her shop, pulled the blinds down, calculated that she had enough left-over osso bucco for Mrs Lionel as well as herself, fed Sunny (*well, about time*, the cat said with her look), and found her coat. The late-afternoon chill was on Mulbury as they set out on the gravel path around the town. Rosemary flicked the hood of her coat up, fake fur tickling her cheeks.

'You need one of these.' Jasper touched his hat.

'Where did you get it?'

'It's a re-creation of Patti's. She gave it to me this morning. A birthday gift.'

'It's your birthday?'

'Not yet. She was getting in ahead of everyone else, she said.' Jasper's long stride faltered. 'You don't think she thinks...'

'Jasper, you are perfectly well again. Once you get your strength back to normal, you'll forget you were ever sick.'

He nodded, but chewed his lip. 'I'd like to forget it.'

'Does it still worry you?'

'I feel haunted by it.'

Rosemary stepped a little closer to him, so her arm brushed his. Jasper had been about as sick as you could get and survive. At one stage, the residents of Mulbury had gathered in the hospital waiting room, ready for a requiem that never, thankfully, happened. He had survived his pneumonia, and very well indeed, with no residual issues except fatigue. She glanced at his face. Too pale. 'Are you eating properly?'

'Yes, Mum.' He chuckled. 'Actually, probably not. I started off okay when I got home, and people had been so lovely that I had a stack of frozen meals for weeks. I'm okay when I'm cooking for other people—Monday dinners, you know—but it's harder when it's only myself. But then again, I'm not the only one in town who usually eats alone.'

'You are welcome to eat with me any night.'

Under his hat, Jasper's face flushed. 'Thank you, Rosemary. I'll take you up some nights. The main problem is that I have had little appetite. Certainly not in the last couple of days.'

'Why?'

They had walked another one hundred metres before he answered. 'Helena.'

'Your sister who thinks you're cursed? Has she been to see you?'

'Indirectly.' He plunged his hands into his coat pocket. 'She's the one who broke my window.'

'What, she forgot how to knock?'

He laughed mirthlessly. 'Helena doesn't have any manners and what she thinks is hers she takes.'

'She took that book. Why?'

'Evidence.'

'Jasper, this is absurd. You think your sister did criminal damage to your property because she wanted a tatty copy of a space cowboy book?'

'Space *Western*, Rosemary. And yes, that's right. Oh, I can't prove it, but it's what Helena would do.' He shook his head slightly. 'She has a mean streak.'

They were heading up the incline past the Mayoral residence, and Jasper puffed. Rosemary kept quiet, slowing her pace to match his, until they'd rounded the corner and were on the flat again. 'There's more to this story, isn't there?'

He nodded, face crimson now with effort.

'Do you want to talk about it? Not now, not while we're

walking. Perhaps later.' Rosemary did some calculations in her head. Leftover osso bucco for three? Yes, with extra vegetables and lots of couscous. 'I'm having dinner with Mrs Lionel. Why don't you come along? She can show you her hands.'

'Her hands?' Jasper frowned. 'What happened?'

Rosemary told the story of the lye. As she did, Jasper's steps lengthened again, and he pulled his hands out of his pockets. His face had returned to his normal colour— slightly pink—and he nodded vigorously at Rosemary's idea of voluntary assistance for *The Green Mulbury*.

'Is Mrs Lionel alright? I mean, in herself?'

'Not yet. She sees it as a failing.'

'Oh.' Jasper slowed and stopped to view Mulbury from their vantage spot. 'I will always consider Mrs Lionel one of the most successful people I know.'

'Tell her that. She needs to hear it.'

They stood side by side for a while, the town spread before them. Wood heaters had started for the evening and the air had tufts of smoke wending their way through the rooftops. Goldmarket Square was lit by soft streetlights. When it was darker, they would spotlight The Exceptional Tree. It dominated the Square and their view, its vast branches reaching up towards the stars.

Jasper sighed. 'Beautiful, isn't it?'

'You are glad you moved here.'

'Not one single regret. Well, one.' He reached up for his hat again. 'I gave away a stylish fedora, thinking it would be out of place here. I should have kept it.'

'You thought you were heading for hillbilly life.'

'Something like that. Far from it, isn't it?'

Rosemary watched the patchwork of red brick buildings below. 'Yes. Very much.'

'What about you? Do you have any regrets coming here?'

'Only that it wasn't sooner.'

Jasper hesitated. 'It was Alasdair's idea, wasn't it?'

'Yes. He was the tree changer.' Rosemary pulled her jacket up a little to combat the cold creeping in around her neck. 'He wanted a shoemaker's shop.'

'He was a shoemaker by trade?'

'No. He was a dreamer.' She gave Jasper a wry smile. 'Business and dreaming don't go together well.'

'So did your shop start off selling shoes?'

She shook her head. 'We started from our home, which then was on the road to Big Town. Not long after, I bought my shop from an older couple who sold bric-à-brac. It was a musty, run-down place, and I hadn't the chance to get it going. Then Alasdair's shoes didn't work out.'

'You weren't running your shop when he-'

'No. But I sold the house and moved into the shop. Which I'd mostly done already.'

Jasper lowered his voice. 'How difficult that must have been for you.'

'The shop took off and never faltered.'

'I didn't mean that.'

'I know.'

'Do you think about him much?'

The most recent Alasdair dream came back, flooding her with the ghostly feeling of loss. Rosemary squared her shoulders under her coat. 'We all have trials to get through.'

Jasper nodded, putting his hands up to his mouth to blow warm air on them.

Rosemary stepped forward. 'Let's keep going.'

They walked along the top of the town and started back toward Barry's closed garage. Hardly anyone was still out and about. One car pulled out into the street and drove slowly away. Another was parked on that patch of grass at the back of Barry's. Rosemary studied it as she went by, but she didn't recognise it. They crossed the road and turned the corner, going past *Patricia's* with its latest display of an unusual tulle dress with—really?—a rugby top sewn into it, and came to *The Read Mulbury*.

Jasper glanced at his watch. 'Forty-five minutes. Not too bad.'

'It's very good. How do you feel?'

He shook his legs out. 'A little tired but okay.'

Rosemary reached for the shop keys in her pocket. 'Dinner at six-thirty. Come to Mrs Lionel's.'

'Alright.'

Rosemary turned to go and felt his hand on her jacket sleeve. 'What is it?'

'Oh. Nothing.' He let her arm go. 'Thanks for coming with me.'

'Let's make it a regular walk and get you strong again.'

He smiled. 'I'd like that.'

She left him, only glancing back once as she unlocked her own door. He was still standing there, hands back in his coat pockets. She gave him a short wave, but didn't wait to see if he replied.

Sunny was curled on the couch. She stretched a paw out to Rosemary as she stroked the stripe on her head as if to say, *don't disturb me.* Rosemary stoked the wood heater, turning the overhead fan on to blow the warm air down from the ceiling, and prepared dinner. Just before six-thirty, she put it all into one cast-iron pot and carried it next door to Mrs Lionel's.

The Green Mulbury shop door was unlocked. Rosemary

let herself in awkwardly, hands wrapped in a pair of oven gloves. 'Only me,' she called into the dimness.

'We're in here,' said a deep voice.

She followed it to the lounge room, expecting to see Jasper next to Mrs Lionel on the couch with wine glasses at the ready. Instead, a broad older man stood as she came in, tugging at his suit coat to bring its edges together. 'Geoffrey,' Rosemary said. 'What are you doing here?'

'He came to see me, dear,' said Mrs Lionel.

Rosemary put the pot inside the oven and set it on low to keep dinner warm. 'The real reason?'

'It's been a long time.' Geoffrey reached over to shake Rosemary's hand. 'I don't seem to get to the country very often any more.'

'It's kind of you to send work Ronnie's way.'

'He's a good lad. Different from his welder brother.'

Rosemary bristled. 'Ronnie has his own talents.'

'Doggedness being one, I'd say. It's a good skill.' Geoffrey sat down again. 'I was here on business and thought I'd say hello to my old neighbour.'

'Geoffrey's parents had the farm next to mine,' explained Mrs Lionel.

'That's right.' Rosemary sat as well. 'I remember now. But you were here on business?'

'The old bloke you found.' Geoffrey nodded at Mrs Lionel. 'We had something to follow up. Then I sent the young constable with me away for half an hour.'

'You've discovered who the fellow is?'

'No.' Geoffrey's face grew grim. 'Just where he was killed.'

'In the back of Richard Hubbard's car.'

Geoffrey's bushy eyebrows shot up. 'You knew?'

'I guessed.'

'Can you guess who did it then?'

'No. Can you?'

'The matter is under investigation.' Geoffrey stood, leaning over to take one of Mrs Lionel's bandaged hands in both his big hands. 'Lovely to see you, Dorothea. Take care, now.'

Rosemary showed the police officer to the door. 'You haven't made any arrests.'

Geoffrey shook his head. 'Not yet. Bye, Rosemary.' He left for the waiting unmarked car.

'Who was that?'

Jasper appeared along the dim footpath, staring as Rosemary gave Geoffrey a short wave. 'Ronnie's uncle.'

'Oh.' Jasper started. 'And who's this?'

Rosemary swung around to see where he was pointing. The evening was dark and all she could see were the silhouettes of a group of people. It wasn't until they ran up, bunched together but with blonde hair flying, that she could say, 'I think the sisters have some news for us.'

TWENTY-SIX

Holly and Hannah had Heather between, an arm looped through hers on either side. Hannah scowled, Holly chewed her lip, but Heather was distant. *Although,* thought Rosemary, *at least she doesn't appear to be as scared as she had been.* 'Come inside,' she said, holding the door to *The Green Mulbury* wide. 'We're about to have dinner.'

'Food?' Hannah's face brightened. 'Have you enough for us as well?'

Rosemary opened her mouth to say no, but Jasper touched her arm. 'I'll duck over to Roman's,' he whispered. 'He'll at least have some soup.'

Rosemary nodded and gestured to the sisters to go inside. She watched for a moment as Jasper crossed the road, long legs carrying him quickly, then followed the sisters in.

Inside, Heather was beside Mrs Lionel, holding the bandaged hands tenderly. Holly tugged at her younger sister to let go, but the older woman shook her head. 'It's alright,' she mouthed at Holly. 'She's soft as a feather.'

Holly nodded and sank down onto the floor, her back against the couch. Hannah followed suit.

'What's happened?' asked Rosemary

'We had a police officer-'

'-Dad's car-'

'-stolen, hot-wired-'

'-not literally hot-wired but-'

'-blood on the back seat-'

'-Exceptional Tree-'

Rosemary held up her hand. 'Wait.' The noise stopped. 'One at a time.'

'I'm oldest,' said Holly quickly.

'I'm fastest,' said Hannah.

'A man was in the car.'

Heather's voice was almost too quiet to hear, but it had the effect of halting her sisters in their tracks. They leaned towards her.

'Go on, Heather,' Rosemary said.

'A man...' her voice trailed away as she gently stroked the backs of Mrs Lionel's hand.

'Tell us more, dear.' Mrs Lionel leaned forward to give Heather a kiss on the top of her blonde head.

'The man had my knife.'

Such a long silence followed that Rosemary eventually said, 'What knife was that?'

Heather shook her head.

Mrs Lionel leaned down to Heather. 'It's alright, dear. You don't have to tell us until you're ready.'

Hannah laid her cheek momentarily on Sunny's head. 'For a moment I thought she was back.'

'What knife did she mean?' said Rosemary.

'A fleshing knife,' said Holly. 'Part of the taxidermy kit Dad gave her a long time ago. She's never used it. You don't need a fleshing knife for birds. There were a bunch of tools she never used, and they were in this bag.'

'How did the police have them, dear?' said Mrs Lionel.

'They were in the back of the car,' said Rosemary. 'Barry said there was a bag of tools in there.'

'Yes, that's right.' Hannah sighed. 'The blood in the car was from the old man you found, Mrs Lionel.'

Rosemary nodded slowly. 'That's where he'd been killed.'

'They think Heather did it.'

Holly scowled. 'They didn't say that, Hannah.'

'Well, it's obvious. Dad's car, Heather's knife. What else could they think?'

'If they had really thought that, they would have taken Heather in for questioning, surely.' Mrs Lionel smiled at the daydreaming Heather.

'He was assessing her,' said Hannah. 'I could see that from the way he watched her.'

'Geoffrey is a detective.' Mrs Lionel shrugged a shoulder. 'It's what he does.'

'Well, he was alright. Quite kind, really.' Hannah wriggled to sit more comfortably. 'I didn't like the other one. Too judgemental.'

'I don't think he'd ever seen anyone like Heather before.' Holly reached up and patted Heather's leg. 'Let's face it, she is unusual.'

'She's not unusual,' said Mrs Lionel quickly. 'She's *Heather*.'

'*We* know what you mean.' Holly put her head back to rest on the couch. 'But others wouldn't.'

The door croaked open and a few moments later, Jasper appeared holding a pot with hands in oven gloves. 'He gave us the lot,' he said, putting the pot on a mat on the table. 'Minestrone.'

'Excellent.' Hannah leapt up. 'I'm starving.'

They gathered around the table to slurp on soup and eat Rosemary's osso bucco. Somewhere from the depths of Mrs Lionel's freezer came a loaf of cornbread which Jasper thawed, then cut into thick slices. Heather sat next to Mrs Lionel, tenderly feeding her with a large spoon. Rosemary smiled to herself as the older woman tried to protest before giving into Heather's ministrations. They caught each other's eyes. Mrs Lionel gave a helpless shrug and Rosemary an understanding nod.

'What do we do, Rosemary?' said Hannah, finishing her soup and pushing her bowl forward. 'They might blame Heather.' She glanced at her sister, who was carrying Mrs Lionel's empty crockery to the sink. 'She wouldn't survive a trial, let alone anything else.'

'It won't come to that,' said Mrs Lionel.

'Won't it?' Holly put her spoon down even though she hadn't finished. 'I think it might.'

'They have a crime scene in the car,' said Rosemary, linking her hands together and putting her elbows on the table. 'And one under The Exceptional Tree. They have another at the back of your property.'

Holly nodded. 'Where the car was stolen.'

'They'll be looking closely at those three areas. There will be evidence that Heather was in all of them.'

'We've all been in that car at some stage.' Hannah shook her head. 'But Heather hasn't been near The Exceptional Tree for ages.'

'Not that you know, but she has been exploring Mulbury in her quest for dead birds. How else do you explain the necklace I found?'

'Rosemary,' said Heather, clutching the bird around her neck. Someone had strung it on a black book lace.

'It's likely that the police have other leads that they aren't telling us,' Rosemary said. 'Ronnie couldn't find anything to identify the dead man, so they'll go to the next level.'

'Which is what?'

'No idea. I'm not a police officer.'

Holly picked up her spoon again. 'So, what you're saying is that you don't think we have to worry about Heather?'

'I'm not saying that at all.'

Holly put her spoon down.

'I think, dear,' said Mrs Lionel, glaring at Rosemary, 'that what Rosemary is saying is there's no firm evidence yet and the police will concentrate on finding some before they make any accusations.'

Holly stared into her bowl for a moment before eating again.

'Anyone for dessert?' Jasper asked, pushing his chair back.

'I don't have any, dear,' said Mrs Lionel.

'I'm going to whip up golden syrup dumplings if that's okay with you.'

'Oh yes, that would be lovely. I have a new jar of syrup in the pantry.'

'I'll help.' Rosemary stood, stacked the rest of the empty bowls, and followed Jasper behind the kitchen counter. She heard Holly ask Mrs Lionel about her hands, and the tale of the lye started again. 'Kind of you to make dessert,' she said to Jasper.

'When I was a teenager, I used to make it all the time. Iris and I loved golden syrup dumplings. Mum and Helena weren't so keen. They were more of the "I'll have a little slice of apple, is all I need" types.'

'Not big sweet eaters.'

'Not big eaters, full stop.' Jasper hunted in a cupboard until he found the right sized saucepan. 'Still. More for us, Dad would say.'

'Are your parents still alive?'

Jasper shook his head. 'You?'

'No.'

'Siblings?'

Rosemary shook her head.

'You can have Helena any time.'

'I'm fine by myself.'

Rosemary didn't miss Jasper's glance but ignored it. She leaned back on the bench to watch him create. Once he had the ingredients, he whipped the dumplings up in such a practiced manner that she wondered whether his father had eaten anything but golden syrup dumplings. Soon they bubbled on the stove, Jasper prodding them occasionally to push them under the liquid.

'Jasper,' Rosemary said, 'what makes you think it was Helena who broke your window and stole your book?'

Jasper stirred for a moment. 'I'd phoned her. To talk, you know.'

'About anything specifically?'

'Hey, Jasper,' said Hannah. 'Are they ready yet? They smell amazing.'

'Nearly.' Jasper kept his head down.

'We can talk later if you like,' said Rosemary quietly. 'If you want to, that is.'

He nodded. 'Thanks. In fact, thanks for everything.'

'What everything?'

'Walking with me. Talking with me.'

'You don't have to thank me for that.'

'It's not only that. You visited the hospital, too. And made me dinners when I got back. And looked after the shop.'

'We all looked after your shop.'

'But you kept the accounts up to date. Thank you.'

'It wasn't hard.'

'Rosemary.' Jasper pointed the wooden spoon at her, but crammed it back in the saucepan when syrup threatened to drip. 'I'm trying to say thank you.'

'Yes. And you did.'

'You're meant to say *thank you* back.'

'Am I?'

'Yes. It shows me you understand my gratitude.'

Rosemary said nothing.

'Okay, so, once again.' He paused in his prodding. 'I'm very grateful that you are my friend.'

'Thank you.' There was a drop of syrup that had somehow made its way onto his chin. She wiped it off with a fingertip. 'It's my pleasure.'

'Jasper,' said Hannah, now sitting at the table. 'Are they ready yet?'

Jasper turned his reddened face back to the stove. 'Five minutes. Want to get some bowls out?'

With Hannah clattering around beside them, Rosemary knew that the conversation was over. She fetched cream and spoons and thought about what Jasper had said. Had she done for him anything more than she'd done for anyone else? She'd also visited Jules in the hospital that time she'd had her gallbladder removed, although Jules hadn't been in as long as Jasper. She'd done other shops' bookwork before, although mainly Mrs Lionel's and occasionally Rakisha's, if the curly-haired woman begged enough. Perhaps she'd done more for Jasper, introducing him to an updated software package and setting it up, so he only had to learn the basics when he started back in his shop. She'd meant what she'd said. It had been a pleasure to help Jasper out.

A little image of Alasdair arrived in her head, bold and handsome. She blinked it away.

They ate golden syrup dumplings and cream until they were groaning. Jasper ended up making two lots, and it impressed even Rosemary how much Hannah Hubbard could eat. After dinner, they sat around the warm lounge room, Holly and Heather tackling the dishes, while Jasper leaned back on the couch with a sigh.

Rosemary watched as Heather floated back in and sat on the floor with her head resting on Mrs Lionel's leg. The young woman turned to look at Rosemary. There was a flicker of concern in her eyes, but whether that was for Mrs Lionel or for her own fate, Rosemary couldn't be sure.

TWENTY-SEVEN

Ronnie arrived in Mulbury around eight-thirty in the morning. Rosemary had started some cider with the leftover apples and was studying its sugar levels when he knocked at her door. She waved him in. The bell jangled furiously as he threw back the door under the weight of a large box. 'Sorry,' he said. 'I brought you a few things from Honey. Old jars, mainly.'

Rosemary directed him to the floor behind the couch. 'Put them down and I'll sort them out.'

'Right.' Ronnie staggered in and thumped the box down. 'I've got a few of my things in there to work on at Mrs Lionel's. She doesn't open until ten o'clock, Honey said.'

'Correct.'

'Okay.' Ronnie glanced around at the table.

'You can set up here for starters, if you like.'

'Oh, great, thanks, Rosemary. I'll get us coffee if you like.'

'Where are you going?'

'What about Franco's?'

'He doesn't do coffee, only pastries.'

'Oh. It's only that Rakisha's coffee...'

'Is revolting.' Rosemary folded her arms. 'Go to Kelly's. I'll be fine with my percolator.'

'Are you sure?'

'Yes.'

Ronnie nodded and patted his pockets for his wallet. 'I'll be back soon.'

While she waited, Rosemary went back to her cider. Ronnie's satchel fell with a clunk to the floor from where he had hung it on the back of a chair, spilling papers onto the floor. She knelt to pick them up, noting the printed reference to the national online archive website in the header.

The door jangled and Ronnie came back clutching a coffee in one hand and a paper bag in the other. He smiled at Rosemary. 'I got you a raspberry slice.'

'There was no need.'

'There was, actually.' Ronnie carried the bag into the house and set it on the kitchen bench before ripping it open. The slice was a perfect square, coconut evenly browned and biscuit base golden. In between, the layer of raspberry jam sat thick and rich. 'Do you recognise it?'

'Kelly has a reputation for making a winning raspberry slice.'

'She charges like she does.' Ronnie chuckled. 'But what do you think makes the slices perfect?'

'Her cooking skills?'

'That probably helps, but I think the defining factor would be the jam. It is a *raspberry* slice, after all.'

'What's your point, Ronnie?'

'It's your jam.' Ronnie took a knife from the block and deftly cut the slice in two. 'She tried to hide it, but I could see it on the shelf at the back of her preparation area. Your labels stand out. She's making a profit because of your product.'

'Kelly has never come in here and bought jam or anything else.'

'Well, she wouldn't have to. Someone else could easily do that for her. I bet she says to customers, "Oh, I'm so busy, I never have time to get extra jam" and they say, "While you're making my coffee, I'll get some for you" and she says, "I'd be ever so grateful but please don't tell Rosemary because she would be mightily offended if she knew I don't have the time to visit her right now" and they'll say, "Oh, we wouldn't dream of making trouble for you, so she'll never know who the jam is for".'

As Ronnie's charade became noisier, Sunny stood up from her spot on the windowsill, the hairs along her spine upright. When Ronnie finished, the cat sank back on her haunches, although her tail waved slowly back and forth. Rosemary settled her with a look.

'You learn something every day,' she said, taking the slice and biting it in half. Ronnie had been right. It was perfect, but mainly because the jam was sensationally summery in her mouth.

Ronnie pulled his satchel towards him and tugged at the papers inside. 'I've been doing some research.'

Rosemary nodded.

'You were right. *Button Menswear* came up a few times in my searches. Photos, you know. The shop front and the street. I need to keep searching, though. I only did images to start. Is it okay if I sit here for a while and use your internet?'

'Of course.'

Rosemary left Ronnie to his research and went back into the shop. The sun had angled in again from the skylight and highlighted the slightly darker patch of wood created from the mass of chutney that had hit it not that long ago. The shelf was again fixed to the wall and jars lined it, but for a moment Rosemary heard the crash and could see the splintered mess oozing its way across the floor.

Ronnie's shout pulled her out of her reverie. 'What is it?' she asked, hurrying back into the house.

Ronnie's face was blotchy again. He pushed his laptop around so she could see the screen. 'I've found the owner of *Button Menswear*. Well, sort of.'

Rosemary leaned across until she could read the 1984 news article Ronnie had found. '"Tailor shop terminated,"' she read, and stopped. 'This article wasn't in a major newspaper.'

'No.' Ronnie shrugged. 'A local rag, probably one of those free weekly news sheets. You see what it says here? "Popsy's shop, empty now for twelve months, has sold, along with his remaining valuable collection of tie pins, cufflinks and buttons. Locals will always remember Popsy's cheery manner and excellent tailorship".' He leaned back. 'Not a lot of help except to know that this Popsy must have made the dead man's suit before the shop closed.'

Rosemary agreed, but a screech of brakes and a heavy crash snapped their attention to the road.

An old station wagon, its front now crumpled against the bus stop signpost, skewed across the asphalt. A figure lay on the centre white line, wild greying hair spread around her like froth on a beach.

'Rakisha.'

'Oh no.'

Ronnie was directly behind Rosemary as they ran out the door. She glanced at the car as she passed, but the driver was already out and standing over the blinking form of Rakisha on the ground. 'What do you think you were doing, Keesh?' she heard him say.

'Out of the way, Barry,' Rosemary said, kneeling beside Rakisha and scanning her for obvious injuries.

'Are you hurt?' asked Ronnie, squatting down on her other side.

'No, I don't think so, darling.' Rakisha lifted her head to search for Barry. 'How do I tell?'

'Do you have any pain?'

'She *is* a pain,' said Barry, crossing his arms over his squat chest. 'Dashing out in front of me. I almost hit her.'

'The car didn't hit her?' Ronnie frowned. 'Are you sure?'

'Of course, I'm sure.' Barry pointed at his crashed car. 'I swerved away from the silly woman and look where that's got me.'

'It didn't hit me,' said Rakisha. 'I think I slipped. I'm not in any pain, darling. I think I might lie here a while, though.'

'Do you mind if I check you aren't hurt?' Rosemary said.

'Go ahead, darling.'

Rosemary felt Rakisha's arms and legs and ran her hand around the back of her head as far as possible without moving her. There were no points of pain or any blood. She noticed that Rakisha's sandals were undone. 'You probably tripped on your own shoes.'

'Do you think?' Rakisha bent a knee up and felt for her foot. 'Oh, these tricky things. I don't do them up, they're too hard to reach.' She reached her hands up. 'Pull me up, Barry darling.'

Clearly, Barry was not pleased, either at being Rakisha's darling or her pull rope. He took her hands, though, and eased her up, settling her on her feet before letting go and wiping his hands on his trousers. 'Tell me what you were doing in the middle of the road?'

'I needed to talk to you, darling. I was trying to catch your attention.'

'You got my attention, all right. What do you want to talk to me about?'

Rakisha cast a glance at Rosemary and Ronnie. 'Perhaps you could help me back to my shop?'

'Not likely. Look at my car. I need to do something about this first.'

'In a little while, darling? Come and talk to me?'

Barry was already gone. He stood next to the dented bonnet, scratching his head. The pole was embedded into the car but had not, as far as Rosemary could tell, invaded the radiator. 'You need to come and sit with me for a while, Rakisha,' she said. 'We'll monitor you in case you hit your head.'

'But Barry...'

'It's not the best time for him to be talking to you,' said Ronnie. 'How about I lock up your shop for the time being and you go with Rosemary?'

Rakisha shook her head slowly, but pulled a set of keys from her apron pocket and gave them to Ronnie. She allowed Rosemary to take her arm, and they walked carefully around the stationary station wagon and into *The Preserved Mulbury*. Rosemary sat Rakisha on the couch and made tea. Sunny glared at her from the windowsill as if to say, *not another one.*

Rosemary put a teaspoon of sugar into Rakisha's tea and

cooled it enough that the woman could drink it straight away. She studied her closely as she offered it to her, but Rakisha seemed her normally vague self. Still, she may have been dazed or going into shock, so Rosemary sat opposite her to watch.

Ronnie came back in a few minutes later. Silently, he handed Rakisha's keys back to her and went straight to the table to rummage through his paperwork. Rosemary raised her eyebrows at him, but he gave a slight shake of his head and put his head down to work.

'Everything okay with the shop, darling?' Rakisha asked, her gaze out the window.

Ronnie kept his head down. 'Yes.'

'My life is that shop.' Rakisha sighed.

'Is business good, Rakisha?' Rosemary leaned forward a little. 'Shops are expensive things to keep going.'

'Business? Oh, darling, it's not about the business.' Rakisha sighed. 'It's about a state of being. I *am* that shop with its dedication to good and wholesome products, and its light-on-the-ground philosophy. I demonstrate, darling, that you can have a café that serves wonderfully nutritious articles without robbing Earth of her natural resources.'

'Very important factors.'

'Oh, yes, so it's much more than a shop.' Rakisha sighed again, this time long and low and ending in a moan. 'Such a shame I struggle to pay the bills.'

'Business isn't good then.'

'It's not about the business...' but Rakisha's voice was suddenly not so confident. 'That's what I wanted to say to Barry.'

Rosemary sat a little straighter. She heard Ronnie do the same as his chair squeaked. 'What about Barry?'

'He has these ideas. Not my ideas. If they help me pay the bills, though, I guess the darling's on the right track.'

'What track would that be, Rakisha?'

Rakisha stared at Rosemary with unexpectedly clear eyes. 'He wants me to sell his buttons.'

TWENTY-EIGHT

Rosemary glanced at Ronnie, who again gave a brief headshake. 'Buttons?'

'Yes, darling.' Rakisha held her thumb and forefinger out to show the size. 'Darling little things. I thought I could weave them into a necklace or choker, but Barry said, no, they'll sell alright piece by piece to the right buyer.'

'Have you?' said Ronnie. 'Sold any?'

'Not yet, darling. He only gave them to me just then. I had an idea, you see, of giving one away with every tenth granola purchase and wanted to talk to him about it. That's why…' She put a delicate finger to her head. 'I slipped. Now he's cross, isn't he, darlings? Cross because he hit that pole.'

'He'll get over it.' Rosemary glanced out the window where she could see Barry driving away. 'I'm sure he has good friends who are panel beaters.'

Rakisha nodded, then put her hands to her head to arrange her flyaway hair. 'I'm okay now, Rosemary, darling. I'll go back to the shop and start the morning again.'

'Rosemary will take you across,' said Ronnie loudly,

standing up suddenly and making the chair tip. He caught it before it crashed to the ground. 'Just in case.'

Rakisha rose stiffly. 'Really, there's no need.'

'Yes, there is.' Ronnie's eyes widened at Rosemary.

'I'll walk with you,' said Rosemary. 'Just in case.'

Rakisha flapped her hands around but didn't protest. She went back through *The Preserved Mulbury*, Rosemary a few steps behind with Ronnie still making strange, silent gestures at her. She nodded to him that she got it and jangled out the door to Goldmarket Street.

Rakisha made for the bus stop pole and touched it tentatively. It was still serving its purpose, although now at a forty-five-degree angle. As she wandered across to the Square, Rosemary followed her zigzag pattern. She put a hand up to halt the one meandering car on the road as Rakisha went by, apologising to the driver through the open window, but he smiled it away, casual, carefree tourist written on every inch of his cheerful face.

The Sweet Potato was dark. Ronnie must have turned the lights out and locked it up, thought Rosemary. And shut the curtains. She frowned as Rakisha fumbled with the keys and finally pushed the door open to step through. Rosemary flicked a light on as she entered, then immediately turned it off again as the interior lit up and could be seen through the glass door panel.

'Oh dear,' said Rakisha, staring at the ceiling. 'There must be something going on with the electricity. I wonder if I should call someone.'

'I wouldn't,' said Rosemary hastily. 'Give it a bit of time.'

'I could open the curtains.'

'Are these the buttons that Barry gave you to sell?'

'Yes. I put them out on the table to make a nice display, but then I had that good idea to make them bonus gifts with other purchases. Well, darling, you know what happened next.'

'You went outside to find Barry. Do you think anyone came into the shop before Ronnie locked it up?'

'I hadn't opened yet, darling. Do you think I've missed some customers?'

'Not yet.'

'Good.' Rakisha came to stand next to the table. 'Aren't they the most gorgeous things?'

Rosemary bent over the table to study them more closely. There were about thirty buttons sewn to a felt sheet, each one beautifully painted in enamel depicting brightly coloured butterflies. She touched one with a finger, feeling its hard surface. *Ivory*, she thought. *Illegal to sell, even secondhand.* 'Rakisha, where did Barry say he got these?'

'He didn't, darling. He only wondered whether he could sell them through my shop. Said they suited my aesthetic.'

'Aesthetic?'

'Not actually the word that Barry used. He said something more along the lines of *they suit your bohemian cafe.* She stared for a moment at Rosemary. 'Not the word *bohemian*, darling. More along the lines of *hovel*, but I knew what he meant. He's not one for getting the words right, but he's a dear darling. So much like Peter Petal...' Rakisha drifted off behind the counter and turned her coffee machine on.

Rosemary had no idea who Peter Petal was, but doubted that anyone who Rakisha had known in the past would be like Barry Holden. She touched the smallest of the buttons and felt a layer of dirt. She resisted the urge to touch any more. These would need expert attention.

'Rakisha, you won't get much for them in this condition.'

'Oh.' Rakisha ground some beans with a mortar and pestle. 'Barry said that buyers liked them like that. I suggested cleaning them, darling, but he wouldn't have a bar of it. You agree with me, though, don't you? I could make them so nice and shiny.'

'You know who would do a lovely job on these?'

'*I* could, you know. I'm ever such a careful person.'

Rosemary dared not glance at Rakisha's crumb-laden counter. 'Mrs Lionel is our expert Mulbury cleaner. She would be the one to ask.'

'Oh, yes, Mrs Lionel. What a darling old woman. I'll ring Barry now and ask.'

Rosemary tried not to show the bristles that happened with the words *darling old woman* and held up her hand. 'Don't worry Barry. He's got enough to do at the moment with his car. I'll take them over to Mrs Lionel and have them back before Barry even notices.'

'Wait a moment, darling.' Rakisha stepped out from where the coffee machine hummed and rummaged in her apron pocket. 'Barry said he had someone coming to look at them... tomorrow. See?' She handed Rosemary a piece of paper that read *2pm Friday*.

'We'll have it sorted by then. Do you have the bag they came in?'

'They were in a tube like the ones you store half-finished jigsaws in. I threw it in the recycling. Here.' She reached beneath the counter and pulled out a calico bag emblazoned with *The Sweet Potato* logo of two crossed tubers. 'Have this.'

Rosemary took the bag, carefully rolled the felt, and

placed it in the bag. It left a pile of silt behind them on the table.

'Barry said not to put them out in full view of people.' Rakisha ran her finger through the dust. 'Now I see why. No one would want such dirty buttons.'

'Did Barry say how much he was selling them for?'

Rakisha shook her head. 'He took some photos to show a button expert today.'

'A button expert?'

'I imagine they're a haberdasher. Oh.' Rakisha's eyes widened. 'He could have had Patti look at them.'

'But he thought of someone else.'

'Someone in the city, I think. That was who he was off to see when his car ran off the road.'

Ran off the road to avoid you, thought Rosemary. 'How are you feeling after your fall this morning?'

'Completely forgotten about it, darling.' Rakisha rubbed her buttock.

'You'll be alright by yourself?'

'Oh, yes. I've got a new recipe to try today. Vegan apple and peanut tart.'

'Sounds delicious.'

'I'll save you a piece for when you bring those back.'

Rosemary twisted the top of the calico bag and clasped it in her hand as she nodded to Rakisha and left *The Sweet Potato* for *The Green Mulbury*. Ronnie must have seen her through the window and came out of *The Preserved Mulbury* just as she reached the footpath. She held the bag up. He nodded, and together they opened the croaking door into Mrs Lionel's shop.

'In here, Ronnie,' called Mrs Lionel from the kitchen. 'I'm making a pot of tea.'

'Put out another cup,' said Rosemary.

'You here too, Rosemary? Lovely.'

They entered the room and Rosemary put the bag of buttons carefully on the kitchen counter. 'Let me help you,' said Ronnie and took the kettle off the older woman.

'You've changed your bandages.'

Mrs Lionel held up her hands so that Rosemary could see that they were now bound in bindings applied in a neat crossover. 'The others were far too bulky. At least I can use a knife and fork by myself now.'

'Heather will be disappointed.'

'She's a dear girl.'

'She's very fond of you.'

'As I am of her.' She pushed a tray of cups and a milk jug towards Rosemary. 'Take that to the table, dear. Then you can show me what's in that bag.'

Ronnie poured tea as Rosemary explained the morning's events. She untwisted *The Sweet Potato* bag as she spoke, pulled out the felt and placed it in front of Mrs Lionel. The older woman leaned down to blow the dust from one. When Rosemary finished, she nodded. 'I think you're correct, dear. Hand-painted ivory. They could be very old. A very unusual thing for a mechanic to have.'

'Barry gave them to Rakisha to sell on his behalf.'

'Goodness.' Mrs Lionel drummed her fingers on the table. 'I used to think Barry a good, hard-working man.'

'Have you known him long?' asked Ronnie, peering more closely at the array of buttons.

'Long enough. He's never lived in Mulbury, but he attends most Monday dinners.' Mrs Lionel narrowed her eyes at Rosemary. 'You're the shrewd one. What are your thoughts?'

'Similar to yours. Barry is hardly likely to come across valuable antique buttons in his business.' Rosemary frowned. 'What I really don't like is how he's involved Rakisha.'

'She's a bit too trusting. Never had decent intuition, poor dear.'

'What will you do now?' Ronnie touched a button depicting a yellow butterfly. 'Time to call the police. We could contact Uncle Geoffrey.'

'We should,' said Mrs Lionel. 'I'd like to avoid getting Rakisha into trouble.'

'She'll be in trouble with Barry when he gets back and finds out what she's done. We'd better keep an eye on her today.'

'Lucky we had you on the case, Ronnie, dear.' Mrs Lionel patted the young man's forearm with a padded hand.

Ronnie's entire face went crimson. 'Do you think I should ring Uncle Geoffrey now?'

'That would be best.'

Ronnie stepped out onto the balcony to call, leaving Mrs Lionel and Rosemary staring at the buttons. 'Where did Barry get them, do you think?' asked Mrs Lionel.

'I have a few thoughts about that.'

'I know you do. Will you share them?'

'Not quite yet.' Rosemary smiled at her friend. 'I need to check the recycling first.'

TWENTY-NINE

It was lunchtime when Jules arrived at Patricia's for her fitting. She waited until Patti finished with a couple of smiling customers and went with her into the kitchen.

'This is so exciting, Jules.' Patti clapped her hands. 'I hope you don't mind being in here. Gerry's having a little catnap on the bed.'

Jules glanced around at the tiny but neat kitchen, nodding approval at the various pots arranged on the stove. 'Not at all, Patti. I'm happy anywhere.'

'Oh, you're so wonderful.' Patti held up a length of white material. 'Here it is, doesn't look like much.'

'It will be glorious.'

Patti set to work, using a thin tape measure around Jules before measuring and pinning the cloth together.

'Bit of excitement this morning,' Jules said.

Patti's mouth was full of pins. She didn't even glance up as she concentrated on getting the sleeve length correct on Jules's slender arm.

'Barry nearly ran over Rakisha.'

Patti stabbed her excess pins into a pincushion. 'Oh dear, I didn't know.'

'Really?'

Patti straightened and looked at Jules with slightly misty eyes from her close work. 'No, I had a lovely morning thinking about this design and didn't hear a thing outside.' She stepped back and held up a mirror so Jules could see her own reflection. 'What do you think?'

Jules turned this way and that, noting how the white material, a mishmash of the old serviettes from *The Leftover Restaurant* and scraps of linen, draped around her shoulders and nipped in at the waist before flaring quietly over her hips. 'It's lovely, Patti. It makes me feel special.' She fingered a square of material that was pinned to make a breast pocket. 'This is the original piece? The one that started you thinking?'

Patti nodded. 'I thought I might find some similar cloth to work in but, really, it has a quality of its own. Such a funny little thing to find in the gutter.'

'Your finds *are* funny things. But the way you work them is magic.' Jules traced a finger over the edge of the pocket. 'It's embroidered.'

'Yes. A little looped blue thread around the edge and some initials in the corner.'

Jules craned to see. 'Oh, look. Is that right?'

Patti beamed. 'I wasn't going to tell you. I wanted you to find them yourself.'

'J. C. My initials.' She shook her head at Patti. 'You put them there, didn't you?'

'No, I didn't, you see. Isn't it wonderful? I hadn't noticed until I'd washed the hanky. I bleached it carefully, of course, and then the letters stood out. *J. C.* Jules Capriccio.' Patti clasped her hands together. 'It was destiny.'

Jules studied herself in the mirror again, turning her shoulders this way and that. 'Wait until Roman sees this. When did you say it would be ready?'

'Soon.'

'Tomorrow?'

'Well, I'll try. I haven't any other orders to finish.' Patti pulled a wicker basket from under the shop counter and held out a few garments for Jules to see. 'I need to wash these finds. I have a group of young things coming from the city to see what I have.' She blushed. 'They said they've heard about what I do. I really think it was the tulle and rugby top that did it.'

'Yes.' Jules eyed the mannequin in the window that wore the astonishing combination. 'I can see how that would attract a certain crowd. Shall I slip this off now?'

'Let me alter a few pins to make it easier for you.'

Jules stood still while Patti fussed with pin placement. 'Do you ever think about the origin of these things you find and who they belonged to?'

'Yes, all the time.' Patti stepped back to take the shirt as it came off. 'For example, do the garments belong to someone who hasn't realised they've lost them because they already have so many clothes? Or were they sorrowfully missed because that's all the person had to wear?' She sat down suddenly. 'I mean, someone like the old man in the Square. Mrs Lionel said that he'd probably lived rough for a very long time. I bet he didn't have many spare clothes. He would have been devastated to lose even a handkerchief.'

'You wonder what people's stories are, don't you? Especially those people we don't always see even though they live right under our noses.'

Patti nodded. 'Oh, yes. I sometimes think about all the horrible things that could happen that would mean *us* living on the street instead of in our lovely homes. Losing our business, losing our partners, losing our health...'

'Take nothing for granted.' Jules pulled her old shirt and jacket back on.

'Oh, I never do.' Patti set the basket upright. 'That's why it's such a glorious thing.'

'What is?'

'To take these lost and discarded items and give them new life.'

'If only they could tell us why they were lost and discarded.' Jules reached out to stroke her new shirt's pinned pocket. 'I wonder what this would say.'

'"*I have accidentally fallen out of my master's top pocket.*"'

'Pardon?'

Patti indicated the material Jules was still touching. 'This piece was for show. It was aged, but not used. More like a keepsake than an actual handkerchief. A pocket square.'

The door to the shop opened in a whoosh, making Jules and Patti look toward it. It was hard to see who was under the impressive pile of garments. Patti spotted her first. 'Kelly. Goodness me, what have you got there?' She hurried forward with another wicker basket.

'Clothes for you.' Kelly let the garments cascade into the basket. 'As ordered.'

'Where did all those come from?' Jules stepped to the basket and pulled at a random article. 'Is this a dressing gown?'

'Smoking jacket, if you don't mind.' Kelly pushed the basket away with one foot. 'I could kill for a drink, Patti. Got anything interesting?'

'My Melbourne Moments Tea leaves arrived yesterday.'

'That's not really what I mean, but it will do.' Kelly lifted her hair away from the back of her neck to cool it. 'Melbourne Moments Tea? How does it differ from Sydney Moments Tea?'

'Cooler, more layered.' Patti put a light hand on Jules. 'Tea for you, too?'

'Lovely,' said Jules to Patti, who walked on light feet to her kitchen. 'Tell me, Kelly. Where did you get these?'

'Patti likes me to trawl through the streets when I visit the city. Mostly, though, these old things come from op shops. She doesn't use everything, but I give her a great selection.'

'That's very kind of you.'

Kelly laughed and let her hair fall back around her shoulders. 'Don't sound so surprised, Jules. I can be nice sometimes.'

Jules shook her head slightly, hiding the movement with another rummage through the basket. 'Well, I'm glad it's up to Patti to decide what to do with these. I wouldn't know where to start.'

'She's clever, that one.'

'Two nice things in one day.'

'Oh, hilarious.' Kelly sat herself down on one of Patti's waiting chairs. 'Anyway, what are you doing?'

'Patti's making me a shirt.'

'Lucky you.' Kelly yawned. 'I'm not sure that I'd wear one of Patti's creations.'

'No.' Jules tilted her chin pointedly at Kelly's black trousers and pale blue T-shirt. 'You've been in the city. Visiting?'

'Sort of. Sourcing some things for the café. I saw Darren.'

'Has he finished his report on The Exceptional Tree?'

'Yes.' Kelly's face tightened. 'There's a bit of bad news in there.'

'Oh, it will mortify the town.'

'Don't say anything yet. The report has to go to the local council for discussion.'

Jules nodded. 'A wait-and-see situation.'

'What is?' said Patti brightly, carrying a tray of tea.

'Oh.' Jules tapped the basket with her foot. 'What you'll do with these.'

'Yes, I have to wait and see what comes to mind.' Patti grinned. 'And isn't that wonderful?'

RONNIE CAME BACK into *The Green Mulbury* with a strange look on his face. 'Everything alright, dear?' asked Mrs Lionel.

'I've been talking to Uncle Geoffrey.'

'We know,' said Rosemary impatiently. 'And?'

'Remember the dressmaker I spoke to who knew of *Button Menswear* but not the name of the proprietor? Well, she's actually something of an expert in antique clothing.'

'As was Mrs Tasher,' said Mrs Lionel.

Ronnie shook his head. 'This woman had a strange phone call from a man who wanted to know the value of some old buttons. She made an appointment to see him today.'

'Was it Barry, dear?'

Ronnie shrugged. 'He gave his name as Garry.'

Rosemary rolled her eyes. 'How original.'

'Anyway,' continued Ronnie, 'he showed her photographs, and she recognised some designs, in particular the painting of the banded peacock butterfly. She'd only seen this butterfly once in a valuable collection of buttons many years ago.'

'Where was this collection?'

Ronnie grinned. 'Ah, you see, it was owned by the tailor who owned *Button Menswear*.'

'They were stolen from his shop, dear?'

'Well, she didn't know for sure, as they legally sold some collections when the shop closed, but she thought it suspicious enough to contact the police. Apparently, it's a very rare collection and Garry was acting strangely. *And* she remembered the name of the tailor. She called him Pop C.'

'Popsy? The man from your article?'

'Yes, and no. The article spelled it P.O.P.S.Y. but the dressmaker was insistent that it was Pop C.' Ronnie pointed through the wall to *The Preserved Mulbury*. 'As in Sunny.'

For a moment, Mrs Lionel looked puzzled. 'Ah, I get it. C for cat.'

'That's it.'

'You told Geoffrey that we have the buttons?'

Ronnie nodded. 'He said to keep them safe while he investigated further.'

Rosemary walked to the window. The usual array of tourists filled Goldmarket Square, and wandered around pointing at the Victorian Goldfields buildings. 'Did the dressmaker know why the shop shut?'

'Uncle Geoffrey didn't say.'

'Ask her,' said Rosemary. 'You have her number from the first time you spoke.'

Ronnie's face transitioned through its unique range of red. 'Good idea. Maybe seeing the photographs Garry gave her has sparked her memories.' He disappeared outside again to make the call.

'In the meantime,' said Mrs Lionel, 'I think I'd better

put these somewhere safe.' She rolled the felt up and placed it carefully in *The Sweet Potato* bag.

'Do you have somewhere in mind?'

'Oh, yes.' The older woman smiled and tapped the side of her nose. 'In the-'

Ronnie burst back into the shop, sending the frog into an excited volley of croaking. 'Polly remembered.'

'Polly, dear?'

'Polly the dressmaker.' Ronnie raised his phone. 'I'd forgotten her name, but luckily it was in my contacts. *Button Menswear* closed because Pop C disappeared the year before, presumed dead.'

Mrs Lionel glanced at Rosemary. 'The tailor disappeared?'

'They did not find him, despite the family keeping up the search for decades. His wife sold the shop and all the things in it, but Polly was pretty sure this button collection was too valuable to be sold as goods and chattels. She thought it might have ended up in a museum, but apparently not.' Ronnie scratched his head. 'How did Barry get hold of it?'

'Rosemary knows,' said Mrs Lionel.

Ronnie's hand fell away. 'You do?'

Rosemary said nothing.

'I don't think she'll tell us until she's sure.' Mrs Lionel picked up the bag of buttons. 'So, what's next?'

'I reckon I can find out Pop C's real name now,' said Ronnie. 'Polly gave me the contact details for her disguising.'

'Sorry, dear, what did you say?'

'*Disguising*. That's what Polly called her dressmaker friends group.'

'It's a collective noun,' said Rosemary. 'An unusual one at that.'

Ronnie frowned, then shook his head. 'Anyway, I'm going to ring in when they meet tomorrow and ask them some questions.'

'Good work, Ronnie.' Mrs Lionel patted him on the arm.

'It's also time,' said Rosemary, 'for you, Ronnie, to go back into the case of the dead man under The Exceptional Tree and have another think.'

'But I've written my report and given it to Uncle Geoffrey.'

'You may have an amendment.'

'Really? Oh.' Ronnie mottled again. 'You think the old dead man is the tailor?'

Rosemary shrugged. 'Let's see how the jigsaw pieces fit together.'

'Okay.' Ronnie slid his phone back into his pocket. 'If you don't mind, Mrs Lionel, I'll head back to Big Town now. I was going to help you with the shop.'

'Plenty of time for that later, dear.'

Rosemary watched as Ronnie ploughed through the door again, setting the frog into a frenzy, and went to his car.

'It would be wonderful to know who the old fellow was,' said Mrs Lionel thoughtfully. 'It wouldn't seem such a lonely death then.'

'It will be even better,' said Rosemary, running her hand through the hanging herbs above her, 'when we know who murdered him.'

Gerry Yale was late getting out of bed. It had something to do with Patti getting up so early. She'd woken him, not on purpose, but with the cheery way she'd swung her legs out and almost galloped to the bathroom for a quick shower. He'd fallen back to sleep with the drone of the water but was awake again as she emerged smelling like roses and humming as she chose her day's outfit. A glance at the clock told him it was five o'clock.

At eight o'clock, he woke again. The house was quiet. He sat up, straining to hear something. There it was, the faint humming. Patti was in the shop, probably seated in the space behind the counter where she'd set up her sewing tools. He got out of bed, pulled on a caramel velour dressing gown that Patti had found in a caravan cupboard during their last holiday, and padded out to see her.

'Oh, hello, sweetie,' she said. 'What do you think?' She held up a garment for Gerry to see.

'Ah, it's... white, isn't it? I mean, very white. Hard to keep clean.'

Patti giggled and shook her head. 'It's not to wear while

doing the gardening, Gerry. This is for Jules. If anyone can keep a white shirt clean, it's Jules.'

'Yes, you're right there.' Gerry pulled up a chair and sat down. 'You were up early.'

'Oh, I'm sorry, I woke you, didn't I? I was sound asleep and then, suddenly, I wasn't. This shirt has been on my mind. I've got a few more stitches, and it's finished. I thought I'd run it over to Jules before the shop opens.'

'Don't rush. I can open the shop.'

'I know you can, you lovely man. I'm expecting a few buses today. Young people from the university.'

'Young people?'

'Yes, but that's not what they're called these days. I can't remember the word. Hippies?'

'I think the term *hippies* applies to older people now.'

'Dipsters? Oh, I can't remember. Anyway, *young people*. I have a range of new things for them to see.' She indicated a row of neatly folded garments on the floor.

'Now, Patti, make sure they can pay you properly. Young people may not afford what you should charge. All these hours you put into sewing.' Gerry peered at the shirt. 'This, for example. If you were being paid by the hour, this would be worth its weight in gold.'

Patti leaned over to stroke Gerry's stubbly cheek. 'You're such a businessman, sweetie. This is not purely about money, now, is it?'

Gerry shook his head. Patti's eyes were bright, full of energy and ideas. It made him tired sometimes just to look at her. 'I know it isn't. For you. Lucky you have me to balance these books, or you'd probably work for nothing.'

'Oh, I'm not that silly. But you do a wonderful job of keeping the accounts. Are we going along okay?'

'Yes, we are, because of your incredible talent, going really well.'

Patti laughed. 'Oh, that's great. I keep a bit of a tally in my head, you know. Balancing the costs of this darling shop to what I take during the day. I thought we were pretty even.'

'Do you want to know exactly how we're going?'

Patti's hand shot out to land on Gerry's chest. 'No. Don't tell me. All I need to know is that I can keep doing what I'm doing, that *Patricia's* is surviving. If I think about money, then all this...' she held up the shirt '... will be sewn with dollars in mind. It'll make my stitches wobbly.'

Gerry nodded again. 'If you ever need to know, it's all in the software.' He put a hand on the laptop shelved under the counter. 'Anyway.' He stood up. 'I imagine you have had nothing to eat yet. I'm going to make your breakfast.'

'I'll be about five minutes and then I'll be finished.'

'Perfect.' He tightened the cord on his gown. 'I'll get on to it.'

It was more like fifteen minutes before Patti appeared. She bounced in, cheeks glowing, obviously thrilled at finishing Jules's shirt. Gerry set a plate of mushrooms and bacon on sourdough in front of her, smiling at her squeal of delight. As he turned back to the frying pan to do himself an egg to top his breakfast, he couldn't help but think that there was one thing he really excelled at and that was the ability to cook breakfast in a bathrobe.

Patti left for Jules' once breakfast was done, leaving Gerry to clean up the kitchen and himself. As he hung his bath towel on the clothes horse set up on his balcony, he saw Jasper Lu leaning over the rail of his porch, peering into Rosemary Exeter's yard. It was awkward catching your neighbour out like that. Gerry banged the clothes horse onto the boards of the deck and coughed loudly. It worked. Jasper turned at the noise.

'Hello, Gerry.'

'Ah, Jasper. Didn't see you there.'

'How's your morning going?'

'So far, so good. Yours?'

'Should be fine. Haven't really got going yet.'

Gerry nodded. 'It'll be busy enough soon enough.'

'Yes. I'd better get my skates on.' Jasper lifted his hand and disappeared through his glass doors.

Gerry took a moment to pretend to study the rusting nails on his balcony rail, leaning far enough over to see Rosemary in her backyard tending to the flock of ducks and chickens that she kept in her orchard. She was a fine-looking woman—tall and elegant—and he understood Jasper's yearning. For that's what it was. Gerry knew about yearning. It had taken him years to catch Patti's eyes, but it had been worth every minute. Patti was the bright star in Gerry's sky.

He left the railing and sat for a moment on an outdoor chair to tie his brogues. A few cars were making their way to Big Town, rumbling down Low Road at sensible speeds until they hit the higher speed zone and could zoom away. When Patti had suggested taking over the little shop, Gerry baulked at the thought of it being on the corner, especially on the main road out of Mulbury. Never having lived in a little country town before, he had no idea that morning traffic would comprise three cars heading out and one coming in. The only person he knew who drove from Big Town to Mulbury to work was Barry, and Gerry did not know why. Barry could have set up his mechanic shop anywhere he wanted. It seemed such a long drive to do each day if you didn't have to.

He finished his shoes and sat back. *Speaking of Barry, he thought, I haven't seen him since he'd picked up that box to take to the op shop.* Gerry usually left the shop when Patti was doing a fitting, standing on the pavement outside or taking a stroll up and down. He could hear the work of the garage from where he was, sounds he didn't quite understand, lots of banging and hissing. People came and went regularly, dropping off their vehicles. Barry was the sort of bloke who'd stand and talk and charge by the hour for doing so. He knew all the gossip and happenings of the town that way. Gerry frowned, trying to remember the last time he'd seen Barry chin-wagging with customers.

Barry slid from his mind as he stood up. Inside, there was work to be done. Patti had packaged Jules' shirt neatly in tissue paper and then in a fancy white box finished with a broad pink ribbon. While Patti was no doubt the clever, creative one, Gerry was an excellent cleaner-uperer. He entered the shop and started tidying the leftover threads and paper Patti had left in her haste to show Jules her handiwork.

Half an hour later and the shop was as neat—Gerry chuckled at the thought—as a pin. He opened the blinds, dusted the front display, and flipped over the 'open' sign. The door squealed as he opened it to test its unlocked status and he thought, once again, how he should oil those beautiful brass hinges. As he closed the door, he glimpsed a young man walking across the Square. Not that it was so unusual to see someone heading for a café, but the man's coat was hitched right up to his ears and he had a large navy-blue beanie pulled hard down on his forehead. Clearly, he was cold.

Gerry frowned. Of course, it was completely different for someone who'd eaten a hearty breakfast, had a hot shower, and only ventured outside to tie his shoelaces, but the sun was lighting the Square and was surprisingly warm for a near-winter day. Perhaps the young man had been sitting in the shade somewhere? Or maybe he was very thin. Gerry had heard that thin people felt the cold. He put a hand unconsciously on his rounded belly.

The young man went first to *The Sweet Potato,* but Rakisha obviously wasn't up yet. He continued to Kelly's and pushed open the door. Gerry couldn't see inside the café from where he stood, so he shrugged and went back to the shop counter to fire up the till.

Moments later, the door squealed, and Patti came in. Her face was flushed from her walk and her eyes were bright. Gerry felt his knees buckle a little. 'Hello, dearest,' he said. 'Was she pleased?'

'*Pleased* wasn't the word for it, Gerry.' Patti spun around, her navy skirt fanning out and brushing against the row of coats in the centre of the shop. 'She loved it. No, she said she was *ecstatic*. Ecstatic, Gerry. Isn't that lovely?'

'Yes, my word, very lovely.'

Patti stopped spinning and put her hands to her cheeks. 'I mustn't get carried away.' She patted her face and let her hands drop. 'On to the next thing.' She glanced down at the row of garments on the floor. 'I'll get freshened up and work on these.'

'I'll get you a cup of tea.'

'Oh, you are wonderful, Gerry.' Patti skipped across and planted a red lipstick kiss on her husband's cheek. 'I'll be back in a moment.'

Gerry hurried back to the kitchen and prepared tea in the rose teapot that Patti loved so much. He set it down on the edge of Patti's now clear work bench behind the counter and went to arrange a rack of skirts outside. The rack caught on the step of the shop, and he jiggled it without success.

'I can help you.'

Gerry twisted to see the beanie-clad young man. He stood, still hunched in his large, downy coat, clutching a large coffee and a brown paper bag. His eyebrows were raised, questioning.

'Thank you,' said Gerry. 'That would be very useful.'

The young man put his purchases on the ground and stepped closer to lift the end of the rack clear. Gerry caught a whiff of unwashed body and noticed the takeover of stubble on the young man's face. They wheeled the rack to its place on the pavement, and Gerry grounded it with a few small sandbags.

'Thank you. Much easier with two.'

The young man smiled back at him. His eyes, though, were troubled. 'How is your shop doing? You know, with sales and that. Money coming in.'

Gerry paused, then decided the question was innocent. After all, the man seemed genuinely interested. 'My wife is wonderfully talented. The success of the shop is all because of her.'

The young man nodded. 'So, it's had no other boost? No lucky finds that have helped it along the way?'

Gerry frowned. 'Patti finds many old clothes, if that's what you mean. They aren't *lucky* finds. They're dreadful. She *makes* them lovely. This shop started from bare bones, and she has built it up.'

The young man nodded, pulling his coat up a bit more.

'Would you like to come inside to eat your breakfast?' Gerry pointed to the coffee and paper bag. 'Much warmer. You do look cold.'

The young man blinked, then shook his head. 'Thank

you. I'm okay, though. I'll sit in the sun to warm up.' He gave a little laugh. 'It's always like this in the morning.'

Gerry raised a hand in farewell as the young man went around the corner and down the road towards Big Town. It wasn't until he reflected on what the young man had said that he realised how peculiar it sounded. Not, 'I'm always like this in the morning' but 'It's always like this'.

I do not know, thought Gerry, *what that means.*

THIRTY-ONE

Rakisha hadn't slept well. Peter Petal was back in her dreams, as annoying as a blowfly. His image seemed to stick at age twenty-five when he was at his most charming. Now and then, the image blurred to have Barry's face insert itself onto Peter's youthful body. It was disconcerting, and she kept waking up with a jolt.

The other thing on her mind was the bag of buttons. She needed them back today, but wasn't sure whether Mrs Lionel had finished with them. There seemed to have been a bit of excitement in *The Green Mulbury* yesterday with that young Ronnie Whatshisname dashing in and out of the shop, but it had been a grinding day for Rakisha and she couldn't spare the time among the pounding of beans and crushing of herbs to find out what was going on. She supposed that she'd have to go over and fetch the buttons before she opened *The Sweet Potato*.

She yawned and stretched, reluctant to move out of the cosy bed. The little house had a lovely aroma of sandal-wood, and it made her dreamy. And sad. She hadn't seen any of her friends from the old days for years. They'd drifted off like autumn leaves caught in the wind, including Rakisha, who'd landed in Mulbury almost by default. Her car had run out of petrol and there she'd stayed.

The alarm rang again. This time when she went to silence it, she knocked it clean off the bedside table and there was no excuse now not to get up. She slid out of the warm cocoon of blankets, shut down the clock with a tap of her foot, and dressed in mauve layers. A cup of legume coffee later, and it was time to see Mrs Lionel.

It was later than Rakisha had realised. All the shops along Goldmarket Street were open, with a trickle of customers wandering in and out. She'd missed the early morning coffee types but still had a chance with those who waited until morning tea to quench their caffeine-like longings. Even so, she hurried over the road, ignoring the bus stop pole, which leaned at a jaunty angle, and pushed through the door of *The Green Mulbury*. The frog croaked importantly, and she shrieked.

'Rakisha,' said Mrs Lionel, emerging from the entrance to her house. 'How are you, dear?'

'Oh, I'm fine, darling.' Rakisha put her hand on her chest and tried to slow her heart rate. 'I don't suppose you've thought about getting a different type of animal to sit at your doorway?'

'Percy had that job.' Mrs Lionel glanced back at the faded dog bed near the couch. 'He is a little yappy, so now I deploy him to other duties.'

Rakisha eyeballed the older woman and wondered why, when she asked a serious question, people responded as if the matter wasn't important. Mrs Lionel's dog had been dead for quite a while now, so it was no joke. She tossed her hair back. 'Well, darling, a frog certainly wouldn't suit my shop.'

Mrs Lionel shook her head. 'I imagine it wouldn't. Have you come in for a cup of tea and a chat?'

'No, thank you, darling. No time for a chat today. I've come for my bag of buttons.'

'Bag of-? Ah, I see.'

'Rosemary Exeter said you were going to clean them for me. Which is, darling, very kind of you.'

'They aren't quite ready, Rakisha. Could I bring them over to you a bit later?'

Rakisha's hair had flopped forward over her shoulders. She pushed it back irritably. 'Barry said the buyer would come at two o'clock.'

'Lots of time, then, for me to bring them across to you.' Mrs Lionel smiled. 'That also gives you time to open *The Sweet Potato* and get going for the day.'

Rakisha glanced back to the Square. A minibus had pulled up and a group of eager tourists were already milling about The Exceptional Tree. 'Yes, darling, I suppose you're right. I couldn't get up this morning and now I'm running late.'

'Well, you head off and I'll be over shortly.' Mrs Lionel walked over to the door and bent down to the frog. 'I've turned him off for you so you can escape silently.'

There it was again, Rakisha thought. A little joke that she didn't find funny at all. Despite that, Mrs Lionel's smile was warm, and she gave Rakisha a hug on the way out. Mrs Lionel smelled of lavender and lemons. Rakisha clasped the fragrance to herself as she crossed the road safely and walked across the Square.

Inside, *The Sweet Potato* was its safe, familiar self. Rakisha pulled the rough cotton curtains back from the windows and twisted them into knots to keep them back. She rubbed at a dirty patch on the glass with her sleeve, making a mental note to wash the windows when she had a chance. The two tiny tables inside, with the rattan tops and chairs, were packed with condiments. Rakisha straightened their bamboo placemats and went behind the counter to start the coffee machine.

It was as she was setting out the day's bean brownies in the display cabinet that the door groaned open a crack. A man entered quickly and closed the door behind him with a bang.

'Barry, petal. I mean, darling. Need a coffee before you start work?'

'Listen, Keesh, I need the tube back.'

Rakisha blinked at the man in front of her. There was something blurry about him. Perhaps it was the obvious three-day growth on his pale face or the way his collar was askew, and his shirt hung out of his jumper, as if he'd dressed in the dark and in a hurry. He was also slightly bent over and kept glancing furtively out of the window. 'Barry, darling, you look like you're trying to hide.'

'What? No. No. Hide from what?' He gave a hollow chuckle. 'I need my tube back.'

'You mean the darling little buttons?' Rakisha slipped a brownie into a paper bag. 'I haven't got them.'

Barry straightened slightly, his mouth open. 'You haven't got them?'

'No, darling, they're with Mrs Lionel. She's giving the sweet little things a clean and then she'll run them over to me in time for the buyer.'

'They're at...? I need them *now*.'

'That's what I said to Mrs Lionel this morning.' Rakisha had to shout over the sound of frothing soy milk. 'She'll bring them over in time for your two o'clock person. She's such a kind woman. Here.' She finished preparing Barry's coffee and brought it and the brownie around the front of the counter. 'I made you-'

The door was groaning closed.

Rakisha put her things down on one table and leaned across to see out the window. Barry was walking—no, scurrying—across the Square to *The Green Mulbury*, which, she could see, was swarming with people. Two buses had pulled up and Rakisha saw a pack of tourists strolling purposely across the Square to the cafes within it. The morning tea mob, she thought.

It was busy for a good hour or so. Barry's coffee went cold, and she hoisted it into the compost bucket once it did to make way for an arthritic woman who wanted to sit at the table. The brownie stayed on the table for a little longer until the same woman pocketed it as she left. Rakisha didn't have time to worry. Some people visiting were those of her own heart, and conversation flowed around caffeine substitutes, healthy sugars, and gluten-free flours. It was, she thought to herself later, a delightful morning.

The buses left before lunchtime, heading to the next little tourist village for lunch. Rakisha scanned the remaining food she had left on display and figured that lunch would be light for most of the buses' passengers. She was wiping the tables when she remembered Barry's buttons.

Through the window, she couldn't see anyone in *The Green Mulbury*. She squinted. No, she was wrong. There was Barry, his figure stooped, in the centre of the shop talking to Mrs Lionel. Not talking, exactly. Shaking his finger at. Mrs Lionel had her arms crossed and her feet apart, as if bracing herself against his words. Several times, she shook her head, and each time she did, Barry stepped closer to her. *Oh dear,* thought Rakisha, *seems as if she might have lost the buttons.*

There was nothing to do but flip her closed sign over and hurry across the Square to *The Green Mulbury*. Barry now had Mrs Lionel up against the wall of her shop, but the older woman was staring defiantly into his face. 'It isn't here,' she was saying firmly as Rakisha pushed the door open. The frog croaked. 'Not here,' said Mrs Lionel again.

'Hello, darlings,' said Rakisha. 'Is something the matter?'

Barry turned to her, and she stepped back involuntarily. His eyes were panicky, darting this way and that, and his hair was all over the place as if he'd run his hands over and over his head.

'Goodness,' she said. 'You don't look well at all.'

'Keesh,' said Barry in a strangled voice, 'she doesn't have it. Where is it?'

'Where is what, Barry, darling?'

'The tube, Keesh. The one I left with you.'

'In the recycling bin.'

Barry's mouth dropped open and he struggled to talk. 'The buttons...'

'I put the buttons in a bag, darling. Much nicer than that horrible old thing.'

'Whatever, Keesh. Where are they?'

Rakisha frowned. Mrs Lionel had stepped away from her position against the shelf, which left Barry standing twisted and miserable alone. 'Here,' she said. 'The buttons are being cleaned.'

'They did not need to be cleaned.' Barry clenched his fists and brought them down to thump on his own legs.

'Listen here, Barry,' said Mrs Lionel coldly. 'You can stop that rot. That tube was stolen property, and you were trying to make money out of it.'

'The tube?' said Rakisha, trying to catch on.

'The buttons, you stupid-'

'Cut that out,' said Mrs Lionel as if Barry were a naughty dog. 'And keep Rakisha out of this. What do you think would have happened to her if your person had taken them? She'd be an accessory.' She leaned over and poked Barry hard in the arm. 'You can do what you like to yourself, Barry Holden, but don't bring others into it.'

Rakisha wriggled. The air in the shop was too frosty. 'I'm not sure, darlings,' she said, 'that I understand what's going on.'

'That's the best way to be, dear.' Mrs Lionel smiled encouragingly in her direction. 'How about you go back to *The Sweet Potato,* and I'll sort Barry out?'

Rakisha knew that Mrs Lionel could sort anything out, but something felt wrong about leaving the shop and stepping lightly back to the café. She shook her head and stood her ground.

Barry studied Rakisha long and hard. His hands gradually softened, as did his tightly held shoulders. In fact, his whole body slumped down, including his face, which went slack. Slowly, he sighed. One last glance at Mrs Lionel, another stare into Rakisha's eyes, and he slouched out of the shop, the frog croaking a farewell as he ran back towards the garage.

Rakisha raised her eyebrows at Mrs Lionel, who smiled again and said, 'Cup of tea?'

Even though she didn't drink the stuff, Rakisha nodded. As she followed Mrs Lionel into the kitchen, a thought dawned on her. Barry Holden was not the least like Peter Petal.

THIRTY-TWO

At five minutes to two o'clock, Rosemary Exeter went to stand on the pavement outside *The Preserved Mulbury*. It was a glorious day. A cerulean-coloured sky stretched across the town, and people shed their coats in the buttercup sunshine. It was one of those days that slowed people down, that made them forget everyday worries and be more concerned about soaking up warmth. Rosemary smiled at the small throng of people gathering in the Square. They sat on the park benches and gazed up at The Exceptional Tree as if they'd seen nothing so, well, *exceptional*.

At one minute to two o'clock, a dark figure appeared amongst the sunshine seekers. He wore a blue shirt, one that would no doubt pick up the vibrant colour of his eyes, and a pair of black jeans. He glanced at the names of the shops in the Square, saw *The Sweet Potato*, and made a beeline for it.

Rosemary crossed the road and approached him from the front. 'Hello again, Mr Cambridge.'

The man stopped. 'Ah. The pickle lady.'

'I get called various things, but that's a new one.'

'Did you give my message to my son?'

'He knows you've been in Mulbury.'

'And then he went to ground, I suppose.'

'He said he would be back.'

Joey Cambridge dropped his gaze to the ground. 'I was harsh the other day. I thought you were harbouring him.'

'Not intentionally.'

He stood straight. 'My temper has never been good.'

'It's caused you problems in the past.'

He frowned and folded his arms across his chest. 'Yes.'

'Including the estrangement of your son.'

'That wasn't me. He stole money from my business.' Joey dropped his arms and thrust his hands into his jeans' pockets. 'I nearly lost the entire venture. Took me years to recover. He's a scoundrel.'

'He's still your son.'

Joey's gaze blazed into her. 'Oh, I see. You've got a child who's never done you wrong, haven't you? You would not know the *hurt* a child can inflict on a parent. You have no idea.'

His shout made tourist heads turn, but Rosemary put out a reassuring hand to them. 'You're correct. My child has done nothing that hurt me more than her. I don't have any idea what you've gone through.' She stepped toward him. 'But what did that leave him?'

'What do you mean?'

'You say he stole your money. What happened next?'

'He lost it all. Every cent.' Joey rubbed one hand through his hair. 'I had nothing. He had nothing. He disappeared, and I never wanted to see him again.'

'Until now. How did you know he was in Mulbury?'

'The postcard, the one that was in my mother's box of special keepsakes.' Joey ran his hand over his face. 'I knew it was the last contact my mother had with my father, but no one knew the location of the picture on the front. My dear mother...' He sighed. 'She still knew it was special and kept it close to her bedside. It was only when I gathered her things together that I saw it was missing.'

'You didn't know where the picture was, either.'

'Not until I thought about it more. I collect taxidermy. I visited here a little while ago to buy a bird.'

'Heather's eagle.'

'Heather is the young female taxidermist? Her father sold it on her behalf.'

Rosemary held back her snort.

Joey went on without noticing. 'It came to me as I drove away from my mother's nursing home. The postcard she loved so much had disappeared. Every time I visited her during her last years, she'd point out every detail on it. I knew that picture well, but it didn't click in place until she'd died. The picture was this.' He flung his hand towards the shops on Goldmarket Road. 'It was Mulbury.'

'So, you came to see what the cross meant.'

'Yes, but it made no sense. That shop...' He pointed towards *Patricia's*. '... High-end fashion. Nothing like it would have been here in 1983. But then I wondered whether Marc would work out the photograph as well. And he did.' Joey dropped his gaze to the ground before straightening, his face stormy. 'He's at it again, don't you see? His terrible, dishonest ways.' He glanced towards *The Sweet Potato*. 'My mother died after many years of suffering dementia, and somehow he found out. He went through her things before I could get there and took that postcard and anything of value. Including the rest of my father's collections, the ivory buttons.'

'You have evidence of that?'

'It's for sale, isn't it? Came up through a friend of a

friend of a friend.' Joey smiled mirthlessly. 'I kept a vague eye on my father's interest areas as I grew up. As did Marc, but not for the same reason, I suspect. My father's disappearance meant he never became the world expert couturier he should have been, which was a sore point for a family that was devastated he was never located. Marc only saw the dollars in the things that were left behind. When I heard of this unique collection's sale, I knew immediately that it must have been my father's.'

'Marc's not the one selling it.'

He shook his head. 'He must be. Who else would have taken the collection from my mother's things?'

'The collection wasn't among your mother's estate.'

Joey's face darkened. 'How would you-?' He stopped as another figure appeared at the edge of the Square. With his olive-green coat done up to his neck, and hands thrust into his pockets, Marc Cambridge looked like he'd stepped into the wrong film set. A few sun-warmed tourists glanced at him, but they mostly ignored him as he went to stand in a patch of sunlight near the corner of the Square. 'Ah. See?'

'He's not here to sell your buttons.' Rosemary nodded towards another man scuttling across the Square, his hands plunged into the pockets of his overalls. '*He* is.'

'Him?' Joey watched as Barry Holden ploughed past them and entered *The Sweet Potato*. 'Who is he?'

'Our mechanic.'

'Then why is Marc here?'

'For this.' Rosemary reached into the inside pocket of her jacket and pulled out the postcard with the cross pressed into Mrs Tasher's haberdashery. 'He lost it and *he...*' Rosemary indicated *The Sweet Potato* as Barry stormed out again, followed by a frowning Rakisha '... found it.'

'What is wrong with you, darling?' Rakisha was

shouting as she clutched at Barry's arm. 'They are pretty buttons, but really not your sort of thing. You shouldn't be carrying on like this.'

But Barry had halted in the middle of the Square, his eyes on the police car that was winging its way around the corner of the road from Big Town.

THIRTY-THREE

Barry shook at Rakisha, but her grip was fierce. His eyes
were wide and his face the shade of the grey gravel of Goldmarket Square as he stared at the large shape of Geoffrey
stepping from the police car. His expression didn't change
even when the junior constables with the older police
officer went towards Marc Cambridge, surrounding the
man and talking rapidly to him.

The sight of a police drama enthralled the tourists.
They came out of the shops and gathered under The Exceptional Tree. With their exit, the shop owners followed. Mrs
Lionel crossed the Square to stand near Rosemary, her grim
gaze on Joey Cambridge. Jasper emerged from his bookshop
at the same time as Patti and Gerry came from *Patricia's*
with Jules at their side wearing a bright white shirt. Kelly
ran out of her café and shooed the gawping tourists from
under the Tree to stand in the winter shine. Only Franco
kept working, the rich fragrance of his pies drifting into
the air.

'Are you alright, Rosemary?' Jasper said, coming to
stand with her and frowning at Joey Cambridge.

'I'm perfectly fine.'

He lowered his voice. 'What's going on?'

'A couple of things. The police have located a murderer and a thief, but they aren't the same person.'

Joey turned slowly to Rosemary, obviously finding it hard to tear his gaze away from the police handcuffing his son. 'Murderer? I don't understand.'

Rosemary smiled sadly at him. 'I'm so sorry.'

'Who is he supposed to have murdered?'

Rosemary shook her head. 'This is the point where you talk to the police.'

He stared at her for a long moment, shock widening his eyes and draining colour from his face, before striding over to the police car. He stopped a metre short of his son, who glanced up and let his head droop again. Joey Cambridge reached out to his son, but let his hand fall clear of its mark.

'That,' said Jasper quietly, 'is one of the saddest sights I have ever witnessed.'

A commotion from the edge of the Square heralded the Hubbard sisters, Heather in the middle pulling her sisters along in her haste. The silver bird dangled from her open-necked shirt.

'Oh, no,' said Hannah as they arrived at Rosemary, waving frantically at the police. 'Have they come for Heather?'

'No.' Rosemary straightened the little bird at Heather's neck. 'The only thing your sister is guilty of is being kind to an old man.'

Hannah frowned at Holly. 'Huh?'

'Rosemary will explain,' said Holly, putting an arm around her taller sister. 'I'm sure of it.'

'Let's see how things work out first,' said Rosemary, looking at Mrs Lionel. 'Have you got it?'

Mrs Lionel held up a bag decorated with the two-tubered logo of *The Sweet Potato* and a long carrot peeling. She flicked the peel off. 'Barry didn't think to hunt for this in my compost bin.'

'Just as he didn't think to get this from Rakisha's recycling bin.' Rosemary reached into her bag and pulled out a battered cardboard tube.

'What is that?' asked Hannah.

'It's one of those things that you put half-finished jigsaws in,' said Holly. 'You know, when you put the pieces on felt and roll it up. Why have you got that, Rosemary?'

'It was what the button collection was in.'

'Rosemary,' said Gerry, noticing the tube and hurrying over. 'That thing was in the box of toys I gave to Barry.'

'Yes,' said Rosemary.

'What are you doing with it?'

'It held a valuable collection of buttons intended for Mrs Tasher's evaluation.'

'I beg your pardon?'

'Ah,' said Mrs Lionel. 'The tailor from *Button Menswear* came to Mulbury to have it evaluated, but it was Scarlet Tuesday. He never got the chance to return home.'

'We're speculating,' said Rosemary, 'although I think it's likely.'

'They hid the collection in the cellar to keep it safe,' said Gerry, running a hand over his face. 'And then that poor haberdasher, Mrs Tasher, perished in the fires trying to flee. Oh dear, that's a terrible irony.'

'So,' said Mrs Lionel, 'what happened to the tailor?'

Rosemary said nothing but tipped her head towards Geoffrey, who had taken Joey Cambridge aside.

'Hey,' said Hannah. 'Is that the man Heather's scared of?'

Rosemary studied the youngest Hubbard sister. Heather was playing with the silver fairy wren, her eyes on Rosemary. 'That's Joey Cambridge, Heather. He's not who you saw, though.'

Heather shook her head. 'Joe,' she said.

'Yes,' said Rosemary. 'You saw Joe, not Joey.'

'Who's Joe?' asked Hannah.

Rosemary took a step back and craned her neck to see Ronnie stepping out of his car. He hurried towards her with his head turned towards his Uncle Geoffrey and nearly tripped on the gutter. 'Ronnie will tell us.'

'Go on,' said Hannah as Ronnie arrived, panting. 'Who is he?'

'Sorry?' Ronnie scanned the people in the Square. 'Who is who?'

'How did you go with the meeting of the disguising?' said Rosemary.

'Good, in the end.' Ronnie swept the hair from his forehead. 'They were in for a chat, but they finally got to it. The tailor from *Button Menswear* was Joseph Cambridge.'

'Joseph Cambridge?' Hannah grabbed Heather's arm. 'Joe?'

'Joe,' said Heather.

'Cambridge, dear?' said Mrs Lionel. 'As in, *Marc* Cambridge?'

Ronnie pulled his phone out and held it out so the others could see the archived article from the state library. 'Yes, Joseph Cambridge was a tailor who went missing at the time of Scarlet Tuesday. Here's a picture of his wife and little son, Joey. And...' he flicked the picture forward '... here's one of Joey Cambridge all grown up telling journalists they'd found no trace of his father. He's holding his son's hand. *Marc's* hand.'

'I get it,' said Jasper, watching as Geoffrey ordered his constables to put Marc in the car. 'The old man Mrs Lionel found under The Exceptional Tree was Joseph Cambridge, the tailor.'

Jules put her hand to her head. 'He was that young man's grandfather?'

Instead of answering, Rosemary leaned forward to stare at Jules' shirt. She reached out a finger and touched the shirt's pocket. 'J. C.'

'Oh,' said Jules, putting her hand down to smooth the fabric. 'Isn't it wonderful? Patti styled it out of scrap linen.'

'It was destiny, wasn't it, Jules?' Patti smiled. 'J. C. was embroidered on the piece I found in the gutter. Jules Capriccio.' She froze suddenly. 'No. Not Jules Capriccio. *Joseph Cambridge.*' Her face blanched. 'That pocket square belonged to the old man?'

'We believe so, dear.' Mrs Lionel put a gentle hand on Patti's arm. 'And you have turned it into a beautiful garment as a tribute.'

'I don't get it,' said Hannah. 'The dead man was murdered by...'

'His grandson.' Rosemary reached out to touch Heather's sleeve. 'The old man was sleeping in your father's car, which Heather knew. Marc tried to steal it.'

'Why?' said Jasper. 'He already had a car. We saw it that night after dinner.'

'In the short time we've known him,' said Rosemary, 'he's had two cars, a red sedan and a brown one. Two cars in two weeks. Marc had made a habit of stealing cars, probably as their fuel ran out. Richard's was going to be another he took, but it was occupied. Heather saw the tousle between the men. She probably saw the car drive away, but it stopped near Barry's. I imagine Heather followed and was in time to see Joseph lying like he was asleep in the Square.' She patted Heather. 'You put that feather in Joe's pocket.'

'Joe,' said Heather, her eyes bright. 'Blue-eyed Joe. My friend.'

'I don't get it,' said Hannah, rubbing her head through her unruly hair. 'Why didn't you tell us that a man was sleeping in Dad's car?'

'Because,' said Heather clearly, staring directly at her sister, 'you would have told him to go away.'

Hannah's mouth dropped open. Holly chuckled. 'Heather's right, Han. You *would* have.'

Hannah stared at her sisters, then nodded. 'You're right, Heather. I probably would have.'

'Poor Hannah,' said Heather, patting her sister's hand. 'There, there.'

Jasper leaned over to Rosemary. 'Did Marc know that the old man was his grandfather?'

'Not then,' said Rosemary. 'Perhaps now.'

The group fell silent as they watched Marc bundled into the police car. Joey Cambridge was talking earnestly to one constable, who kept shaking his head. Joey grabbed at his arm, and the other police officers closed in on him until he stepped back, his body folding in until he sat heavily on the ground. An officer crouched down with him, but Joey turned his head, his sobs clearly heard across the Square.

'This is dreadful,' said Jules.

'And now they're going for Barry,' said Holly.

Geoffrey had turned his attention to the stunned Barry Holden, who still had Rakisha clinging to his arm.

'Okay,' said Gerry, throwing up his hands. 'What's Barry in trouble for? And why's he got Rakisha by the arm?'

'He's let her go now,' said Patti. 'Rakisha. Sweetie. Come over here.'

'Oh, darlings,' said Rakisha, after she'd weaved her way unsteadily to them. 'Barry is in *enormous* trouble.'

'Can we sit down somewhere?' Patti was as ready to drop as Rakisha. 'This is quite shocking.'

'Over here,' called Kelly, waving towards the outside tables of *Mullings of Mulbury*.

Rosemary followed her friends, turning once to see Barry packed into another police car. Geoffrey saw her watching and strode over.

'Geoffrey,' said Mrs Lionel, 'are you able to tell us anything?'

'I'm sorry, Dorothea,' Geoffrey said grimly. 'I can't say much. We have two men helping us with enquires related to alleged murder and alleged theft. I will call on whoever knows anything to give statements later.' He nodded at the small crowd, kept his gaze on Rosemary for a moment longer, then went back to his team.

'That leaves it up to you, Rosemary,' said Hannah, as she watched the police officer directing Joey Cambridge into the police car that also contained his son. 'What's up with Barry?'

'I'd be guessing.'

'Tell us anyway.' Hannah sat down on the edge of Holly's chair, forcing her older sister over. 'Otherwise, we'll make it up and it'll be worse than anything you could say.'

Rosemary checked with Mrs Lionel, who gave a brief shrug. 'A possible scenario would go like this. Barry discovers a car in his driveway on the morning Mrs Lionel discovered Joseph Cambridge in the Square. Not only a car, but a postcard which has dropped on the ground, getting a patch of particularly sticky red mud on it. He pockets it, not thinking much, but noticing that there is a cross on Mrs Tasher's haberdashery. That makes him keep the card rather than throw it out.' She paused, but the faces in front of her were expectant.

'When Gerry asks Barry to take the box of toys from the cellar to Big Town, something happens. Maybe Barry drops the box, and the jigsaw tube opens. Maybe he likes jigsaws and keeps it. Whatever it was, Barry discovers that the tube was full of intricately painted buttons. It dawns on him that the cross showing the old haberdashery and the buttons in the cellar of that same shop are an unusual coincidence and that he might have discovered something important. And valuable.'

'And so the silly man tried to sell them.' Gerry shook his head.

'But there was a second card,' said Ronnie. 'Where did that come from?'

'Was it Barry?' said Jasper. 'Trying to provide a distraction?'

'That's my guess.' Rosemary waited until the police cars left and the Square quietened. 'He found out that Marc was looking for a postcard and delivered one. Replica cards are easy to find around Mulbury. He made it look old and put it in my shop because he knew Marc had been in there.'

'You think he put the original card there as well?'

'Yes.'

'He should have burned it,' said Jasper. 'Got rid of the evidence.'

'I suspect he thought that the rediscovery of a card would deflect any suspicion,' said Mrs Lionel thoughtfully. 'After all, he'd taken the buttons so there was nothing left to find at the place the cross showed.'

A stillness settled over the residents of Mulbury until

Kelly brought out coffee for everyone, which was welcomed by most as the sun started its decline towards a cool evening.

'The postcard,' said Ronnie eventually. 'That was the reason Marc and Joey came back to Mulbury, but why was Joseph here?'

'Perhaps he's always been here.' Rosemary leaned back in her chair. 'People who sleep rough are often very good at keeping out of sight.'

'Or not being seen,' said Mrs Lionel, setting her cup back in its saucer. 'Which says more about us than them.'

'Crumbs,' said Hannah. 'I feel bad.'

'The old man had an injury to his skull,' continued Mrs Lionel. 'Perhaps it happened here in Mulbury as the fires hit the town? He was with Mrs Tasher, having his collection evaluated. They tried to flee. Poor Mrs Tasher didn't make it. Joseph Cambridge may have been hurt so badly he couldn't remember who he was.'

'The emergency treatment shelter,' said Gerry. 'He may have been a patient in there.'

'And then what?' said Holly. 'He just wandered off?'

'It was chaos.' Gerry rubbed a hand over his face. 'Mrs Lionel said that Mulbury was like a refugee camp. He could have disappeared, and no one noticed.'

'Confused and homeless, and no one helped him.' Hannah put her cup down with a shaking hand. 'It's so sad.'

'I suppose,' said Mrs Lionel, 'we'll never know the complete story.'

'Goodness,' said Jules, her hand on the pocket of her new shirt, 'we'll need a week to recover from this.'

'A week?' Gerry fanned himself with a serviette. 'More than that. But at least we know Mulbury is unlikely to have a murder linked to it again.'

Rosemary watched as the Mulburians around her nodded solemnly. *I'm not so certain,* she thought. *That old man's death under the beautiful Exceptional Tree feels like the start of something and not the finish.*

THIRTY-FOUR

After the excitement of the afternoon, the evening felt long awaited. Mrs Lionel declined Rosemary's offer of dinner and instead went to the Hubbards'. 'Heather is making risotto,' Mrs Lionel said.

'Heather makes risotto?'

'Oh yes. It's the one recipe she can make.' Mrs Lionel beamed. 'I'm going to love it.'

Rosemary was sure she would.

Honey rang as Rosemary packed up the shop for the night. 'Mum? Are you okay? Ronnie just got home, and he told me what happened. It sounds incredible.'

Rosemary locked her door and headed into the house to light the fire. Sunny curled around her legs as she squatted in front to pile kindle in, the phone balanced on a block of wood. 'It all happens in Mulbury, Honey.'

'Sounds like it. Is Heather alright again?'

'Yes. Once the circumstances of the poor man's death were made clear, she was back with us. She's even making dinner for Mrs Lionel.'

'Well, that's a huge relief.'

A soft rap at Rosemary's door made her glance up. She made out the outline of Jasper Lu outside the door. 'I have to go, Honey.'

'Right, Mum. Love you.'

'Love you, too.' Rosemary smiled, finished the call, and opened the door to Jasper. 'Hello. Are you okay?'

'Yes.' Jasper rubbed his arms. 'Do you think I could come in?'

Rosemary backed away from the door to let the man in, and then directed him to the lounge, where it was already warmer. He settled onto the couch even before Rosemary could say anything else, putting a bag of books on the floor. 'What a day.'

'Yes.' She waited for him to say more. When he didn't, she sat down and folded her hands in her lap. Sunny jumped up beside her but didn't curl into her usual crescent. The cat stared at Jasper as well, tail twitching. 'You've got something to tell me.'

'You don't want to hear my story.'

'Don't go all drama queen on me, Jasper Lu. Tell me if you want or not. Your choice.'

He laughed. 'Now who's the drama queen? Okay, I'll tell you. Want a cup of tea to go with it?'

'Of course.'

Ten minutes later, and tea was made. Rosemary sat on the couch with Jasper, Sunny curled up on a cushion between them.

'It goes like this,' Jasper said.

Rosemary sipped her scalding brew. 'What does?'

'My story.'

She smiled behind her mug.

Jasper shook his head. 'Remember that I found the first? *Forces and Horses*? And the shop window was broken, and a copy stolen. I think it was Helena.'

'It wasn't Helena.'

'No?'

'It was Marc. He did it to make it seem as if someone was robbing the shops. He searched Patti's quite thoroughly looking for the buttons.'

'Oh.' Jasper shook his head. 'How do you know it wasn't Helena?'

Rosemary reached for the books on the coffee table and held them up. 'I took three books from your shop.'

'But you're holding four.'

She handed him the tattiest. 'Marc put it here when he was talking with Ronnie.'

'Oh, wow,' said Jasper, taking the book in both hands. '*Forces and Horses*. I thought it was Helena rubbing it in.'

'Rubbing what in?'

'Well.' He put the book down. 'You see, I rang Helena after I read the acknowledgement.'

'Why?'

'Because of what it said.'

'To H, I, J and K.'

'You knew?'

'I read it as well.'

Jasper reached for his bag and withdrew the precious first. He lifted Sunny on her cushion to his other side, getting a baleful hiss from the indignant cat, and squeezed in next to Rosemary. He pressed his warm leg next to hers.

'It was the acknowledgement in this very book that gave it away.' He opened *Forces and Horses* and carefully passed it to her.

'Gave what away?'

He pointed at the page. 'See? *To H, I, J and K.*'

'Yes.' Rosemary tapped the print. 'Does that mean something?'

'Not to others. It was *our* family code. I'm J, obviously. My sisters are Helena and Iris.'

Rosemary tipped her head. 'And who is K?'

Jasper scratched his chin. 'Our father. Chris.'

'With a K?'

'That was the odd thing. My father's name starts with a C. It sounds like a K. It works better in the acknowledgement as a K.'

'But why are you, your sisters and your father in a book by T. G. G. Duncan?'

Jasper took a deep breath in and let it out slowly. 'Because T. G. G. Duncan was my mother.'

Rosemary looked at Jasper, whose face turned a pleasing shade of pink. 'This acknowledgement makes you think your mother wrote these books.'

Jasper folded his hair behind both ears. 'Yes, yes, I do. H, I, J. It's us, see?'

'No. This could be another family with a code. Was your mother's maiden name Duncan?'

'No. She used Lu like the rest of us.'

'It's a long bow to draw, Jasper.'

He shook his head vigorously. 'No, no, it isn't. You see, I've read T. G. G. Duncan but never the acknowledgement page. I was sitting here one night, flicking through the book and remembering those amazing scenes when Captain Kesper beats his foes by hurling into hyperspace, when I saw this.' He lifted the book to showcase the acknowledgement.

'Is that all you've got to go on?'

'Well, no.' His face warmed further. 'I searched for her photo on the internet. T. G. G. Duncan always wore dark glasses and a broad-brimmed hat, but now I look closely I can see the family resemblance.' He put a hand on his nose. 'We all have the same shape.'

Rosemary studied Jasper's nose, which seemed a pleasant but ordinary straight slope. 'Wouldn't discovering your mother's talent have been a lovely surprise?'

'Yes, yes, it was. It was quite wonderful.' He glanced at her. 'Why do you say that as if it wasn't?'

'Because you discovered something else that night, as well.'

He froze, blinked a few times, then shook his head. 'How could you possibly know that?'

'Your reaction to the window break-in. You immediately thought it was Helena.'

He didn't look aggrieved. 'I did, I really did. Well, it was the K.' He tapped the page. 'It took me a while to work it out.'

'You don't think they put the K there because it worked better.'

'No.'

'She's dedicated this to someone else.' Rosemary shrugged. 'Is that such a bad thing? This could be a friend or a relative. Why is it such a big deal?'

'I rang my sister. I rang Helena.' He chewed his lip for a moment. 'After I told her about the acknowledgement, it confirmed her already held (but secretly kept) suspicion that T. G. G. Duncan was our mother, too. Helena is quite a bit older than me or Iris. She remembers our mother sitting at a typewriter every spare moment she got.' He lowered the book. 'I don't. She'd stopped by the time I'd been born.' He grimaced.

'Why the face?'

'Because Helena laughed at the K.'

'Laughed?'

'Yes, her nasty, cruel laugh. The one she reserves for me.'

'Why would she laugh at you?'

Jasper hooked hair behind his ear. 'She thought the K *vindicated* her. It showed something that she was always telling me.'

'Which was?'

'My father *wasn't* my father. That the K was another man. That *K* is my father, and not *Chris*, her father.'

Rosemary sat silently.

Jasper shook his head. 'You don't believe any of this.'

'I didn't say that.'

'You don't need to.' He chewed his lip for a moment. 'T. G. G. Duncan didn't publish any more books after 1965. That's the year I was born. Do you think she stopped writing because of me?'

Rosemary contemplated the man in front of her. One side of his hair remained hooked behind his ear, leaving a strand sticking out almost sideways, and his eyes searched hers earnestly. She resisted the urge to pat the wayward strand down. 'Jasper, you know nothing for certain. Did your father treat you any differently from your siblings?'

Jasper shook his head. 'No. My father—the one that I grew up with—was a sweet man, kindly. I had a simple and beloved childhood. Except, perhaps, for Helena's constant bullying.' He put the book down. 'I think she's suspected something about my heritage for a long time. She always looked after Iris like a big sister should. She treated me worse than a dog. There was something there that I didn't know.'

Rosemary put her hand on the book. 'I'm sorry, Jasper, but I don't really understand. Your mother and father are both gone now. You are an adult man that doesn't have to listen to his big sister. Does it really matter?'

'Yes, Rosemary, it does.' Jasper tugged the book away. 'I feel *wronged*.'

Rosemary tried to visualise how it would feel to find out that you were someone else's child. 'I'm sorry,' she said. 'I had no right to say that. Of course, it matters, I can see you think that.'

He kept his eyes on the book but gave a small smile. 'Let's just say that I didn't know how I would feel about it until it happened to me.'

'Just because Helena suspected something when she was a little girl, doesn't mean it was true.'

'I have proof of a sort.'

'What is that?'

'My sisters are blonde.'

'What does that prove?'

'Rosemary, look at me. My hair is black, pitch black. Well, my hair *was* black.' He patted his head where some silver threads ran along the length of his long hair. 'I look completely different to Helena and Iris.'

'That doesn't mean much. Lots of people don't look like their parents.'

'Helena always took great delight in pointing it out.' He put the book on his legs and his head back on the couch. 'She says it's why I have the curse. That it came from my father.'

They sat for a moment; the silence only broken by the occasional crackling of the fire. Jasper's fingers were drumming the top of the book. She lifted his hands away and gently extracted the hardback to place on the table before it was ruined. His hand tightened around hers. 'Jasper,' she said after a moment. 'I'm sorry, I can't.'

'I know.' He gave her hand a warm squeeze and let go. 'You're not ready.'

His leg no longer felt comfortable against hers. She stood up suddenly, the movement making Sunny grunt. 'More tea?'

Jasper stood, too. 'I'm sorry, Rosemary.'

She put her hand up. 'It's not your fault, Jasper.' She rounded the couch and stopped. 'One thing, though.'

His look was hopeful. 'Yes?'

'You've been saying that you're feeling better. Will this discovery hold your recovery back?'

'Oh.' His face fell. 'No, I don't think so. It's the start of another conundrum, though, a bit like my sickness. This time it's who *is* my actual father?' He gave a short laugh. 'But what makes me really feel better is that my mother was a wonderful person.'

'Because she wrote these books?'

'She was a wonderful person before I knew about the books. We all loved her, even cranky Helena.' He ran a hand through his hair. 'She was an *author*, Rosemary. My life has been in books and now I discover my mother—my clever, beautiful mother—was a writer. Don't you think that's amazing?'

I think it was amazing that she was able to hide so much from you, she thought, but what could she do but smile at the obvious delight in his face? 'It's great, Jasper. More than that. It's perfect.'

He smiled. 'All the rest can wait.'

Rosemary heard the meaning in his voice and said nothing.

Jasper cleared his throat. 'Does anyone ever ask you whether you're okay? You seem to spend a lot of time asking others.'

Rosemary thought for a moment. 'I'm sure they do. Mrs Lionel is always looking out for me.'

'You are great friends.'

'Yes, we are.'

'Ever since...?' Jasper's gaze dropped.

'Out with it, Jasper.'

'Alasdair.' He breathed out sharply.

'Yes, especially since Alasdair.'

'You see,' said Jasper carefully, 'I've never really known what happened there.'

'With Alasdair?'

'Yes, with Alasdair.'

A quiet fell. Rosemary closed her eyes for a moment and when she opened them again, there was Jasper Lu, hair falling over his kind, dark eyes, a charming shade of red flooding his cheeks.

'I didn't mean to pry...'

'It's not prying. It's curiosity. I get it, I really do. But I don't enjoy talking about it.'

'I'm sorry, I shouldn't have...'

Rosemary held up her hand. 'It's fine, really. Some people know, some people *think* they know.' She took a big breath and let it swoop out. 'Alasdair disappeared. One day he packed some things and left.'

'He's missing?'

'No, they found him.' She shrugged.

'He's dead?'

'We thought so at first. We even had a memorial for him, you might have heard about that.' Rosemary thought briefly about the encounter with the besotted Darren and shook her head. 'No. Alasdair is very much alive.'

'Oh.' Jasper nodded, and it went on for a long time. 'He'll be back then.'

'No, he has no intention of returning. Not to Mulbury. Not to me. Not even to Honey.' Rosemary stroked Sunny's head. 'Is that what you wanted to know?'

'I suppose it was. But why would he leave like that? Had something happened?'

'That,' said Rosemary, 'is the biggest mystery of all. Although Kelly Flanagan believes it is something to do with me being a cold and dispassionate person.'

Jasper's forehead creased. 'I don't see you as that. Not at all.' When she said nothing further, he sighed. 'I'm sorry, once again.'

'No need to be. It's not your fault, as it wasn't mine or Honey's. The police said it happens more than you think. People want a new life, so they get one.' She pulled her braid over her shoulder and smoothed it. 'I don't talk about it, not even with Honey. Let's drop it now.'

Jasper's shoulders wriggled. He started nodding again, caught himself, and stopped, casting his eyes around the coffee table as if searching for something else to talk about. She was slightly disappointed when, instead of starting a lively conversation about the exploits of one of his Regency romance heroines or the benefits of buying antique books as an investment, he stood up and clapped his hands together.

'I'd better go,' he said. 'Leave you in peace.'

They walked together to the door. Rosemary opened it but Jasper paused. He took one of her hands lightly. 'I'm sorry about Alasdair,' he said quietly.

'I'm not,' she said, surprising herself. 'Not any more.'

He let her hand go slowly, sliding his fingers out of hers. 'See you tomorrow.'

'Yes.'

'A walk, perhaps? I've got to beat my curse with exercise.'

She smiled. 'I don't believe in curses.'

'I do.' He shook his head, then regarded her with his head tilted. 'Strangely, though, not half as much when you're around.'

He waved as he left, so she waved back, feeling a ridiculous amount of anticipation about strolling up the hill with Jasper Lu to overlook Mulbury in its soft autumn light.

She'd only just settled back on the couch, Sunny once again beside her, when the phone rang.

'Honey Blossom.'

'Sorry, Mum, but I didn't ask before.'

'Ask what?'

'What you're making now.'

'I'm not making anything, Honey. It's evening.'

'But what's next? What will you be making tomorrow?'

Rosemary glanced around her cosy house, her gaze falling on the last of the apples in a bowl on the kitchen counter. 'I'll be stewing apples,' she said. 'It's my turn to make dinner Monday night. I thought I'd do an apple crumble.'

'Pink Lady apples? Brisk and sweet, I know.'

'Yes. They make a sharp apple base for the crumble.'

'Ginger in the crumble?'

'Yes. Mixed spice and ginger.'

'I can smell it, you know.'

'Honey, I haven't started cooking it yet.'

'I can. The apples warm the air, and the ginger in the crumble makes it sharp. It's like being in a country kitchen with a jug of thick fresh cream waiting on the counter. I can even smell the richness of the cream.'

'Honey, you're quite mad, did you know that?'

Honey laughed, the warm laugh of apple crumble browning in the oven. 'See you soon, Mum. Love you.'

'Love you, Honey.'

As she ended the call, Rosemary Exeter put her head back against the couch, pulled Sunny on to her lap, and closed her eyes contentedly. What more could a person want than a loving daughter, a warm cat and the smell of apples stewing on the stove?

ACKNOWLEDGMENTS

Thanks to my ever patient gardener husband who grows the fruits and vegetables we seem to be constantly preserving, and which gave me the idea for The Preserved Mulbury.

Thanks also to my editorial team and ARC readers who help me see what I should be seeing but just can't.

All remaining errors are entirely my own.

ABOUT THE AUTHOR

Juno Harvey lives in Victoria, Australia, with her family.
She makes jam on the weekends and works in a university
during the week.

Want to join Juno's Reader's Team?
Go to www.junoharvey.com and receive a free book!

https://www.junoharvey.com/

Books of light...and shade.